CLASSIC LOVE STORIES

More short stories available
from Macmillan Collector's Library

CLASSIC
LOVE STORIES

Edited and introduced by
BECKY BROWN

MACMILLAN COLLECTOR'S LIBRARY

This collection first published 2024 by Macmillan Collector's Library
an imprint of Pan Macmillan
The Smithson, 6 Briset Street, London EC1M 5NR
EU representative: Macmillan Publishers Ireland Ltd,
1st Floor, The Liffey Trust Centre, 117–126 Sheriff Street Upper,
Dublin 1, DO1 YC43
Associated companies throughout the world
www.panmacmillan.com

ISBN 978-1-0350-1490-3

Introduction copyright © Becky Brown 2024
Selection and arrangement copyright © Macmillan Publishers International Ltd. 2024

The Permissions Acknowledgements on p. 351 constitute an extension of this copyright page.

1 3 5 7 9 8 6 4 2

A CIP catalogue record for this book is available from the British Library.

Casing design and endpaper pattern by Andrew Davidson
Typeset in Plantin by Jouve (UK), Milton Keynes
Printed and bound in China by Imago

Visit www.panmacmillan.com to read more
about all our books and to buy them.

Contents

Introduction

BECKY BROWN

In some ways, short stories might seem a funny place to find love. When we think about classic literature's great romances, it is almost inevitably novels and their slowly developed characters and relationships that will spring to mind – *Pride and Prejudice*'s Mr Darcy and Elizabeth Bennet, perhaps, or *Lady Chatterley's Lover*'s Constance and Oliver. Over the stately course of a novel, we have the luxury of lingering in a slow burn; we can travel through meetings and partings, tender moments and misunderstandings, passions and rages. We see our lovers within the elaborate tapestry of their lives and society, and we are given an intimate understanding of the stakes – of the personal and social barriers – that litter the bumpy road to true love (or perhaps to something else entirely).

But the authors of the short stories in this volume do not have the luxury of time – of an extended word count – to examine the many facets of a relationship. Instead, they must rely on the cold plunge, on the immediate immersion of the reader in a moment between two people. These intimate dioramas are as diverse as they are fascinating. We witness couples sharing beginnings, middles and ends. From Dostoevsky's detailed portrait of the earliest pangs of adult feeling breaking into the simpler world of childhood in *A Little Hero*, to Zora Neale Hurston's *The Gilded Six Bits*, in which passion, infidelity and redemption are woven into the fabric of a marriage, and Carson McCullers' exceptional *A Tree. A Rock. A Cloud.*, in which a man who has long since been abandoned by his wife explains the 'science of love' to a stranger.

Some choose to throw us into a single moment, mere hours or days, and rely on literary ingenuity to construct the rest of the life we cannot see. Elizabeth Taylor's *Flesh*, in which two middle-aged people have a clumsy holiday affair, is a masterclass in the unseen – hinting only gently at the lives they led, and the lives they'll go back to. Others give a distillation, the arc of a whole life in miniature, as in F. Scott Fitzgerald's *The Lees of Happiness*, a tender and humane examination of ideal love subjected to the cruelties of day-to-day life.

This crafted brevity, this artful concision, often allows for a solitary component of love to be turned carefully under the writer's microscope. Dorothy Edwards and H.G. Wells both scrutinise the infatuation of an older man with a younger woman, the former with compassion, the latter with gleeful malice – and yet both are a delight to read. Kate Chopin and D. H. Lawrence examine something much more animal; a sensory, unarticulated yearning, an almost primal desire. For Chopin, this is acted out against the constraints of a convent, with the titular lilacs exchanged between two women who can never be together. Lawrence's intimacy, on the other hand, is flesh-on-flesh, urgent and even senseless. For every similarity each story shares, there is a world of difference.

In the fourteen stories in this volume, we can traverse centuries and continents, cultures and ideologies. We meet with tragedy and humour, philosophy and frivolity. But uniting it all is always a spark of connection between two people, and a story that will mend or break your heart.

CLASSIC LOVE STORIES

ANTON CHEKHOV

The Lady with the Dog

1

It was said that a new person had appeared on the sea-front: a lady with a little dog. Dmitri Dmitritch Gurov, who had by then been a fortnight at Yalta, and so was fairly at home there, had begun to take an interest in new arrivals. Sitting in Verney's pavilion, he saw, walking on the sea-front, a fair-haired young lady of medium height, wearing a *béret*; a white Pomeranian dog was running behind her.

And afterwards he met her in the public gardens and in the square several times a day. She was walking alone, always wearing the same *béret*, and always with the same white dog; no one knew who she was, and everyone called her simply "the lady with the dog."

"If she is here alone without a husband or friends, it wouldn't be amiss to make her acquaintance," Gurov reflected.

He was under forty, but he had a daughter already twelve years old, and two sons at school. He had been married young, when he was a student in his second year, and by now his wife seemed half as old again as he. She was a tall, erect woman with dark eyebrows, staid and dignified, and, as she said of herself, intellectual. She read a great deal, used phonetic spelling, called her husband, not Dmitri, but Dimitri, and he secretly considered her unintelligent, narrow, inelegant, was afraid of her, and did not like to be at home. He had begun being unfaithful to her long ago—had been unfaithful to her often, and, probably on that account, almost always spoke ill of women, and when they were talked about in his presence, used to call them "the lower race."

It seemed to him that he had been so schooled by bitter experience that he might call them what he liked, and yet he could not get on for two days together without "the lower race." In the society of men he was bored and not himself, with them he was cold and uncommunicative; but when he was in the company of women he felt free, and knew what to say to them and how to behave; and he was at ease with them even when he was silent. In his appearance, in his character, in his whole nature, there was something attractive and elusive which allured women and disposed them in his favour; he knew that, and some force seemed to draw him, too, to them.

Experience often repeated, truly bitter experience, had taught him long ago that with decent people, especially Moscow people—always slow to move and irresolute—every intimacy, which at first so agreeably diversifies life and appears a light and charming adventure, inevitably grows into a regular problem of extreme intricacy, and in the long run the situation becomes unbearable. But at every fresh meeting with an interesting woman this experience seemed to slip out of his memory, and he was eager for life, and everything seemed simple and amusing.

One evening he was dining in the gardens, and the lady in the *béret* came up slowly to take the next table. Her expression, her gait, her dress, and the way she did her hair told him that she was a lady, that she was married, that she was in Yalta for the first time and alone, and that she was dull there . . . The stories told of the immorality in such places as Yalta are to a great extent untrue; he despised them, and knew that such stories were for the most part made up by persons who would themselves have been glad to sin if they had been able; but when the lady sat down at the next table three paces from him, he remembered these tales of easy conquests, of trips to the mountains, and the tempting thought of a swift, fleeting love affair, a romance with an unknown woman, whose name he did not know, suddenly took possession of him.

He beckoned coaxingly to the Pomeranian, and

when the dog came up to him he shook his finger at it. The Pomeranian growled, Gurov shook his finger at it again.

The lady looked at him and at once dropped her eyes.

"He doesn't bite," she said, and blushed.

"May I give him a bone?" he asked; and when she nodded he asked courteously, "Have you been long in Yalta?"

"Five days."

"And I have already dragged out a fortnight here."

There was a brief silence.

"Time goes fast, and yet it is so dull here!" she said, not looking at him.

"That's only the fashion to say it is dull here. A provincial will live in Belyov or Zhidra and not be dull, and when he comes here it's 'Oh, the dulness! Oh, the dust!' One would think he came from Grenada."

She laughed. Then both continued eating in silence, like strangers, but after dinner they walked side by side; and there sprang up between them the light jesting conversation of people who are free and satisfied, to whom it does not matter where they go or what they talk about. They walked and talked of the strange light on the sea: the water was of a soft

4

warm lilac hue, and there was a golden streak from the moon upon it. They talked of how sultry it was after a hot day. Gurov told her that he came from Moscow, that he had taken his degree in Arts, but had a post in a bank; that he had trained as an opera-singer, but had given it up, that he owned two houses in Moscow ... And from her he learnt that she had grown up in Petersburg, but had lived in S——since her marriage two years before, that she was staying another month in Yalta, and that her husband, who needed a holiday too, might perhaps come and fetch her. She was not sure whether her husband had a post in a Crown Department or under the Provincial Council—and was amused by her own ignorance. And Gurov learnt, too, that she was called Anna Sergeyevna.

Afterwards he thought about her in his room at the hotel—thought she would certainly meet him next day; it would be sure to happen. As he got into bed he thought how lately she had been a girl at school, doing lessons like his own daughter; he recalled the diffidence, the angularity, that was still manifest in her laugh and her manner of talking with a stranger. This must have been the first time in her life she had been alone in surroundings in which she was followed, looked at, and spoken to merely from a secret motive which she could hardly fail to guess.

He recalled her slender, delicate neck, her lovely grey eyes.

"There's something pathetic about her, anyway," he thought, and fell asleep.

2

A week had passed since they had made acquaintance. It was a holiday. It was sultry indoors, while in the street the wind whirled the dust round and round, and blew people's hats off. It was a thirsty day, and Gurov often went into the pavilion, and pressed Anna Sergeyevna to have syrup and water or an ice. One did not know what to do with oneself.

In the evening when the wind had dropped a little, they went out on to the groyne to see the steamer come in. There were a great many people walking about the harbour; they had gathered to welcome someone, bringing bouquets. And two peculiarities of a well-dressed Yalta crowd were very conspicuous: the elderly ladies were dressed like young ones, and there were great numbers of generals.

Owing to the roughness of the sea, the steamer arrived late, after the sun had set, and it was a long time turning about before it reached the groyne. Anna Sergeyevna looked through her lorgnette at the steamer and the passengers as though looking for acquaintances, and when she turned to Gurov her eyes were shining. She talked a great deal and asked disconnected questions, forgetting next moment what she had asked; then she dropped her lorgnette in the crush.

The festive crowd began to disperse; it was too dark to see people's faces. The wind had completely dropped, but Gurov and Anna Sergeyevna still stood as though waiting to see someone else come from the steamer. Anna Sergeyevna was silent now, and sniffed the flowers without looking at Gurov.

"The weather is better this evening," he said. "Where shall we go now? Shall we drive somewhere?"

She made no answer.

Then he looked at her intently, and all at once put his arm round her and kissed her on the lips, and breathed in the moisture and the fragrance of the flowers; and he immediately looked round him, anxiously wondering whether anyone had seen them.

"Let us go to your hotel," he said softly. And both walked quickly.

The room was close and smelt of the scent she had bought at the Japanese shop. Gurov looked at her and thought: "What different people one meets in the world!" From the past he preserved memories

7

of careless, good-natured women, who loved cheerfully and were grateful to him for the happiness he gave them, however brief it might be; and of women like his wife who loved without any genuine feeling, with superfluous phrases, affectedly, hysterically, with an expression that suggested that it was not love nor passion, but something more significant; and of two or three others, very beautiful, cold women, on whose faces he had caught a glimpse of a rapacious expression—an obstinate desire to snatch from life more than it could give, and these were capricious, unreflecting, domineering, unintelligent women not in their first youth, and when Gurov grew cold to them their beauty excited his hatred, and the lace on their linen seemed to him like scales.

But in this case there was still the diffidence, the angularity of inexperienced youth, an awkward feeling; and there was a sense of consternation as though someone had suddenly knocked at the door. The attitude of Anna Sergeyevna—"the lady with the dog"—to what had happened was somehow peculiar, very grave, as though it were her fall—so it seemed, and it was strange and inappropriate. Her face drooped and faded, and on both sides of it her long hair hung down mournfully; she mused in a dejected attitude like "the woman who was a sinner" in an old-fashioned picture.

"It's wrong," she said. "You will be the first to despise me now."

There was a water-melon on the table. Gurov cut himself a slice and began eating it without haste. There followed at least half an hour of silence.

Anna Sergeyevna was touching; there was about her the purity of a good, simple woman who had seen little of life. The solitary candle burning on the table threw a faint light on her face, yet it was clear that she was very unhappy.

"How could I despise you?" asked Gurov. "You don't know what you are saying."

"God forgive me," she said, and her eyes filled with tears. "It's awful."

"You seem to feel you need to be forgiven."

"Forgiven? No. I am a bad, low woman; I despise myself and don't attempt to justify myself. It's not my husband but myself I have deceived. And not only just now; I have been deceiving myself for a long time. My husband may be a good, honest man, but he is a flunkey! I don't know what he does there, what his work is, but I know he is a flunkey! I was twenty when I was married to him. I have been tormented by curiosity; I wanted something better. 'There must be a different sort of life,' I said to myself. I wanted to live! To live, to live! ... I was fired by curiosity ... you don't understand it, but, I swear to God, I could not control myself; something happened to me: I could not be restrained. I told my husband I was ill, and came here ... And here I have been walking about as though I were dazed, like a mad creature; ... and now I have become a vulgar, contemptible woman whom anyone may despise."

Gurov felt bored already, listening to her. He was irritated by the naïve tone, by this remorse, so unexpected and inopportune; but for the tears in her eyes, he might have thought she was jesting or playing a part.

"I don't understand," he said softly. "What is it you want?"

She hid her face on his breast and pressed close to him.

"Believe me, believe me, I beseech you ..." she said. "I love a pure, honest life, and sin is loathsome to me. I don't know what I am doing. Simple people say: 'The Evil One has beguiled me.' And I may say of myself now that the Evil One has beguiled me."

"Hush, hush! ..." he muttered.

He looked at her fixed, scared eyes, kissed her, talked softly and affectionately, and by degrees she was comforted, and her gaiety returned; they both began laughing.

Afterwards when they went out there was not a soul on the sea-front. The town with its cypresses had quite a deathlike air, but the sea still broke noisily on the shore; a single barge was rocking on the waves, and a lantern was blinking sleepily on it.

They found a cab and drove to Oreanda.

"I found out your surname in the hall just now: it was written on the board—Von Diderits," said Gurov. "Is your husband a German?"

"No; I believe his grandfather was a German, but he is an Orthodox Russian himself."

At Oreanda they sat on a seat not far from the church, looked down at the sea, and were silent. Yalta was hardly visible through the morning mist; white clouds stood motionless on the mountain-tops. The leaves did not stir on the trees, grasshoppers chirruped, and the monotonous hollow sound of the sea, rising up from below, spoke of the peace, of the eternal sleep awaiting us. So it must have sounded when there was no Yalta, no Oreanda here; so it sounds now, and it will sound as indifferently and monotonously when we are all no more. And in this constancy, in this complete indifference to the life and death of each of us, there lies hid, perhaps, a pledge of our eternal salvation, of the unceasing movement of life upon earth, of unceasing progress towards perfection. Sitting beside a young woman who in the dawn seemed so lovely, soothed and spell-bound in these magical surroundings—the sea, mountains, clouds, the open sky—Gurov thought how in reality everything is beautiful in this world when one reflects: everything except what we think or do ourselves when we forget our human dignity and the higher aims of our existence.

A man walked up to them—probably a keeper—looked at them and walked away. And this detail seemed mysterious and beautiful, too. They saw a steamer come from Theodosia, with its lights out in the glow of dawn.

"There is dew on the grass," said Anna Sergeyevna, after a silence.

"Yes. It's time to go home."

They went back to the town.

Then they met every day at twelve o'clock on the sea-front, lunched and dined together, went for walks, admired the sea. She complained that she slept badly, that her heart throbbed violently; asked the same questions, troubled now by jealousy and now by the fear that he did not respect her sufficiently. And often in the square or gardens, when there was no one near them, he suddenly drew her to him and kissed her passionately. Complete idleness, these kisses in broad daylight while he looked round in dread of someone's seeing them, the heat, the smell of the sea, and the continual passing to and fro before him of idle, well-dressed, well-fed people, made a new man of him; he told Anna Sergeyevna how beautiful she was, how fascinating. He was impatiently passionate, he would not move a step away from her, while she was often pensive and continually urged him to confess that he did not respect her, did not love her in the least, and thought of her as nothing but a common woman. Rather late almost every evening they drove somewhere out of town, to Oreanda or to the waterfall; and the expedition was always a success, the scenery invariably impressed them as grand and beautiful.

They were expecting her husband to come, but a letter came from him, saying that there was something wrong with his eyes, and he entreated his wife to come home as quickly as possible. Anna Sergeyevna made haste to go.

"It's a good thing I am going away," she said to Gurov. "It's the finger of destiny!"

She went by coach and he went with her. They were driving the whole day. When she had got into a compartment of the express, and when the second bell had rung, she said:

"Let me look at you once more ... look at you once again. That's right."

She did not shed tears, but was so sad that she seemed ill, and her face was quivering.

"I shall remember you . . . think of you," she said. "God be with you; be happy. Don't remember evil against me. We are parting for ever—it must be so, for we ought never to have met. Well, God be with you."

The train moved off rapidly, its lights soon vanished from sight, and a minute later there was no sound of it, as though everything had conspired together to end as quickly as possible that sweet delirium, that madness. Left alone on the platform, and gazing into the dark distance, Gurov listened to the chirrup of the grasshoppers and the hum of the telegraph wires, feeling as though he had only just waked up. And he thought, musing, that there had been another episode or adventure in his life, and it, too, was at an end, and nothing was left of it but a memory . . . He was moved, sad, and conscious of a slight remorse. This young woman whom he would never meet again had not been happy with him; he was genuinely warm and affectionate with her, but yet in his manner, his tone, and his caresses there had been a shade of light irony, the coarse condescension of a happy man who was, besides, almost twice her age. All the time she had called him kind, exceptional, lofty; obviously he had seemed to her different from what he really was, so he had unintentionally deceived her . . .

Here at the station was already a scent of autumn; it was a cold evening.

"It's time for me to go north," thought Gurov as he left the platform. "High time!"

3

At home in Moscow everything was in its winter routine; the stoves were heated, and in the morning it was still dark when the children were having breakfast and getting ready for school, and the nurse would light the lamp for a short time. The frosts had begun already. When the first snow has fallen, on the first day of sledge-driving it is pleasant to see the white earth, the white roofs, to draw soft, delicious breath, and the season brings back the days of one's youth. The old limes and birches, white with hoarfrost, have a good-natured expression; they are nearer to one's heart than cypresses and palms, and near them one doesn't want to be thinking of the sea and the mountains.

Gurov was Moscow born; he arrived in Moscow on a fine frosty day, and when he put on his fur coat and warm gloves, and walked along Petrovka, and when on Saturday evening he heard the ringing of the bells, his recent trip and the places he had seen lost all charm for him. Little by little he became absorbed in Moscow life, greedily read three newspapers a day, and declared he did not read the Moscow papers on principle! He already felt a longing to go to restaurants, clubs, dinner-parties, anniversary celebrations, and he felt flattered at entertaining distinguished lawyers and artists, and at playing cards with a professor at the doctors' club. He could already eat a whole plateful of salt fish and cabbage . . .

In another month, he fancied, the image of Anna Sergeyevna would be shrouded in a mist in his memory, and only from time to time would visit him in his dreams with a touching smile as others did. But more than a month passed, real winter had come, and everything was still clear in his memory as though he had parted with Anna Sergeyevna only the day before. And his memories glowed more and more vividly. When in the evening stillness he heard from his study the voices of his children, preparing their lessons, or when he listened to a song or the organ at the restaurant, or the storm howled in the chimney, suddenly everything would rise up in his memory: what had happened on the groyne, and the early morning with the mist on the mountains, and the steamer coming from Theodosia, and the kisses. He would pace a long time about his room, remembering it all and smiling; then his memories passed into dreams, and in his fancy the past was mingled with what was to come. Anna Sergeyevna did not visit him in dreams, but followed him about everywhere like a shadow and haunted him. When he shut his eyes he saw her as though she were living before him, and she seemed to him lovelier, younger, tenderer than she was; and he imagined himself finer than he had been in Yalta. In the evenings she peeped out at him from the bookcase, from the fireplace, from the corner—he heard her breathing, the caressing rustle of her dress. In the street he watched the women, looking for someone like her.

He was tormented by an intense desire to confide his memories to someone. But in his home it was impossible to talk of his love, and he had no one outside; he could not talk to his tenants nor to anyone at the bank. And what had he to talk of? Had he been in love, then? Had there been anything beautiful, poetical, or edifying or simply interesting in his relations with Anna Sergeyevna? And there was nothing for him but to talk vaguely of love, of woman, and no one guessed what it meant; only his wife twitched her black eyebrows, and said: "The part of a lady-killer does not suit you at all, Dimitri."

One evening, coming out of the doctors' club

with an official with whom he had been playing cards, he could not resist saying:

"If only you knew what a fascinating woman I made the acquaintance of in Yalta!"

The official got into his sledge and was driving away, but turned suddenly and shouted:

"Dmitri Dmitritch!"

"What?"

"You were right this evening: the sturgeon was a bit too strong!"

These words, so ordinary, for some reason moved Gurov to indignation, and struck him as degrading and unclean. What savage manners, what people! What senseless nights, what uninteresting, uneventful days! The rage for card-playing, the gluttony, the drunkenness, the continual talk always about the same thing. Useless pursuits and conversations always about the same things absorb the better part of one's time, the better part of one's strength, and in the end there is left a life grovelling and curtailed, worthless and trivial, and there is no escaping or getting away from it—just as though one were in a madhouse or a prison.

Gurov did not sleep all night, and was filled with indignation. And he had a headache all next day. And the next night he slept badly; he sat up in bed, thinking, or paced up and down his room. He was sick of his children, sick of the bank; he had no desire to go anywhere or to talk of anything.

In the holidays in December he prepared for a journey, and told his wife he was going to Petersburg to do something in the interests of a young friend— and he set off for S——. What for? He did not very well know himself. He wanted to see Anna Ser-geyevna and to talk with her—to arrange a meeting, if possible.

He reached S——in the morning, and took the best room at the hotel, in which the floor was covered with grey army cloth, and on the table was an inkstand, grey with dust and adorned with a figure on horseback, with its hat in its hand and its head broken off. The hotel porter gave him the necessary information; Von Diderits lived in a house of his own in Old Gontcharny Street—it was not far from the hotel: he was rich and lived in good style, and had his own horses; everyone in the town knew him. The porter pronounced the name "Dridirits."

Gurov went without haste to Old Gontcharny Street and found the house. Just opposite the house stretched a long grey fence adorned with nails.

"One would run away from a fence like that," thought Gurov, looking from the fence to the win-dows of the house and back again.

He considered: to-day was a holiday, and the

husband would probably be at home. And in any case it would be tactless to go into the house and upset her. If he were to send her a note it might fall into her husband's hands, and then it might ruin everything. The best thing was to trust to chance. And he kept walking up and down the street by the fence, waiting for the chance. He saw a beggar go in at the gate and dogs fly at him; then an hour later he heard a piano, and the sounds were faint and indistinct. Probably it was Anna Sergeyevna playing. The front door suddenly opened, and an old woman came out, followed by the familiar white Pomeranian. Gurov was on the point of calling to the dog, but his heart began beating violently, and in his excitement he could not remember the dog's name.

He walked up and down, and loathed the grey fence more and more, and by now he thought irritably that Anna Sergeyevna had forgotten him, and was perhaps already amusing herself with someone else, and that that was very natural in a young woman who had nothing to look at from morning till night but that confounded fence. He went back to his hotel room and sat for a long while on the sofa, not knowing what to do, then he had dinner and a long nap.

"How stupid and worrying it is!" he thought when he woke and looked at the dark windows: it was already evening. "Here I've had a good sleep for some reason. What shall I do in the night?"

He sat on the bed, which was covered by a cheap grey blanket, such as one sees in hospitals, and he taunted himself in his vexation:

"So much for the lady with the dog . . . so much for the adventure . . . You're in a nice fix . . ."

That morning at the station a poster in large letters had caught his eye. "The Geisha" was to be performed for the first time. He thought of this and went to the theatre.

"It's quite possible she may go to the first performance," he thought.

The theatre was full. As in all provincial theatres, there was a fog above the chandelier, the gallery was noisy and restless; in the front row the local dandies were standing up before the beginning of the performance, with their hands behind them; in the Governor's box the Governor's daughter, wearing a boa, was sitting in the front seat, while the Governor himself lurked modestly behind the curtain with only his hands visible; the orchestra was a long time tuning up; the stage curtain swayed. All the time the audience were coming in and taking their seats Gurov looked at them eagerly.

Anna Sergeyevna, too, came in. She sat down in the third row, and when Gurov looked at her his heart contracted, and he understood clearly that for him there was in the whole world no creature so near, so precious, and so important to him; she, this little woman, in no way remarkable, lost in a provincial crowd, with a vulgar lorgnette in her hand, filled his whole life now, was his sorrow and his joy, the one happiness that he now desired for himself, and to the sounds of the inferior orchestra, of the wretched provincial violins, he thought how lovely she was. He thought and dreamed.

A young man with small side-whiskers, tall and stooping, came in with Anna Sergeyevna and sat down beside her; he bent his head at every step and seemed to be continually bowing. Most likely this was the husband whom at Yalta, in a rush of bitter feeling, she had called a flunkey. And there really was in his long figure, his side-whiskers, and the small bald patch on his head, something of the flunkey's obsequiousness; his smile was sugary, and in his buttonhole there was some badge of distinction like the number on a waiter.

During the first interval the husband went away to smoke; she remained alone in her stall. Gurov, who was sitting in the stalls, too, went up to her and said in a trembling voice, with a forced smile:

"Good evening."

She glanced at him and turned pale, then glanced

again with horror, unable to believe her eyes, and tightly gripped the fan and the lorgnette in her hands, evidently struggling with herself not to faint. Both were silent. She was sitting, he was standing, frightened by her confusion and not venturing to sit down beside her. The violins and the flute began tuning up. He felt suddenly frightened; it seemed as though all the people in the boxes were looking at them. She got up and went quickly to the door; he followed her, and both walked senselessly along passages, and up and down stairs, and figures in legal, scholastic, and civil service uniforms, all wearing badges, flitted before their eyes. They caught glimpses of ladies, of fur coats hanging on pegs; the draughts blew on them, bringing a smell of stale tobacco. And Gurov, whose heart was beating violently, thought:

"Oh, heavens! Why are these people here and this orchestra! . . ."

And at that instant he recalled how when he had seen Anna Sergeyevna off at the station he had thought that everything was over and they would never meet again. But how far they were still from the end!

On the narrow, gloomy staircase over which was written "To the Amphitheatre," she stopped.

"How you have frightened me!" she said,

breathing hard, still pale and overwhelmed. "Oh, how you have frightened me! I am half dead. Why have you come? Why?"

"But do understand, Anna, do understand ..." he said hastily in a low voice. "I entreat you to understand ..."

She looked at him with dread, with entreaty, with love; she looked at him intently, to keep his features more distinctly in her memory.

"I am so unhappy," she went on, not heeding him. "I have thought of nothing but you all the time; I live only in the thought of you. And I wanted to forget, to forget you; but why, oh why, have you come?"

On the landing above them two schoolboys were smoking and looking down, but that was nothing to Gurov; he drew Anna Sergeyevna to him, and began kissing her face, her cheeks, and her hands.

"What are you doing, what are you doing!" she cried in horror, pushing him away. "We are mad. Go away to-day; go away at once ... I beseech you by all that is sacred, I implore you ... There are people coming this way!"

Someone was coming up the stairs.

"You must go away," Anna Sergeyevna went on in a whisper. "Do you hear, Dmitri Dmitritch? I will come and see you in Moscow. I have never been happy; I am miserable now, and I never, never shall be happy, never! Don't make me suffer still more! I swear I'll come to Moscow. But now let us part. My precious, good, dear one, we must part!"

She pressed his hand and began rapidly going downstairs, looking round at him, and from her eyes he could see that she really was unhappy. Gurov stood for a little while, listened, then, when all sound had died away, he found his coat and left the theatre.

4

And Anna Sergeyevna began coming to see him in Moscow. Once in two or three months she left S——, telling her husband that she was going to consult a doctor about an internal complaint—and her husband believed her, and did not believe her. In Moscow she stayed at the Slaviansky Bazaar hotel, and at once sent a man in a red cap to Gurov. Gurov went to see her, and no one in Moscow knew of it.

Once he was going to see her in this way on a winter morning (the messenger had come the evening before when he was out). With him walked his daughter, whom he wanted to take to school: it was on the way. Snow was falling in big wet flakes.

"It's three degrees above freezing-point, and yet

it is snowing," said Gurov to his daughter. "The thaw is only on the surface of the earth; there is quite a different temperature at a greater height in the atmosphere."

"And why are there no thunderstorms in the winter, father?"

He explained that, too. He talked, thinking all the while that he was going to see *her*, and no living soul knew of it, and probably never would know. He had two lives: one, open, seen and known by all who cared to know, full of relative truth and of relative falsehood, exactly like the lives of his friends and acquaintances; and another life running its course in secret. And through some strange, perhaps accidental, conjunction of circumstances, everything that was essential, of interest and of value to him, everything in which he was sincere and did not deceive himself, everything that made the kernel of his life, was hidden from other people; and all that was false in him, the sheath in which he hid himself to conceal the truth—such, for instance, as his work in the bank, his discussions at the club, his "lower race," his presence with his wife at anniversary festivities— all that was open. And he judged of others by himself, not believing in what he saw, and always believing that every man had his real, most interesting life under the cover of secrecy and under the cover of night. All personal life rested on secrecy, and possibly it was partly on that account that civilized man was so nervously anxious that personal privacy should be respected.

After leaving his daughter at school, Gurov went on to the Slaviansky Bazaar. He took off his fur coat below, went upstairs, and softly knocked at the door. Anna Sergeyevna, wearing his favourite grey dress, exhausted by the journey and the suspense, had been expecting him since the evening before. She was pale; she looked at him, and did not smile, and he had hardly come in when she fell on his breast. Their kiss was slow and prolonged, as though they had not met for two years.

"Well, how are you getting on there?" he asked. "What news?"

"Wait; I'll tell you directly . . . I can't talk."

She could not speak; she was crying. She turned away from him, and pressed her handkerchief to her eyes.

"Let her have her cry out. I'll sit down and wait," he thought, and he sat down in an arm-chair.

Then he rang and asked for tea to be brought him, and while he drank his tea she remained standing at the window with her back to him. She was crying from emotion, from the miserable consciousness that their life was so hard for them; they could only meet in secret, hiding themselves from people, like thieves! Was not their life shattered?

"Come, do stop!" he said.

It was evident to him that this love of theirs would not soon be over, that he could not see the end of it. Anna Sergeyevna grew more and more attached to him. She adored him, and it was unthinkable to say to her that it was bound to have an end some day; besides, she would not have believed it!

He went up to her and took her by the shoulders to say something affectionate and cheering, and at that moment he saw himself in the looking-glass.

His hair was already beginning to turn grey. And it seemed strange to him that he had grown so much older, so much plainer during the last few years. The shoulders on which his hands rested were warm and quivering. He felt compassion for this life, still so warm and lovely, but probably already not far from beginning to fade and wither like his own. Why did she love him so much? He always seemed to women different from what he was, and they loved in him not himself, but the man created by their imagination, whom they had been eagerly seeking all their lives; and afterwards, when they noticed their mistake, they loved him all the same. And not one of them had been happy with him. Time passed, he had made their acquaintance, got on with them, parted, but he had never once loved; it was anything you like, but not love.

And only now when his head was grey he had fallen properly, really in love—for the first time in his life.

Anna Sergeyevna and he loved each other like people very close and akin, like husband and wife, like tender friends; it seemed to them that fate itself had meant them for one another, and they could not understand why he had a wife and she a husband; and it was as though they were a pair of birds of passage, caught and forced to live in different cages. They forgave each other for what they were ashamed of in their past, they forgave everything in the present, and felt that this love of theirs had changed them both.

In moments of depression in the past he had comforted himself with any arguments that came into his mind, but now he no longer cared for arguments; he felt profound compassion, he wanted to be sincere and tender . . .

"Don't cry, my darling," he said. "You've had your cry; that's enough . . . Let us talk now, let us think of some plan."

Then they spent a long while taking counsel together, talked of how to avoid the necessity for secrecy, for deception, for living in different towns and not seeing each other for long at a time. How could they be free from this intolerable bondage?

"How? How?" he asked, clutching his head. "How?"

And it seemed as though in a little while the solution would be found, and then a new and splendid life would begin; and it was clear to both of them that they had still a long, long way to go, and that the most complicated and difficult part of it was only just beginning.

1899

Flesh

Phyl was always one of the first to come into the hotel bar in the evenings, for what she called her *aperitif*, and which, in reality, amounted to two hours' steady drinking. After that, she had little appetite for dinner, a meal to which she was not used.

On this evening, she had put on one of her beaded tops, of the kind she wore behind the bar on Saturday evenings in London, and patted back her tortoiseshell hair. She was massive and glittering and sunburned – a wonderful sight, Stanley Archard thought, as she came across the bar towards him.

He had been sitting waiting for her. They had found their own level in one another on about the third day of the holiday. Both being heavy drinkers drew them together. Before that had happened, they had looked one another over warily as, in fact, they had all their fellow-guests.

Travelling on their own, speculating, both had watched and wondered. Even at the airport, she had stood out from the others, he remembered, as she had paced up and down in her emerald-green coat. Then their flight number had been called, and they had gathered with others at the same channel, with the same pink labels tied to their hand luggage, all going to the same place; a polite, but distant little band of people, no one knowing with whom friendships were to be made – as like would no doubt drift to like. In the days that followed, Stanley had wished he had taken more notice of Phyl from the beginning, so that at the end of the holiday he would have that much more to remember. Only the emerald-green coat had stayed in his mind. She had not worn it since – it was too warm – and he dreaded the day when she would put it on again to make the return journey.

Arriving in the bar this evening, she hoisted herself up on a stool beside him. 'Well, here we are,' she said, glowing, taking one peanut; adding, as she nibbled, 'Evening, George,' to the barman. 'How's tricks?'

'My God, you've caught it today,' Stanley said, and he put his hands up near her plump red shoulders as if to warm them at a fire. 'Don't overdo it,' he warned her.

'Oh, I never peel,' she said airily.

He always put in a word against the sunbathing when he could. It separated them. She stayed all day by the hotel swimming-pool, basting herself with oil. He, bored with basking – which made him feel dizzy – had hired a car and spent his time driving about the island, and was full of alienating information about the locality, which the other guests – resenting the hired car, too – did their best to avoid. Only Phyl did not mind listening to him. For nearly every evening of her married life she had stood behind the bar and listened to other people's boring chat: she had a technique for dealing with it and a fund of vague phrases. 'Go on!' she said now, listening – hardly listening – to Stanley, and taking another nut. He had gone off by himself and found a place for lunch: *hors d'œuvre*, nice-sized slice of veal, two veg, *crème caramel*, half bottle of rosé, coffee – twenty-two shillings the lot. 'Well, I'm blowed,' said Phyl, and she took a pound note from her handbag and waved it at the barman. When she snapped up the clasp of the bag it had a heavy, expensive sound.

One or two other guests came in and sat at the bar. At this stage of the holiday they were forming into little groups, and this was the jokey set who had come first after Stanley and Phyl. According to them all sorts of funny things had happened during the day, and little screams of laughter ran round the bar.

'Shows how wrong you can be,' Phyl said in a low voice. 'I thought they were ever so starchy on the plane. I was wrong about you, too. At the start, I thought you were ... you know ... one of *those*. Going about with that young boy all the time.'

Stanley patted her knee. 'On the contrary,' he said, with a meaning glance at her. 'No, I was just at a bit of a loose end, and he seemed to cotton-on. Never been abroad before, he hadn't, and didn't know the routine. I liked it for the first day or two. It was like taking a nice kiddie out on a treat. Then it seemed to me he was sponging. I'm not mean, I don't think; but I don't like that – sponging. It was quite a relief when he suddenly took up with the Lisper.'

By now, he and Phyl had nicknames for most of the other people in the hotel. They did not know that the same applied to them, and that to the jokey set he was known as Paws and she as the Shape. It would have put them out and perhaps ruined their holiday if they had known. He thought his little knee-pattings were of the utmost discretion, and she felt confidence from knowing her figure was expensively controlled under her beaded dresses when she became herself again in the evenings. During the day, while sun-bathing, she considered that anything went – that, as her mind was a blank, her body became one also.

The funny man of the party – the awaited climax – came into the bar, crabwise, face covered slyly with his hand, as if ashamed of some earlier misdemeanour. 'Oh, my God, don't look round. Here comes trouble!' someone said loudly, and George was called for from all sides. 'What's the poison, Harry? No, my shout, old boy. George, if you *please*.'

Phyl smiled indulgently. It was just like Saturday night with the regulars at home. She watched George with a professional eye, and nodded approvingly. He was good. They could have used him at the Nelson. A good quick boy.

'Heard from your old man?' Stanley asked her.

She cast him a tragic, calculating look. 'You must be joking. He can't write. No, honest, I've never had a letter from him in the whole of my life. Well, we always saw each other every day until I had my hysterectomy.'

Until now, in conversations with Stanley, she had always referred to 'a little operation'. But he had guessed what it was – well, it always was, wasn't it? – and knew that it was the reason for her being on holiday. Charlie, her husband, had sent her off to recuperate. She had sworn there was no need, that she had never felt so well in her life – was only a bit weepy sometimes late on a Saturday night. 'I'm not really the crying sort,' she had explained to Stanley. 'So he got worried, and sent me packing.'

'You clear off to the sun,' he had said, 'and see what that will do.'

What the sun had done for her was to burn her brick-red, and offer her this nice holiday friend. Stanley Archard, retired widower from Hove.

She enjoyed herself, as she usually did. The sun shone every day, and the drinks were so reasonable – they had many a long discussion about that. They also talked about his little flat in Hove; his strolls along the front; his few cronies at the Club; his sad, orderly and lonely life.

This evening, he wished he had not brought up the subject of Charlie's writing to her, for it seemed to have fixed her thoughts on him and, as she went chatting on about him, Stanley felt an indefinable distaste, an aloofness.

She brought out from her note-case a much-creased cutting from the *Morning Advertiser*. 'Phyl and Charlie Parsons welcome old friends and new at the Nelson, Southwood. In licensed hours only!' 'That was when we changed Houses,' she explained. There was a photograph of them both standing behind the bar. He was wearing a dark blazer with a large badge on the pocket. Sequins gave off a smudged sparkle from her breast, her hair was newly, elaborately done, and her large, ringed hand rested on an ornamental beer-handle. Charlie had his hands in the blazer pockets, as if he were there to do the welcoming, and his wife to do the work: and this, in fact, was how things were. Stanley guessed it, and felt a twist of annoyance in his chest. He did not like the look of Charlie, or anything he had heard about him – how, for instance, he had seemed like a fish out of water visiting his wife in hospital. 'He used to sit on the edge of the chair and stare at the clock, like a boy in school,' Phyl had said, laughing. Stanley could not bring himself to laugh, too. He had leant forward and taken her knee in his hand and wobbled it sympathetically to and fro.

No, she wasn't the crying sort, he agreed. She had a wonderful buoyancy and gallantry, and she seemed to knock years off his age by just *being* with him, talking to him.

In spite of their growing friendship, they kept to their original, separate tables in the hotel restaurant. It seemed too suddenly decisive and public a move for him to join her now, and he was too shy to carry it off at this stage of the holiday, before such an alarming audience. But after dinner, they would go for a walk along the sea-front, or out in the car for a drink at another hotel.

Always, for the first minute or two in a bar, he seemed to lose her. As if she had forgotten him, she would look about her critically, judging the setup, sternly drawing attention to a sticky ring on the counter where she wanted to rest her elbow, keeping a professional eye on the prices.

When they were what she called 'nicely grinned-up', they liked to drive out to a small headland and park the car, watching the swinging beam from a lighthouse. Then, after the usual knee-pattings and neck-strokings, they would heave and flop about in the confines of the Triumph Herald, trying to make love. Warmed by their drinks, and the still evening and the romantic sound of the sea idly turning over down below them, they became frustrated, both large, solid people, she much corseted and, anyhow, beginning to be painfully sunburned across the shoulders, he with the confounded steering-wheel to contend with.

He would grumble about the car and suggest getting out on to a patch of dry barley grass; but she imagined it full of insects; the chirping of the cicadas was almost deafening.

She also had a few scruples about Charlie, but they were not so insistent as the cicadas. After all, she thought, she had never had a holiday-romance – not even a honeymoon with Charlie – and she felt that life owed her just one.

*

After a time, during the day, her sunburn forced her into the shade, or out in the car with Stanley. Across her shoulders she began to peel, and could not bear – though desiring his caress – him to touch her. Rather glumly, he waited for her flesh to heal, told her 'I told you so'; after all, they had not for ever on this island, had started their second, their last week already.

'I'd like to have a look at the other island,' she said, watching the ferry leaving, as they sat drinking nearby.

'It's not worth just going there for the inside of a day,' he said meaningfully, although it was only a short distance.

Wasn't this, both suddenly wondered, the answer to the too-small car, and the watchful eyes back at the hotel. She had refused to allow him into her room there. 'If anyone saw you going in or out? Why, they know where I live. What's to stop one of them coming into the Nelson any time, and chatting Charlie up?'

'Would you?' he now asked, watching the ferry starting off across the water. He hardly dared to hear her answer.

After a pause, she laughed. 'Why not?' she said, and took his hand. 'We wouldn't really be doing any

39

harm to anyone.' (Meaning Charlie.) 'Because no one could find out, could they?'

'Not over there,' he said, nodding towards the island. 'We can start fresh over there. Different people.'

'They'll notice we're both not at dinner at the hotel.'

'That doesn't prove anything.'

She imagined the unknown island, the warm and starlit night and, somewhere, under some roof or other, a large bed in which they could pursue their daring, more than middle-aged adventure, unconfined in every way.

'As soon as my sunburn's better,' she promised. 'We've got five more days yet, and I'll keep in the shade till then.'

A chambermaid advised yoghourt, and she spread it over her back and shoulders as best she could, and felt its coolness absorbing the heat from her skin.

Damp and cheesy-smelling in the hot night, she lay awake, cross with herself. For the sake of a tan, she was wasting her holiday – just to be a five minutes' wonder in the bar on her return, the deepest brown any of them had had that year. The darker she was, the more *abroad* she would seem to have been, the more prestige she could command. All summer, pallid herself, she had had to admire others.

Childish, really, she decided, lying rigid under the sheet, afraid to move, burning and throbbing. The skin was taut behind her knees, so that she could not stretch her legs; her flesh was on fire.

Five more days, she kept thinking. Meanwhile, even this sheet upon her was unendurable.

On the next evening, to establish the fact that they would not always be in to dinner at the hotel, they complained in the bar about the dullness of the menu, and went elsewhere.

It was a drab little restaurant, but they scarcely noticed their surroundings. They sat opposite one another at a corner table and ate shell-fish briskly, busily – he, from his enjoyment of the food; she, with a wish to be rid of it. They rinsed their fingers, quickly dried them and leant forward and twined them together – their large placid hands, with heavy rings, clasped on the table-cloth. Phyl, glancing aside for a moment, saw a young girl, at the next table with a boy, draw in her cheekbones to suppress laughter then, failing, turn her head to hide it.

'At *our* age,' Phyl said gently, drawing away her hands from his. 'In public, too.'

She could not be defiant; but Stanley said jauntily, 'I'm damned if I care.'

At that moment, their chicken was placed before them, and he sat back, looking at it, waiting for vegetables

As well as the sunburn, the heat seemed to have affected Phyl's stomach. She felt queasy and nervy. It was now their last day but one before they went over to the other island. The yoghourt – or time – had taken the pain from her back and shoulders, though leaving her with a dappled, flaky look, which would hardly bring forth cries of admiration or advance her prestige in the bar when she returned. But, no doubt, she thought, by then England would be too cold for her to go sleeveless. Perhaps the trees would have changed colour. She imagined – already – dark Sunday afternoons, their three o'clock lunch done with, and she and Charlie sitting by the electric log fire in a lovely hot room smelling of oranges and the so-called hearth littered with peel. Charlie – bless him – always dropped off among a confusion of newspapers, worn out with banter and light ale, switched off, too, as he always was with her, knowing that he could relax – be nothing, rather – until seven o'clock, because it was

Sunday. Again, for Phyl, imagining home, a little pang, soon swept aside or, rather, swept aside *from*.

She was in a way relieved that they would have only one night on the little island. That would make it seem more like a chance escapade than an affair, something less serious and deliberate in her mind. Thinking about it during the day-time, she even felt a little apprehensive; but told herself sensibly that there was really nothing to worry about: knowing herself well, she could remind herself that an evening's drinking would blur all the nervous edges.

'I can't get over that less than a fortnight ago I never knew you existed,' she said, as they drove to the afternoon ferry. 'And after this week,' she added, 'I don't suppose I'll ever see you again.'

'I wish you wouldn't talk like that – spoiling things,' he said heavily, and he tried not to think of Hove, and the winter walks along the promenade, and going back to the flat, boiling himself a couple of eggs, perhaps; so desperately lost without Ethel.

He had told Phyl about his wife and their quiet happiness together for many years, and then her long, long illness, during which she seemed to be going away from him gradually; but it was dreadful all the same when she finally did.

'We could meet in London on your day off,' he suggested.

'Well, maybe.' She patted his hand, leaving that disappointment aside for him.

There were only a few people on the ferry. It was the end of summer, and the tourists were dwindling, as the English community was reassembling, after trips 'back home'.

The sea was intensely blue all the way across to the island. They stood by the rail looking down at it, marvelling, and feeling like two people in a film. They thought they saw a dolphin, which added to their delight.

'Ethel and I went to Jersey for our honeymoon,' Stanley said. 'It poured with rain nearly all the time, and Ethel had one of her migraines.'

'I never had a honeymoon,' Phyl said. 'Just the one night at the Regent Palace. In our business, you can't both go away together. This is the first time I've ever been abroad.'

'The places I could take you to,' he said.

They drove the car off the ferry and began to cross the island. It was hot and dusty, hillsides terraced and tilled; green lemons hung on the trees.

'I wouldn't half like to actually *pick* a lemon,' she said.

'You shall,' he said, 'somehow or other.'

'And take it home with me,' she added. She would save it for a while, showing people, then cut it up for gin and tonic in the bar one evening, saying casually, 'I picked this lemon with my own fair hands.'

Stanley had booked their hotel from a restaurant, on the recommendation of a barman. When they found it, he was openly disappointed; but she managed to be gallant and optimistic. It was not by the sea, with a balcony where they might look out at the moonlit waters or rediscover brightness in the morning; but down a dull side street, and opposite a garage.

'We don't *have* to,' Stanley said doubtfully.

'Oh, come on! We might not get in anywhere else. It's only for sleeping in,' she said.

'It *isn't* only for sleeping in,' he reminded her.

An enormous man in white shirt and shorts came out to greet them. 'My name is Radam. Welcome,' he said, with confidence. 'I have a lovely room for you, Mr and Mrs Archard. You will be happy here, I can assure you. My wife will carry up your cases. Do not protest, Mr Archard. She is quite able to. Our staff has slackened off at the end of the season, and I have some trouble with the old ticker, as you say in England. I know England well. I am a Bachelor of Science of England University. Once had digs in Swindon.'

A pregnant woman shot out of the hotel porch and seized their suitcases, and there was a tussle as Stanley wrenched them from her hands. Still serenely boasting, Mr Radam led them upstairs, all of them panting but himself.

The bedroom was large and dusty and over-looked a garage.

'Oh, God, I'm sorry,' Stanley said, when they were left alone. 'It's still not too late, if you could stand a row.'

'No. I think it's rather sweet,' Phyl said, looking round the room. 'And, after all, don't blame your-self. You couldn't know any more than me.'

The furniture was extraordinarily fret-worked, as if to make more crevices for the dust to settle in; the bedside-lamp base was an old gin bottle filled with gravel to weight it down, and when Phyl pulled off the bed cover to feel the bed she collapsed with laughter, for the pillow-cases were embroidered 'Hers' and 'Hers'.

Her laughter eased him, as it always did. For a moment, he thought disloyally of the dead – of how Ethel would have started to be depressed by it all, and he would have hard work jollying her out of her dark mood. At the same time, Phyl was wryly imagining Charlie's wrath, how he would have carried on – for only the best was good enough for him, as he never tired of saying.

'He's quite right – that awful fat man,' she said gaily. 'We shall be very happy here. I dread to think who he keeps "His" and "His" for, don't you?'

'I don't suppose the maid understands English,' he said, but warming only slightly. 'You don't expect to have to read off pillow-cases.'

'I'm sure there *isn't* a maid.'

'The bed is very small,' he said.

'It'll be better than the car.'

He thought, 'She is such a woman as I have never met. She's like a marvellous Tommy in the trenches – keeping everyone's pecker up.' He hated Charlie for his luck.

'I shan't ever be able to tell anybody about "Hers" and "Hers",' Phyl thought regretfully – for she dearly loved to amuse their regulars back home. Given other circumstances, she might have worked up quite a story about it.

A tap on the door, and in came Mr Radam with two cups of tea on a tray. 'I know you English,' he said, rolling his eyes roguishly. 'You can't be happy without your tea.'

As neither of them ever drank it, they emptied the cups down the hand basin when he had gone.

Phyl opened the window and the sour, damp smell of new cement came up to her. All round about, building was going on; there was also the whine of a saw-mill, and a lot of clanking from the garage opposite. She leant farther out, and then came back smiling into the room, and shut the window on the dust and noise. 'He was quite right – that barman. You can see the sea from here. It's down the bottom of the street. Let's go and have a look as soon as we've unpacked.'

On their way out of the hotel, they came upon Mr Radam, who was sitting in a broken old wicker chair, fanning himself with a folded newspaper.

'I shall prepare your dinner myself,' he called after them. 'And shall go now to make soup. I am a specialist of soup.'

They strolled in the last of the sun by the glittering sea, looked at the painted boats, watched a man beating an octopus on a rock. Stanley bought her some lace-edged handkerchiefs, and even gave the lace-maker an extra five shillings, so that Phyl could pick a lemon off one of the trees in her garden. Each bought for the other a picture-postcard of the place, to keep.

'Well, it's been just about the best holiday I ever had,' he said. 'And there I was in half a mind not to come at all.' He had for many years dreaded the holiday season, and only went away because everyone he knew did so.

'I just can't remember when I last had one,' she said. There was not – never would be, he knew – the sound of self-pity in her voice.

This was only a small fishing-village; but on one of the headlands enclosing it and the harbour was a big new hotel, with balconies overlooking the sea, Phyl noted. They picked their way across a rubbly car-park and went in. Here, too, was the damp smell of cement; but there was a brightly lighted empty bar with a small dance floor, and music playing.

'We could easily have got in here,' Stanley said. 'I'd like to wring that bloody barman's neck.'

'He's probably some relation, trying to do his best.'

'I'll best him.'

They seemed to have spent a great deal of their time together hoisting themselves up on bar stools.

'Make them nice ones,' Stanley added, ordering their drinks. 'Perhaps he feels a bit shy and awkward, too,' Phyl thought.

'Not very busy,' he remarked to the barman.

'In one week we close.'

'Looks as if you've hardly opened,' Stanley said, glancing round.

'It's not *his* business to get huffy,' Phyl thought indignantly, when the young man, not replying, shrugged and turned aside to polish some glasses. 'Customer's always right. He should know that. Politics, religion, colour-bar – however they argue together, they're all of them always right, and if you know your job you can joke them out of it and on to something safer.' The times she had done that, making a fool of herself, no doubt, anything for peace and quiet. By the time the elections were over, she was usually worn out.

Stanley had hated her buying him a drink back in the hotel; but she had insisted. 'What all that crowd would think of me!' she had said; but here, although it went much against her nature, she put aside her principles, and let him pay; let him set the pace, too. They became elated, and she was sure it would be all right – even having to go back to the soup-specialist's dinner. They might have avoided that; but too late now.

The barman, perhaps with a contemptuous underlining of their age, shuffled through some records and now put on 'Night and Day'. For them both, it filled the bar with nostalgia.

'Come *on*!' said Stanley. 'I've never danced with you. This always makes me feel . . . I don't know.'

'Oh, I'm a terrible dancer,' she protested. The Licensed Victuallers' Association annual dance was the only one she ever went to, and even there stayed in the bar most of the time. Laughing, however, she let herself be helped down off her stool.

He had once fancied himself a good dancer; but, in later years, got no practice, with Ethel being ill, and then dead. Phyl was surprised how light he was on his feet; he bounced her round, holding her firmly against his stomach, his hand pressed to her back, but gently, because of the sunburn. He had perfect rhythm and expertise, side-stepping, reversing, taking masterly control of her.

'Well, I never!' she cried. 'You're making me quite breathless.'

He rested his cheek against her hair, and closed his eyes, in the old, old way, and seemed to waft her away into a different dimension. It was then that he felt the first twinge, in his left toe. It was doom to him. He kept up the pace, but fell silent. When the record ended, he hoped that she would not want to stay on longer. To return to the hotel and take his gout pills was all he could think about. Some intuition made her refuse another drink. 'We've got to go back to the soup-specialist some time,' she said. 'He might even be a good cook.'

'Surprise, surprise!' Stanley managed to say, walking with pain towards the door.

*

Mr Radam was the most abominable cook. They had – in a large cold room with many tables – thin greasy chicken soup, and after that the chicken that had gone through the soup. Then peaches; he brought the tin and opened it before them, as if it were a precious wine, and no hanky-panky going on. He then stood over them, because he had much to say. 'I was offered a post in Basingstoke. Two thousand pounds a year, and a car and a house thrown in. But what use is that to a man like me? Besides, Basingstoke has a most detestable climate.'

Stanley sat, tight-lipped, trying not to lose his temper; but this man, and the pain, were driving him mad. He did not – dared not – drink any of the wine he had ordered.

'Yes, the Basingstoke employment I regarded as not *on*,' Mr Radam said slangily.

Phyl secretly put out a foot and touched one of Stan's – the wrong one – and then thought he was about to have a heart attack. He screwed up his eyes and tried to breathe steadily, a slice of peach slithering about in his spoon. It was then she realised what was wrong with him.

'Oh, sod the peaches,' she said cheerfully, when Mr Radam had gone off to make coffee, which would be the best they had ever tasted, he had promised. Phyl knew they would not complain about the horrible coffee that was coming. The more monstrous the egoist, she had observed from long practice, the more normal people hope to uphold the fabrication – either for ease, or from a terror of any kind of collapse. She did not know. She was sure, though, as she praised the stringy chicken, hoisting the unlovable man's self-infatuation a notch higher, that she did so because she feared him falling to pieces. Perhaps it was only fair, she decided, that weakness should get preferential treatment. Whether it would continue to do so, with Stanley's present change of mood, she was uncertain.

She tried to explain her thoughts to him when, he leaving his coffee, she having gulped hers down, they went to their bedroom. He nodded. He sat on the side of the bed, and put his face into his hands.

'Don't let's go out again,' she said. 'We can have a drink in here. I love a bedroom gin, and I brought a bottle in my case.' She went busily to the wash-basin, and held up a dusty tooth-glass to the light.

'You have one,' he said.

He was determined to keep unruffled, but every step she took across the uneven floorboards broke momentarily the steady pain into burning splinters.

'I've got gout,' he said sullenly. 'Bloody hell, I've got my gout.'

'I thought so,' she said. She put down the glass very quietly and came to him. 'Where?'

He pointed down.

'Can you manage to get into bed by yourself?'

He nodded.

'Well, then!' She smiled. 'Once you're in, I know what to do.'

He looked up apprehensively, but she went almost on tiptoe out of the door and closed it softly.

He undressed, put on his pyjamas, and hauled himself on to the bed. When she came back, she was carrying two pillows. 'Don't laugh, but they're "His" and "His",' she said. 'Now, this is what I do for Charlie. I make a little pillow house for his foot, and it keeps the bedclothes off. Don't worry, I won't touch.'

'On this one night,' he said.

'You want to drink a lot of water.' She put a glass beside him. '"My husband's got a touch of gout," I told them down there. And I really felt quite married to you when I said it.'

She turned her back to him as she undressed. Her body, set free at last, was creased with red marks, and across her shoulders the bright new skin from peeling had ragged, dirty edges of the old. She stretched her spine, put on a transparent nightgown and began to scratch her arms.

'Come here,' he said, unmoving. 'I'll do that.'

So gently she pulled back the sheet and lay down beside him that he felt they had been happily married for years. The pang was that this was their only married night and his foot burned so that he thought that it would burst. 'And it will be a damn sight worse in the morning,' he thought, knowing the pattern of his affliction. He began with one hand to stroke her itching arm.

Almost as soon as she had put the light off, an ominous sound zigzagged about the room. Switching on again, she said, 'I'll get that devil, if it's the last thing I do. You lie still.'

She got out of bed again and ran round the room, slapping at the walls with her *Reader's Digest*, until at last she caught the mosquito, and Stanley's (as was apparent in the morning) blood squirted out.

After that, once more in the dark, they lay quietly. He endured his pain, and she without disturbing him rubbed her flaking skin.

'So this is our wicked adventure,' he said bitterly to the moonlit ceiling.

'Would you rather be on your own?'

'No, no!' He groped with his hand towards her.

'Well, then . . .'

'How can you forgive me?'

'Let's worry about you, eh? Not me. That sort of

thing doesn't matter much to me nowadays. I only really do it to be matey. I don't know . . . by the time Charlie and I have locked up, washed up, done the till, had a bit of something to eat . . .'

Once, she had been as insatiable as a flame. She lay and remembered the days of her youth; but with interest, not wistfully.

Only once did she wake. It was the best night's sleep she'd had for a week. Moonlight now fell over the bed, and on one chalky white-washed wall. The sheet draped over them rose in a peak above his feet, so that he looked like a figure on a tomb. 'If Charlie could see me now,' she suddenly thought. She tried not to have a fit of giggles for fear of shaking the bed. Stanley shifted, groaned in his sleep, then went on snoring, just as Charlie did.

He woke often during that night. The sheets were as abrasive as sandpaper. 'I knew this damn bed was too small,' he thought. He shifted warily on to his side to look at Phyl who, in her sleep, made funny little whimpering sounds like a puppy. One arm flung above her head looked, in the moonlight, quite black against the pillow. Like going to bed with a coloured woman, he thought. He dutifully took a sip or two of water and then settled back again to endure his wakefulness.

'Well, I was happy,' she said, wearing her emerald-green coat again, sitting next to him in the plane, fastening her safety-belt.

His face looked worn and grey.

'Don't mind me asking,' she went on, 'but did he charge for that tea we didn't order?'

'Five shillings.'

'I *knew* it. I wish you'd let me pay my share of everything. After all, it was me as well wanted to go.'

He shook his head, smiling at her. In spite of his prediction, he felt better this departure afternoon, though tired and wary about himself.

'If only we were taking off on holiday now,' he said, 'not coming back. Why can't we meet up in Torquay or somewhere? Something for me to look forward to,' he begged her, dabbing his mosquito-bitten forehead with his handkerchief.

'It was only my hysterectomy got me away this time,' she said.

They ate, they drank, they held hands under a newspaper, and presently crossed the twilit coast of England, where farther along grey Hove was waiting for him. The trees had not changed colour much and only some – she noticed, as she looked down on them, coming in to land – were yellower.

She knew that it was worse for him. He had to return to his empty flat; she, to a full bar, and on a Saturday, too. She wished there was something she could do to send him off cheerful.

'To me,' she said, having refastened her safety-belt, taking his hand again. 'To me, it was lovely. To me it was just as good as if we had.'

F. Scott Fitzgerald

The Lees of Happiness

1

If you should look through the files of old magazines
for the first years of the present century you would
find, sandwiched in between the stories of Richard
Harding Davis and Frank Norris and others long
since dead, the work of one Jeffrey Curtain: a novel
or two, and perhaps three or four dozen short stories. You could, if you were interested, follow them
along until, say, 1908, when they suddenly
disappeared.

When you had read them all you would have
been quite sure that here were no masterpieces –
here were passably amusing stories, a bit out of
date now, but doubtless the sort that would then
have whiled away a dreary half-hour in a dental
office. The man who did them was of good intelli-
gence, talented, glib, probably young. In the samples
of his work you found there would have been nothing to stir you to more than a faint interest in the
whims of life – no deep interior laughs, no sense of
futility or hint of tragedy.

After reading them you would yawn and put the
number back in the files, and perhaps, if you were in

some library reading-room, you would decide that by way of variety you would look at a newspaper of the period and see whether the Japs had taken Port Arthur. But if by any chance the newspaper you had chosen was the right one and had crackled open at the theatrical page, your eyes would have been arrested and held, and for at least a minute you would have forgotten Port Arthur as quickly as you forgot Château Thierry. For you would, by this fortunate chance, be looking at the portrait of an exquisite woman.

Those were the days of 'Florodora' and of sextets, of pinched-in waists and blown-out sleeves, of almost bustles and absolute ballet skirts, but here, without doubt, disguised as she might be by the unaccustomed stiffness and old fashion of her costume, was a butterfly of butterflies. Here was the gaiety of the period – the soft wine of eyes, the songs that flurried hearts, the toasts and the bouquets, the dances and the dinners. Here was a Venus of the hansom cab, the Gibson girl in her glorious prime. Here was . . .

. . . here was, you find by looking at the name beneath, one Roxanne Milbank, who had been chorus girl and understudy in *The Daisy Chain*, but who, by reason of an excellent performance when the star was indisposed, had gained a leading part.

You would look again – and wonder. Why you had never heard of her. Why did her name not linger in popular songs and vaudeville jokes and cigar bands, and the memory of that gay old uncle of yours along with Lillian Russell and Stella Mayhew and Anna Held? Roxanne Milbank – whither had she gone? What dark trapdoor had opened suddenly and swallowed her up? Her name was certainly not in last Sunday's supplement on the list of actresses married to English noblemen. No doubt she was dead – poor beautiful young lady – and quite forgotten.

I am hoping too much. I am having you stumble on Jeffrey Curtains's stories and Roxanne Milbank's picture. It would be incredible that you should find a newspaper item six months later, a single item two inches by four, which informed the public of the marriage, very quietly, of Miss Roxanne Milbank, who had been on tour with *The Daisy Chain*, to Mr Jeffrey Curtain, the popular author. 'Mrs Curtain,' it added dispassionately, 'will retire from the stage.'

It was a marriage of love. He was sufficiently spoiled to be charming; she was ingenuous enough to be irresistible. Like two floating logs they met in a head-on rush, caught, and sped along together. Yet had Jeffrey Curtain kept at scrivening for two-score years he could not have put a quirk into one of his

61

stories weirder than the quirk that came into his own life. Had Roxanne Milbank played three dozen parts and filled five thousand houses she could never have had a role with more happiness and more despair than were in the fate prepared for Roxanne Curtain.

For a year they lived in hotels, travelled to California, to Alaska, to Florida, to Mexico, loved and quarrelled gently, and gloried in the golden triflings of his wit with her beauty – they were young and gravely passionate; they demanded everything and then yielded everything again in ecstasies of unselfishness and pride. She loved the swift tones of his voice and his frantic, if unfounded jealousy. He loved her dark radiance, the white irises of her eyes, the warm, lustrous enthusiasm of her smile.

'Don't you like her?' he would demand rather excitedly and shyly. 'Isn't she wonderful? Did you ever see –'

'Yes,' they would answer, grinning. 'She's a wonder. You're lucky.'

The year passed. They tired of hotels. They bought an old house and twenty acres near the town of Marlowe, half an hour from Chicago; bought a little car, and moved out riotously with a pioneering hallucination that would have confounded Balboa.

'Your room will be here!' they cried in turn.

– And then: 'And my room here!'

'And the nursery here when we have children.'

'And we'll build a sleeping porch – oh, next year.'

They moved out in April. In July Jeffrey's closest friend, Harry Cromwell, came to spend a week – they met him at the end of the long lawn and hurried him proudly to the house.

Harry was married also. His wife had had a baby some six months before and was still recuperating at her mother's in New York. Roxanne had gathered from Jeffrey that Harry's wife was not as attractive as Harry – Jeffrey had met her once and considered her – 'shallow'. But Harry had been married nearly two years and was apparently happy, so Jeffrey guessed that she was probably all right.

'I'm making biscuits,' chattered Roxanne gravely. 'Can your wife make biscuits? The cook is showing me how. I think every woman should know how to make biscuits. It sounds so utterly disarming. A woman who can make biscuits can surely do no –'

'You'll have to come out here and live,' said Jeffrey. 'Get a place out in the country like us, for you and Kitty.'

'You don't know Kitty. She hates the country. She's got to have her theatres and vaudevilles.'

'Bring her out,' repeated Jeffrey. 'We'll have a

colony. There's an awfully nice crowd here already. Bring her out!'

They were at the porch steps now and Roxanne made a brisk gesture towards a dilapidated structure on the right.

'The garage,' she announced. 'It will also be Jeffrey's writing-room within the month. Meanwhile dinner is at seven. Meanwhile to that I will mix a cocktail.'

The two men ascended to the second floor – that is, they ascended halfway, for at the first landing Jeffrey dropped his guest's suitcase and in a cross between a query and a cry exclaimed: 'For God's sake, Harry, how do you like her?'

'We will go upstairs,' answered his guest, 'and we will shut the door.'

Half an hour later as they were sitting together in the library Roxanne reissued from the kitchen, bearing before her a pan of biscuits. Jeffrey and Harry rose.

'They're beautiful, dear,' said the husband, intensely.

'Exquisite,' murmured Harry.

Roxanne beamed.

'Taste one. I couldn't bear to touch them before you'd seen them all and I can't bear to take them back until I find what they taste like.'

'Like manna, darling.'

Simultaneously the two men raised the biscuits to their lips, nibbled tentatively. Simultaneously they tried to change the subject. But Roxanne, undeceived, set down the pan and seized a biscuit. After a second her comment rang out with lugubrious finality: 'Absolutely bum!'

'Really –'

'Why, I didn't notice –'

Roxanne roared.

'Oh, I'm useless,' she cried laughing. 'Turn me out, Jeffrey – I'm a parasite; I'm no good –'

Jeffrey put his arm around her.

'Darling, I'll eat your biscuits.'

'They're beautiful, anyway,' insisted Roxanne.

'They're – they're decorative,' suggested Harry.

Jeffrey took him up wildly. 'That's the word. They're decorative; they're masterpieces. We'll use them.'

He rushed to the kitchen and returned with a hammer and a handful of nails.

'We'll use them, by golly, Roxanne! We'll make a frieze out of them.'

'Don't!' wailed Roxanne. 'Our beautiful house.'

'Never mind. We're going to have the library repapered in October. Don't you remember?'

'Well –'

Bang! The first biscuit was impaled to the wall, where it quivered for a moment like a live thing.

Bang! . . .

When Roxanne returned with a second round of cocktails the biscuits were in a perpendicular row, twelve of them, like a collection of primitive spearheads.

'Roxanne,' exclaimed Jeffrey, 'you're an artist! Cook? – nonsense! You shall illustrate my books!'

During dinner the twilight faltered into dusk, and later it was a starry dark outside, filled and permeated with the frail gorgeousness of Roxanne's white dress and her tremulous, low laugh.

– Such a little girl she is, thought Harry. Not as old as Kitty.

He compared the two. Kitty – nervous without being sensitive, temperamental without temperament, a woman who seemed to flit and never light – and Roxanne, who was as young as spring night, and summed up in her own adolescent laughter.

– A good match for Jeffrey, he thought again. Two very young people, the sort who'll stay very young until they suddenly find themselves old.

Harry thought these things between his constant thoughts about Kitty. He was depressed about Kitty. It seemed to him that she was well enough to come back to Chicago and bring his little son. He was thinking vaguely of Kitty when he said good-night to his friend's wife and his friend at the foot of the stairs.

'You're our first real house guest,' called Roxanne after him. 'Aren't you thrilled and proud?'

When he was out of sight around the stair corner she turned to Jeffrey, who was standing beside her resting his hand on the end of the bannister.

'Are you tired, my dearest?'

Jeffrey rubbed the centre of his forehead with his fingers.

'A little. How did you know?'

'Oh, how could I help knowing about you?'

'It's a headache,' he said moodily. 'Splitting. I'll take some aspirin.'

She reached over and snapped out the light, and with his arm tight about her waist they walked up the stairs together.

2

Harry's week passed. They drove about the dreaming lanes or idled in cheerful inanity upon lake or lawn. In the evening Roxanne, sitting inside, played to them while the ashes whitened on the glowing ends of their cigars. Then came a telegram from Kitty saying that she wanted Harry to come East and get her, so Roxanne and Jeffrey were left alone in that privacy of which they never seemed to tire.

'Alone' thrilled them again. They wandered about the house, each feeling intimately the presence of the other; they sat on the same side of the table like honeymooners; they were intensely absorbed, intensely happy.

The town of Marlowe, though a comparatively old settlement, had only recently acquired a 'society'. Five or six years before, alarmed at the smoky swelling of Chicago, two or three young married couples, 'bungalow people', had moved out; their friends had followed. The Jeffrey Curtains found an already formed 'set' prepared to welcome them; a country club, ballroom and golf links yawned for them, and there were bridge parties, and poker parties, and parties where they drank beer, and parties where they drank nothing at all.

It was at a poker party that they found themselves a week after Harry's departure. There were two tables, and a good proportion of the young wives were smoking and shouting their bets, and being very daringly mannish for those days.

Roxanne had left the game early and taken to perambulation; she wandered into the pantry and found herself some grape juice – beer gave her a headache – and then passed from table to table, looking over shoulders at the hands, keeping an eye on Jeffrey and being pleasantly unexcited and content. Jeffrey, with intense concentration, was raising a pile of chips of all colours, and Roxanne knew by the deepened wrinkle between his eyes that he was interested. She liked to see him interested in small things.

She crossed over quietly and sat down on the arm of his chair.

She sat there five minutes, listening to the sharp intermittent comments of the men and the chatter of the women, which rose from the table like soft smoke – and yet scarcely hearing either. Then quite innocently she reached out her hand, intending to place it on Jeffrey's shoulder – as it touched him he started of a sudden, gave a short grunt, and, sweeping back his arm furiously, caught her a glancing blow on her elbow.

There was a general gasp. Roxanne regained her balance, gave a little cry, and rose quickly to her feet. It had been the greatest shock of her life. This, from Jeffrey, the heart of kindness, of consideration – this instinctively brutal gesture.

The gasp became a silence. A dozen eyes were turned on Jeffrey, who looked up as though seeing Roxanne the first time. An expression of bewilderment settled on his face.

'Why – Roxanne –' he said haltingly.

Into a dozen minds entered a quick suspicion, a rumour of scandal. Could it be that behind the scenes with this couple, apparently so in love, lurked some curious antipathy? Why else this streak of fire, across such a cloudless heaven?

'Jeffrey!' – Roxanne's voice was pleading – startled and horrified, she yet knew that it was a mistake. Not once did it occur to her to blame him or to resent it. Her word was a trembling supplication – 'Tell me, Jeffrey,' it said, 'tell Roxanne, your own Roxanne.'

'Why, Roxanne –' began Jeffrey again. The bewildered look changed to pain. He was clearly as startled as she. 'I didn't intend that,' he went on; 'you startled me. You – I felt as if someone were attacking me. I – how – why, how idiotic!'

'Jeffrey!' Again the word was a prayer, incense offered up to a high God through this new and unfathomable darkness.

They were both on their feet, they were saying goodbye, faltering, apologising, explaining. There was no attempt to pass it off easily. That way lay sacrilege. Jeffrey had not been feeling well, they said. He had become nervous. Back of both their minds was the unexplained horror of that blow – the marvel that there had been for an instant something between them – his anger and her fear – and now to both a sorrow, momentary, no doubt, but to be bridged at once, at once, while there was yet time. Was that swift water lashing under their feet – the fierce glint of some uncharted chasm?

Out in their car under the harvest moon he talked brokenly. It was just – incomprehensible to him, he said. He had been thinking of the poker game – absorbed – and the touch on his shoulder had seemed like an attack. An attack! He clung to that word, flung it up as a shield. He had hated what touched him. With the impact of his hand it had gone, that – nervousness. That was all he knew.

Both their eyes filled with tears and they whispered love there under the broad night as the serene streets of Marlowe sped by. Later, when they went to bed, they were quite calm. Jeffrey was to take a week off all work – was simply to loll, and sleep, and go on long walks until this nervousness left him. When they had decided this safety settled down upon Roxanne. The pillows underhead became soft and friendly; the bed on which they lay seemed wide, and white, and sturdy beneath the radiance that streamed in at the window.

Five days later, in the first cool of late afternoon, Jeffrey picked up an oak chair and sent it crashing through his own front window. Then he lay down on the couch like a child, weeping piteously and begging to die. A blood clot the size of a marble had broken in his brain.

3

There is a sort of waking nightmare that sets in sometimes when one has missed a sleep or two, a feeling that comes with extreme fatigue and a new sun that the quality of the life around has changed. It is a fully articulate conviction that somehow the existence one is then leading is a branch shoot of life and is related to life only as a moving picture or a mirror – that the people, and streets, and houses are only projections from a very dim and chaotic past. It was in such a state that Roxanne found herself during the first months of Jeffrey's illness. She slept only when she was utterly exhausted; she awoke under a cloud. The long, sober-voiced consultations, the faint aura of medicine in the halls, the sudden tiptoeing in a house that had echoed to many cheerful footsteps, and most of all Jeffrey's white face amid the pillows of the bed they had shared – these things subdued her and made her indelibly older. The doctors held out hope, but that was all. A long rest, they said, and quiet. So responsibility came to Roxanne. It was she who paid the bills, pored over his bank book, corresponded with his publishers.

She was in the kitchen constantly. She learned from the nurse how to prepare his meals and after the first month took complete charge of the sickroom. She had had to let the nurse go for reasons of economy. One of the two coloured girls left at the same time. Roxanne was realising that they had been living from short story to short story.

The most frequent visitor was Harry Cromwell. He had been shocked and depressed by the news, and though his wife was now living with him in Chicago he found time to come out several times a month. Roxanne found his sympathy welcome – there was some quality of suffering in the man, some inherent pitifulness that made her comfortable when he was near. Roxanne's nature had suddenly deepened. She felt sometimes that with Jeffrey she was losing her children also, those children that now most of all she needed and should have had.

It was six months after Jeffrey's collapse and when the nightmare had faded, leaving not the old world but a new one, greyer and colder, that she went to see Harry's wife. Finding herself in Chicago with an extra hour before train time, she decided out of courtesy to call.

As she stepped inside the door she had an immediate impression that the apartment was very like some place she had seen before – and almost instantly she remembered a round-the-corner bakery of her childhood, a bakery full of rows and rows of pink frosted cakes – a stuffy pink, pink as a food, pink triumphant, vulgar and odious.

And this apartment was like that. It was pink. It smelled pink!

Mrs Cromwell, attired in a wrapper of pink and black, opened the door. Her hair was yellow, heightened, Roxanne imagined, by a dash of peroxide in the rinsing water every week. Her eyes were a thin waxen blue – she was pretty and too consciously graceful. Her cordiality was strident and intimate, hostility melted so quickly to hospitality that it seemed they were both merely in the face and voice – never touching nor touched by the deep core of egotism beneath.

But to Roxanne these things were secondary; her eyes were caught and held in uncanny fascination by the wrapper. It was vilely unclean. From its lowest hem up four inches it was sheerly dirty with the blue dust of the floor; for the next three inches it was grey, then it shaded off into its natural colour, which was – pink. It was dirty at the sleeves, too, and at the collar, and when the woman turned to lead the way into the parlour, Roxanne was sure that her neck was dirty.

A one-sided rattle of conversation began. Mrs

Cromwell became explicit about her likes and dislikes, her head, her stomach, her teeth, her apartment – avoiding with a sort of insolent meticulousness any inclusion of Roxanne with life, as if presuming that Roxanne, having been dealt a blow, wished life to be carefully skirted.

Roxanne smiled. That kimono! That neck!

After five minutes a little boy toddled into the parlour – a dirty little boy clad in dirty pink rompers. His face was smudgy – Roxanne wanted to take him into her lap and wipe his nose; other parts in the vicinity of his head needed attention; his tiny shoes were kicked out at the toes. Unspeakable!

'What a darling little boy!' exclaimed Roxanne, smiling radiantly. 'Come here to me.'

Mrs Cromwell looked coldly at her son.

'He will get dirty. Look at that face!' She held her head on one side and regarded it critically.

'Isn't he a *darling*?' repeated Roxanne.

'Look at his rompers,' frowned Mrs Cromwell. 'He needs a change, don't you, George?'

George stared at her curiously. To his mind the word rompers connotated a garment extraneously smeared, as this one.

'I tried to make him look respectable this morning,' complained Mrs Cromwell as one whose patience had been sorely tried, 'and I found he didn't have any more rompers – so rather than have him go round without any I put him back in those – and his face –'

'How many pairs has he?' Roxanne's voice was pleasantly curious, 'How many feather fans have you?' she might have asked.

'Oh –' Mrs Cromwell considered, wrinkling her pretty brow. 'Five, I think. Plenty, I know.'

'You can get them for fifty cents a pair.'

Mrs Cromwell's eyes showed surprise – and the faintest superiority. The price of rompers!

'Can you really? I had no idea. He ought to have plenty, but I haven't had a minute all week to send the laundry out.' Then, dismissing the subject as irrelevant – 'I must show you some things –'

They rose and Roxanne followed her past an open bathroom door whose garment-littered floor showed indeed that the laundry hadn't been sent out for some time, into another room that was, so to speak, the quintessence of pinkness. This was Mrs Cromwell's room.

Here the hostess opened a closet door and displayed before Roxanne's eyes an amazing collection of lingerie.

There were dozens of filmy marvels of lace and silk, all clean, unruffled, seemingly not yet touched.

On hangers beside them were three new evening dresses.

'I have some beautiful things,' said Mrs Cromwell, 'but not much of a chance to wear them. Harry doesn't care about going out.' Spite crept into her voice. 'He's perfectly content to let me play nursemaid and housekeeper all day and loving wife in the evening.'

Roxanne smiled again.

'You've got some beautiful clothes here.'

'Yes, I have. Let me show you –'

'Beautiful,' repeated Roxanne, interrupting, 'but I'll have to run if I'm going to catch my train.'

She felt that her hands were trembling. She wanted to put them on this woman and shake her – shake her. She wanted her locked up somewhere and set to scrubbing floors.

'Beautiful,' she repeated, 'and I just came in for a moment.'

'Well, I'm sorry Harry isn't here.'

They moved towards the door.

'– and, oh,' said Roxanne with an effort – yet her voice was still gentle and her lips were smiling – 'I think it's Argile's where you can get those rompers. Goodbye.'

It was not until she had reached the station and

bought her ticket to Marlowe that Roxanne realised it was the first five minutes in six months that her mind had been off Jeffrey.

4

A week later Harry appeared at Marlowe, arrived unexpectedly at five o'clock, and coming up the walk sank into a porch chair in a state of exhaustion. Roxanne herself had had a busy day and was worn out. The doctors were coming at five-thirty, bringing a celebrated nerve specialist from New York. She was excited and thoroughly depressed, but Harry's eyes made her sit down beside him.

'What's the matter?'

'Nothing, Roxanne,' he denied. 'I came to see how Jeff was doing. Don't you bother about me.'

'Harry,' insisted Roxanne, 'there's something the matter.'

'Nothing,' he repeated. 'How's Jeff?'

Anxiety darkened her face.

'He's a little worse, Harry. Dr Jewett has come on from New York. They thought he could tell me something definite. He's going to try and find whether this paralysis has anything to do with the original blood clot.'

Harry rose.

'Oh, I'm sorry,' he said jerkily. 'I didn't know you

expected a consultation. I wouldn't have come. I thought I'd just rock on your porch for an hour –'

'Sit down,' she commanded.

Harry hesitated.

'Sit down, Harry, dear boy.' Her kindness flooded out now – enveloped him. 'I know there's something the matter. You're white as a sheet. I'm going to get you a cool bottle of beer.'

All at once he collapsed into his chair and covered his face with his hands.

'I can't make her happy,' he said slowly. 'I've tried and I've tried. This morning we had some words about breakfast – I'd been getting my breakfast down town – and – well, just after I went to the office she left the house, went East to her mother's with George and a suitcase full of lace underwear.'

'Harry!'

'And I don't know –'

There was a crunch on the gravel, a car turning into the drive. Roxanne uttered a little cry.

'It's Dr Jewett.'

'Oh, I'll –'

'You'll wait, won't you?' she interrupted abstractedly. He saw that his problem had already died on the troubled surface of her mind.

There was an embarrassing minute of vague, elided introductions and then Harry followed the party inside and watched them disappear up the stairs. He went into the library and sat down on the big sofa.

For an hour he watched the sun creep up the patterned folds of the chintz curtains. In the deep quiet a trapped wasp buzzing on the inside of the window pane assumed the proportions of a clamour. From time to time another buzzing drifted down from upstairs, resembling several more larger wasps caught on larger windowpanes. He heard low footfalls, the clink of bottles, the clamour of pouring water.

What had he and Roxanne done that life should deal these crashing blows to them? Upstairs there was taking place a living inquest on the soul of his friend; he was sitting here in a quiet room listening to the plaint of a wasp, just as when he was a boy he had been compelled by a strict aunt to sit hour-long on a chair and atone for some misbehaviour. But who had put him here? What ferocious aunt had leaned out of the sky to make him atone for – what?

About Kitty he felt a great hopelessness. She was too expensive – that was the irremediable difficulty. Suddenly he hated her. He wanted to throw her down and kick at her – to tell her she was a cheat and a leech – that she was dirty. Moreover, she must give him his boy.

He rose and began pacing up and down the room. Simultaneously he heard someone begin walking along the hallway upstairs in exact time with him. He found himself wondering if they would walk in time until the person reached the end of the hall.

Kitty had gone to her mother. God help her, what a mother to go to! He tried to imagine the meeting: the abused wife collapsing upon the mother's breast. He could not. That Kitty was capable of any deep grief was unbelievable. He had gradually grown to think of her as something unapproachable and callous. She would get a divorce, of course, and eventually she would marry again. He began to consider this. Whom would she marry? He laughed bitterly, stopped; a picture flashed before him – of Kitty's arms around some man whose face he could not see, of Kitty's lips pressed close to other lips in what was surely passion.

'God!' he cried aloud. 'God! God! God!'

Then the pictures came thick and fast. The Kitty of this morning faded; the soiled kimono rolled up and disappeared; the pouts, and rages, and tears all were washed away. Again she was Kitty Carr – Kitty

Carr with yellow hair and great baby eyes. Ah, she had loved him, she had loved him.

After a while he perceived that something was amiss with him, something that had nothing to do with Kitty or Jeff, something of a different genre. Amazingly it burst on him at last; he was hungry. Simple enough! He would go into the kitchen in a moment and ask the coloured cook for a sandwich. After that he must go back to the city.

He paused at the wall, jerked at something round, and fingering it absently, put it to his mouth and tasted it as a baby tastes a bright toy. His teeth closed on it – Ah!

She'd left that damn kimono, that dirty pink kimono. She might have had the decency to take it with her, he thought. It would hang in the house like the corpse of their sick alliance. He would try to throw it away, but he would never be able to bring himself to move it. It would be like Kitty, soft and pliable, withal impervious. You couldn't move Kitty; you couldn't reach Kitty. There was nothing there to reach. He understood that perfectly – he had understood it all along.

He reached to the wall for another biscuit and with an effort pulled it out, nail and all. He carefully removed the nail from the centre, wondering idly if he had eaten the nail with the first biscuit.

Preposterous! He would have remembered – it was a huge nail. He felt his stomach. He must be very hungry. He considered – remembered – yesterday he had had no dinner. It was the girl's day out and Kitty had lain in her room eating chocolate drops. She had said she felt 'smothery' and couldn't bear having him near her. He had given George a bath and put him to bed, and then lain down on the couch intending to rest a minute before getting his own dinner. There he had fallen asleep and awakened about eleven, to find that there was nothing in the ice-box except a spoonful of potato salad. This he had eaten, together with some chocolate drops that he found on Kitty's bureau. This morning he had breakfasted hurriedly downtown before going to the office. But at noon, beginning to worry about Kitty, he had decided to go home and take her out to lunch. After that there had been the note on his pillow. The pile of lingerie in the closet was gone – and she had left instructions for sending her trunk.

He had never been so hungry, he thought.

At five o'clock, when the visiting nurse tiptoed downstairs, he was sitting on the sofa staring at the carpet.

'Mr Cromwell?'

'Yes?'

'Oh, Mrs Curtain won't be able to see you at

dinner. She's not well. She told me to tell you that the cook will fix you something and that there's a spare bedroom.'

'She's sick, you say?'

'She's lying down in her room. The consultation is just over.'

'Did they – did they decide anything?'

'Yes,' said the nurse softly. 'Dr Jewett says there's no hope. Mr Curtain may live indefinitely, but he'll never see again or move again or think. He'll just breathe.'

'Just breathe?'

'Yes.'

For the first time the nurse noted that beside the writing-desk where she remembered that she had seen a line of a dozen curious round objects she had vaguely imagined to be some exotic form of decoration there was now only one. Where the others had been, there was now a series of little nail-holes.

Harry followed her glance dazedly and then rose to his feet.

'I don't believe I'll stay. I believe there's a train.'

She nodded. Harry picked up his hat.

'Goodbye,' she said pleasantly.

'Goodbye,' he answered, as though talking to himself, and, evidently moved by some involuntary necessity, he paused on his way to the door and she saw him pluck the last object from the wall and drop it into his pocket.

Then he opened the screen door and, descending the porch steps, passed out of her sight.

5

After a while the coat of clean white paint on the Jeffrey Curtain house made a definite compromise with the suns of many Julys and showed its good faith by turning grey. It scaled – huge peelings of very brittle old paint leaned over backwards like aged men practising grotesque gymnastics and finally dropped to a mouldy death in the overgrown grass beneath. The paint on the front pillars became streaky; the white ball was knocked off the left-hand doorpost; the green blinds darkened, then lost all pretence of colour.

It began to be a house that was avoided by the tender-minded – some church bought a lot diagonally opposite for a graveyard, and this, combined with 'the place where Mrs Curtain stays with that living corpse', was enough to throw a ghostly aura over that quarter of the road. Not that she was left alone. Men and women came to see her, met her downtown, where she went to do her marketing, brought her home in their cars – and came in for a moment to talk and to rest in the glamour that still played in her smile. But men who did not know her no longer followed her with admiring glances in the street; a diaphanous veil had come down over her beauty, destroying its vividness, yet bringing neither wrinkles nor fat.

She acquired a character in the village – a group of little stories were told of her: how when the country was frozen over one winter so that no wagons nor automobiles could travel, she taught herself to skate so that she could make quick time to the grocer and druggist, and not leave Jeffrey alone for long. It was said that every night since his paralysis she slept in a small bed beside his bed, holding his hand.

Jeffrey Curtain was spoken of as though he were already dead. As the years dropped by those who had known him died or moved away – there were but half a dozen of the old crowd who had drunk cocktails together, called each other's wives by their first names, and thought that Jeff was about the wittiest and most talented fellow that Marlowe had ever known. Now, to the casual visitor, he was merely the reason that Mrs Curtain excused herself sometimes and hurried upstairs; he was a groan or a sharp cry borne to the silent parlour on the heavy air of a Sunday afternoon.

He could not move; he was stone blind, dumb and totally unconscious. All day he lay in his bed, except for a shift to his wheelchair every morning while she straightened the room. His paralysis was creeping slowly towards his heart. At first – for the first year – Roxanne had received the faintest answering pressure sometimes when she held his hand – then it had gone, ceased one evening and never come back, and through two nights Roxanne lay wide-eyed, staring into the dark and wondering what had gone, what fraction of his soul had taken flight, what last grain of comprehension those shattered broken nerves still carried to the brain.

After that hope died. Had it not been for her unceasing care the last spark would have gone long before. Every morning she shaved and bathed him, shifted him with her own hands from bed to chair and back to bed. She was in his room constantly, bearing medicine, straightening a pillow, talking to him almost as one talks to a nearly human dog, without hope of response or appreciation, but with the dim persuasion of habit, a prayer when faith has gone.

Not a few people, one celebrated nerve specialist among them, gave her a plain impression that it was futile to exercise so much care, that if Jeffrey had been conscious he would have wished to die, that if his spirit were hovering in some wider air it would agree to no such sacrifice from her, it would fret only for the prison of its body to give it full release.

'But you see,' she replied, shaking her head gently, 'when I married Jeffrey it was – until I ceased to love him.'

'But,' was protested, in effect, 'you can't love that.'

'I can love what it once was. What else is there for me to do?'

The specialist shrugged his shoulders and went away to say that Mrs Curtain was a remarkable woman and just about as sweet as an angel – but, he added, it was a terrible pity.

'There must be some man, or a dozen, just crazy to take care of her ...'

Casually – there were. Here and there someone began in hope – and ended in reverence. There was no love in the woman except, strangely enough, for life, for the people in the world, from the tramp to whom she gave food she could ill afford to the butcher who sold her a cheap cut of steak across the meaty board. The other phase was sealed up somewhere in that expressionless mummy who lay with his face turned ever towards the light as mechanically as a compass needle and waited dumbly for the last wave to wash over his heart.

After eleven years he died in the middle of a May

night, when the scent of the syringa hung upon the window-sill and a breeze wafted in the shrillings of the frogs and cicadas outside. Roxanne awoke at two, and realised with a start she was alone in the house at last.

6

After that she sat on her weather-beaten porch through many afternoons, gazing down across the fields that undulated in a slow descent to the white and green town. She was wondering what she would do with her life. She was thirty-six – handsome, strong and free. The years had eaten up Jeffrey's insurance; she had reluctantly parted with the acres to right and left of her, and had even placed a small mortgage on the house.

With her husband's death had come a great physical restlessness. She missed having to care for him in the morning, she missed her rush to town, and the brief and therefore accentuated neighbourly meetings in the butcher's and grocer's; she missed the cooking for two, the preparation of delicate liquid food for him. One day, consumed with energy, she went out and spaded up the whole garden, a thing that had not been done for years.

And she was alone at night in the room that had seen the glory of her marriage and then the pain. To meet Jeff again she went back in spirit to that wonderful year, that intense, passionate absorption and companionship, rather than looked forward to a problematical meeting hereafter; she awoke often to lie and wish for that presence beside her – inanimate yet breathing – still Jeff.

One afternoon six months after his death she was sitting on the porch, in a black dress which took away the faintest suggestion of plumpness from her figure. It was Indian summer – golden brown all about her; a hush broken by the sighing of leaves; westward a four o'clock sun dripping streaks of red and yellow over a flaming sky. Most of the birds had gone – only a sparrow that had built itself a nest on the cornice of a pillar kept up an intermittent cheeping varied by occasional fluttering sallies overhead. Roxanne moved her chair to where she could watch him and her mind idled drowsily on the bosom of the afternoon.

Harry Cromwell was coming out from Chicago to dinner. Since his divorce over eight years before he had been a frequent visitor. They had kept up what amounted to a tradition between them: when he arrived they would go to look at Jeff; Harry would sit down on the edge of the bed and in a hearty voice ask: 'Well, Jeff, old man, how do you feel today?'

Roxanne, standing beside, would look intently at

Jeff, dreaming that some shadowy recognition of this former friend had passed across that broken mind – but the head, pale, carven, would only move slowly in its sole gesture towards the light as if something behind the blind eyes were groping for another light long since gone out.

These visits stretched over eight years – at Easter, Christmas, Thanksgiving and on many a Sunday, Harry had arrived, paid his call on Jeff, and then talked for a long while with Roxanne on the porch. He was devoted to her. He made no pretence of hiding, no attempt to deepen, this relation. She was his best friend as the mass of flesh on the bed there had been his best friend. She was peace, she was rest; she was the past. Of his own tragedy she alone knew.

He had been at the funeral, but since then the company for which he worked had shifted him to the East and only a business trip had brought him to the vicinity of Chicago. Roxanne had written him to come when he could – after a night in the city he had caught a train out.

They shook hands and he helped her move two rockers together.

'How's George?'

'He's fine, Roxanne. Seems to like school.'

'Of course it was the only thing to do, to send him.'

'Of course –'

'You miss him horribly, Harry?'

'Yes – I do miss him. He's a funny boy –'

He talked a lot about George. Roxanne was interested. Harry must bring him out on his next vacation. She had only seen him once in her life – a child in dirty rompers.

She left him with the newspaper while she prepared dinner – she had four chops tonight and some late vegetables from her own garden. She put it all on and then called him, and sitting down together they continued their talk about George.

'If I had a child –' she would say.

Afterwards, Harry having given her what slender advice he could about investments, they walked through the garden, pausing here and there to recognise what had once been a cement bench or where the tennis court had lain . . .

'Do you remember –'

Then they were off on a flood of reminiscences: the day they had taken all the snapshots and Jeff had been photographed astride the calf; and the sketch Harry had made of Jeff and Roxanne, lying sprawled in the grass, their heads almost touching. There was to have been a covered lattice connecting the barn-studio with the house, so that Jeff could get there on wet days – the lattice had been started, but nothing remained except a broken triangular piece that still adhered to the house and resembled a battered chicken coop.

'And those mint juleps!'

'And Jeff's notebook! Do you remember how we'd laugh, Harry, when we'd get it out of his pocket and read aloud a page of material. And how frantic he used to get?'

'Wild! He was such a kid about his writing.'

They were both silent a moment, and then Harry said: 'We were to have a place out here, too. Do you remember? We were to buy the adjoining twenty acres. And the parties we were going to have!'

Again there was a pause, broken this time by a low question from Roxanne.

'Do you ever hear of her, Harry?'

'Why – yes,' he admitted placidly. 'She's in Seattle. She's married again to a man named Horton, a sort of lumber king. He's a great deal older than she is, I believe.'

'And she's behaving?'

'Yes – that is, I've heard so. She has everything, you see. Nothing much to do except dress up for this fellow at dinner-time.'

'I see.'

Without effort he changed the subject.

'Are you going to keep the house?'

'I think so,' she said, nodding. 'I've lived here so long, Harry, it'd seem terrible to move. I thought of trained nursing, but of course that'd mean leaving. I've about decided to be a boarding-house lady.'

'Live in one?'

'No. Keep one. Is there such an anomaly as a boarding-house lady? Anyway I'd have a negress and keep about eight people in the summer and two or three, if I can get them, in the winter. Of course I'll have to have the house repainted and gone over inside.'

Harry considered.

'Roxanne, why – naturally you know best what you can do, but it does seem a shock, Roxanne. You came here as a bride.'

'Perhaps,' she said, 'that's why I don't mind remaining here as a boarding-house lady.'

'I remember a certain batch of biscuits.'

'Oh, those biscuits,' she cried. 'Still, from all I heard about the way you devoured them, they couldn't have been so bad. I was *so* low that day, yet somehow I laughed when the nurse told me about those biscuits.'

'I noticed that the twelve nail-holes are still in the library wall where Jeff drove them.'

'Yes.'

It was getting very dark now, a crispness settled in the air; a little gust of wind sent down a last spray of leaves. Roxanne shivered slightly.

'We'd better go in.'

He looked at his watch.

'It's late. I've got to be leaving. I go East tomorrow.'

'Must you?'

They lingered for a moment just below the stoop, watching a moon that seemed full of snow float out of the distance where the lake lay. Summer was gone and now Indian summer. The grass was cold and there was no mist and no dew. After he left she would go in and light the gas and close the shatters, and he would go down the path and on to the village. To these two life had come quickly and gone, leaving not bitterness, but pity; not disillusion, but only pain. There was already enough moonlight when they shook hands for each to see the gathered kindness in the other's eyes.

Mr. and Mrs. Dove

Of course he knew—no man better—that he hadn't a ghost of a chance, he hadn't an earthly. The very idea of such a thing was preposterous. So preposterous that he'd perfectly understand it if her father—well, whatever her father chose to do he'd perfectly understand. In fact, nothing short of desperation, nothing short of the fact that this was positively his last day in England for God knows how long, would have screwed him up to it. And even now . . . He chose a tie out of the chest of drawers, a blue and cream check tie, and sat on the side of his bed. Supposing she replied, "What impertinence!" would he be surprised? Not in the least, he decided, turning up his soft collar and turning it down over the tie. He expected her to say something like that. He didn't see, if he looked at the affair dead soberly, what else she could say.

Here he was! And nervously he tied a bow in front of the mirror, jammed his hair down with both hands, pulled out the flaps of his jacket pockets. Making between £500 and £600 a year on a fruit farm in—of all places—Rhodesia. No capital. Not a penny coming to him. No chance of his income increasing for at least four years. As for looks and all that sort of thing, he was completely out of the running. He couldn't even boast of top-hole health, for the East Africa business had knocked him out so thoroughly that he'd had to take six months' leave. He was still fearfully pale—worse even than usual this afternoon, he thought, bending forward and peering into the mirror. Good heavens! What had happened? His hair looked almost bright green. Dash it all, he hadn't green hair at all events. That was a bit too steep. And then the green light trembled in the glass; it was the shadow from the tree outside. Reggie turned away, took out his cigarette case, but remembering how the mater hated him to smoke in his bedroom, put it back again and drifted over to the chest of drawers. No, he was dashed if he could think of one blessed thing in his favour, while she ... Ah! ... He stopped dead, folded his arms, and leaned hard against the chest of drawers.

And in spite of her position, her father's wealth, the fact that she was an only child and far and away the most popular girl in the neighbourhood; in spite of her beauty and her cleverness—cleverness!—it was a great deal more than that, there was really nothing she couldn't do; he fully believed, had it been necessary, she would have been a genius at anything—in spite of the fact that her parents adored her, and she them, and they'd as soon let her go all that way as ... In spite of every single thing you could think of, so terrific was his love that he couldn't help hoping. Well, was it? Or was this queer, timid longing to have the chance of looking after her, of making it his job to see that she had everything she wanted, and that nothing came near her that wasn't perfect—just love? How he loved her! He squeezed hard against the chest of drawers and murmured to it, "I love her, I love her!" And just for the moment he was with her on the way to Umtali. It was night. She sat in a corner asleep. Her soft chin was tucked into her soft collar, her gold-brown lashes lay on her cheeks. He doted on her delicate little nose, her perfect lips, her ear like a baby's, and the gold-brown curl that half covered it. They were passing through the jungle. It was warm and dark and far away. Then she woke up and said, "Have I been asleep?" and he answered, "Yes. Are you all right? Here, let me—" And he leaned forward to ... He bent over her. This was such bliss that he could dream no further. But it gave him the courage to bound downstairs, to snatch his straw hat from the hall, and to say as he closed the front door, "Well, I can only try my luck, that's all."

But his luck gave him a nasty jar, to say the least,

almost immediately. Promenading up and down the garden path with Chinny and Biddy, the ancient Pekes, was the mater. Of course Reginald was fond of the mater and all that. She—she meant well, she had no end of grit, and so on. But there was no denying it, she was rather a grim parent. And there had been moments, many of them, in Reggie's life, before Uncle Alick died and left him the fruit farm, when he was convinced that to be a widow's only son was about the worst punishment a chap could have. And what made it rougher than ever was that she was positively all that he had. She wasn't only a combined parent, as it were, but she had quarrelled with all her own and the governor's relations before Reggie had won his first trouser pockets. So that whenever Reggie was homesick out there, sitting on his dark veranda by starlight, while the gramophone cried, "Dear, what is Life but Love?" his only vision was of the mater, tall and stout, rustling down the garden path, with Chinny and Biddy at her heels . . .

The mater, with her scissors outspread to snap the head of a dead something or other, stopped at the sight of Reggie.

"You are not going out, Reginald?" she asked, seeing that he was.

"I'll be back for tea, mater," said Reggie weakly, plunging his hands into his jacket pockets.

Snip. Off came a head. Reggie almost jumped.

"I should have thought you could have spared your mother your last afternoon," said she.

Silence. The Pekes stared. They understood every word of the mater's. Biddy lay down with her tongue poked out; she was so fat and glossy she looked like a lump of half-melted toffee. But Chinny's porcelain eyes gloomed at Reginald, and he sniffed faintly, as though the whole world were one unpleasant smell. Snip, went the scissors again. Poor little beggars; they were getting it!

"And where are you going, if your mother may ask?" asked the mater.

It was over at last, but Reggie did not slow down until he was out of sight of the house and half-way to Colonel Proctor's. Then only he noticed what a top-hole afternoon it was. It had been raining all the morning, late summer rain, warm, heavy, quick, and now the sky was clear, except for a long tail of little clouds, like ducklings, sailing over the forest. There was just enough wind to shake the last drops off the trees; one warm star splashed on his hand. Ping!— another drummed on his hat. The empty road gleamed, the hedges smelled of briar, and how big and bright the hollyhocks glowed in the cottage gardens. And here was Colonel Proctor's—here it was already. His hand was on the gate, his elbow jogged the syringa bushes, and petals and pollen scattered over his coat sleeve. But wait a bit. This was too quick altogether. He'd meant to think the whole thing out again. Here, steady. But he was walking up the path, with the huge rose bushes on either side. It can't be done like this. But his hand had grasped the bell, given it a pull, and started it pealing wildly, as if he'd come to say the house was on fire. The housemaid must have been in the hall, too, for the front door flashed open, and Reggie was shut in the empty drawing-room before that confounded bell had stopped ringing. Strangely enough, when it did, the big room, shadowy, with someone's parasol lying on top of the grand piano, bucked him up—or rather, excited him. It was so quiet, and yet in one moment the door would open, and his fate be decided. The feeling was not unlike that of being at the dentist's; he was almost reckless. But at the same time, to his immense surprise, Reggie heard himself saying, "Lord, Thou knowest, Thou hast not done *much* for me ..." That pulled him up; that made him realize again how dead serious it was. Too late. The door handle turned. Anne came in, crossed the shadowy space between them, gave him her hand, and said, in her small, soft voice, "I'm so sorry, father is out. And mother is having a day in town, hat-hunting. There's only me to entertain you, Reggie."

Reggie gasped, pressed his own hat to his jacket buttons, and stammered out, "As a matter of fact, I've only come . . . to say good-bye."

"Oh!" cried Anne softly—she stepped back from him and her grey eyes danced—"what a *very* short visit!"

Then, watching him, her chin tilted, she laughed outright, a long, soft peal, and walked away from him over to the piano, and leaned against it, playing with the tassel of the parasol.

"I'm so sorry," she said, "to be laughing like this. I don't know why I do. It's just a bad ha-habit." And suddenly she stamped her grey shoe, and took a pocket-handkerchief out of her white woolly jacket. "I really must conquer it, it's too absurd," said she.

"Good heavens, Anne," cried Reggie, "I love to hear you laughing! I can't imagine anything more——"

But the truth was, and they both knew it, she wasn't always laughing; it wasn't really a habit. Only ever since the day they'd met, ever since that very first moment, for some strange reason that Reggie wished to God he understood, Anne had laughed at him. Why? It didn't matter where they were or what they were talking about. They might begin by being as serious as possible, dead serious—at any rate, as far as he was concerned—but then suddenly, in the middle of a sentence, Anne would glance at him, and a little quick quiver passed over her face. Her lips parted, her eyes danced, and she began laughing.

Another queer thing about it was, Reggie had an idea she didn't herself know why she laughed. He had seen her turn away, frown, suck in her cheeks, press her hands together. But it was no use. The long, soft peal sounded, even while she cried, "I don't know why I'm laughing." It was a mystery . . .

Now she tucked the handkerchief away. "Do sit down," said she. "And smoke, won't you? There are cigarettes in that little box beside you. I'll have one too." He lighted a match for her, and as she bent forward he saw the tiny flame glow in the pearl ring she wore. "It is to-morrow that you're going, isn't it?" said Anne.

"Yes, to-morrow as ever is," said Reggie, and he blew a little fan of smoke. Why on earth was he so nervous? Nervous wasn't the word for it.

"It's—it's frightfully hard to believe," he added.

"Yes—isn't it?" said Anne softly, and she leaned forward and rolled the point of her cigarette round the green ashtray. How beautiful she looked like that!—simply beautiful—and she was so small in that immense chair. Reginald's heart swelled with tenderness, but it was her voice, her soft voice, that made him tremble. "I feel you've been here for years," she said.

Reginald took a deep breath of his cigarette. "It's ghastly, this idea of going back," he said.

"*Coo-roo-coo-coo-coo*," sounded from the quiet.

"But you're fond of being out there, aren't you?" said Anne. She hooked her finger through her pearl necklace. "Father was saying only the other night how lucky he thought you were to have a life of your own." And she looked up at him. Reginald's smile was rather wan. "*I* don't feel fearfully lucky," he said lightly.

"*Roo-coo-coo-coo*," came again. And Anne murmured, "You mean it's lonely.

"Oh, it isn't the loneliness I care about," said Reginald, and he stumped his cigarette savagely on the green ash-tray. "I could stand any amount of it, used to like it even. It's the idea of—" Suddenly, to his horror, he felt himself blushing.

"*Roo-coo-coo-coo! Roo-coo-coo-coo!*"

Anne jumped up. "Come and say good-bye to my doves," she said. "They've been moved to the side veranda. You do like doves, don't you, Reggie?"

"Awfully," said Reggie, so fervently that as he

opened the french-window for her and stood to one side, Anne ran forward and laughed at the doves instead.

To and fro, to and fro over the fine red sand on the floor of the dove house, walked the two doves. One was always in front of the other. One ran forward, uttering a little cry, and the other followed, solemnly bowing and bowing. "You see," explained Anne, "the one in front, she's Mrs. Dove. She looks at Mr. Dove and gives that little laugh and runs forward, and he follows her, bowing and bowing. And that makes her laugh again. Away she runs, and after her," cried Anne, and she sat back on her heels, "comes poor Mr. Dove, bowing and bowing . . . and that's their whole life. They never do anything else, you know." She got up and took some yellow grains out of a bag on the roof of the dove house. "When you think of them, out in Rhodesia, Reggie, you can be sure that is what they will be doing . . ."

Reggie gave no sign of having seen the doves or of having heard a word. For the moment he was conscious only of the immense effort it took to tear his secret out of himself and offer it to Anne. "Anne, do you think you could ever care for me?" It was done. It was over. And in the little pause that followed Reginald saw the garden open to the light, the blue quivering sky, the flutter of leaves on the veranda poles, and Anne turning over the grains of maize on her palm with one finger. Then slowly she shut her hand, and the new world faded as she murmured slowly, "No, never in that way." But he had scarcely time to feel anything before she walked quickly away, and he followed her down the steps, along the garden path, under the pink rose arches, across the lawn. There, with the gay herbaceous border behind her, Anne faced Reginald. "It isn't that I'm not awfully fond of you," she said. "I am. But"—her eyes widened—"not in the way"—a quiver passed over her face—"one ought to be fond of—" Her lips parted, and she couldn't stop herself. She began laughing. "There, you see, you see," she cried, "it's your check t-tie. Even at this moment, when one would think one really would be solemn, your tie reminds me fearfully of the bow-tie that cats wear in pictures! Oh, please forgive me for being so horrid, please!"

Reggie caught hold of her little warm hand. "There's no question of forgiving you," he said quickly. "How could there be? And I do believe I know why I make you laugh. It's because you're so far above me in every way that I am somehow ridiculous. I see that, Anne. But if I were to——"

"No, no." Anne squeezed his hand hard. "It's not that. That's all wrong. I'm not far above you at all.

You're much better than I am. You're marvellously unselfish and ... and kind and simple. I'm none of those things. You don't know me. I'm the most awful character," said Anne. "Please don't interrupt. And besides, that's not the point. The point is"—she shook her head—"I couldn't possibly marry a man I laughed at. Surely you see that. The man I marry—" breathed Anne softly. She broke off. She drew her hand away, and looking at Reggie she smiled strangely, dreamily. "The man I marry——"

And it seemed to Reggie that a tall, handsome, brilliant stranger stepped in front of him and took his place—the kind of man that Anne and he had seen often at the theatre, walking on to the stage from nowhere, without a word catching the heroine in his arms, and after one long, tremendous look, carrying her off to anywhere ...

Reggie bowed to his vision. "Yes, I see," he said huskily.

"Do you?" said Anne. "Oh, I do hope you do. Because I feel so horrid about it. It's so hard to explain. You know I've never—" She stopped. Reggie looked at her. She was smiling. "Isn't it funny?" she said. "I can say anything to you. I always have been able to from the very beginning."

He tried to smile, to say "I'm glad." She went on: "I've never known anyone I like as much as I like you. I've never felt so happy with anyone. But I'm sure it's not what people and what books mean when they talk about love. Do you understand? Oh, if you only knew how horrid I feel. But we'd be like . . . like Mr. and Mrs. Dove."

That did it. That seemed to Reginald final, and so terribly true that he could hardly bear it. "Don't drive it home," he said, and he turned away from Anne and looked across the lawn. There was the gardener's cottage, with the dark ilex-tree beside it. A wet, blue thumb of transparent smoke hung above the chimney. It didn't look real. How his throat ached! Could he speak? He had a shot. "I must be getting along home," he croaked, and he began walking across the lawn. But Anne ran after him. "No, don't. You can't go yet," she said imploringly. "You can't possibly go away feeling like that." And she stared up at him frowning, biting her lips.

"Oh, that's all right," said Reggie, giving himself a shake. "I'll . . . I'll—" And he waved his hand as much as to say "get over it."

"But this is awful," said Anne. She clasped her hands and stood in front of him. "Surely you do see how fatal it would be for us to marry, don't you?"

"Oh, quite, quite," said Reggie, looking at her with haggard eyes.

"How wrong, how wicked, feeling as I do. I

mean, it's all very well for Mr. and Mrs. Dove. But imagine that in real life—imagine it!"

"Oh, absolutely," said Reggie, and he started to walk on. But again Anne stopped him. She tugged at his sleeve, and to his astonishment, this time, instead of laughing, she looked like a little girl who was going to cry.

"Then why, if you understand, are you so un-unhappy?" she wailed. "Why do you mind so fearfully? Why do you look so aw-awful?"

Reggie gulped, and again he waved something away. "I can't help it," he said, "I've had a blow. If I cut off now, I'll be able to——"

"How can you talk of cutting off now?" said Anne scornfully. She stamped her foot at Reggie; she was crimson. "How can you be so cruel? I can't let you go until I know for certain that you are just as happy as you were before you asked me to marry you. Surely you must see that, it's so simple."

But it did not seem at all simple to Reginald. It seemed impossibly difficult.

"Even if I can't marry you, how can I know that you're all that way away, with only that awful mother to write to, and that you're miserable, and that it's all my fault?"

"It's not your fault. Don't think that. It's just Fate." Reggie took her hand off his sleeve and kissed it. "Don't pity me, dear little Anne," he said gently. And this time he nearly ran, under the pink arches, along the garden path.

"*Roo-coo-coo-coo! Roo-coo-coo-coo!*" sounded from the veranda. "Reggie, Reggie," from the garden.

He stopped, he turned. But when she saw his timid, puzzled look, she gave a little laugh.

"Come back, Mr. Dove," said Anne. And Reginald came slowly across the lawn.

The Romance of a Busy Broker

Pitcher, confidential clerk in the office of Harvey Maxwell, broker, allowed a look of mild interest and surprise to visit his usually expressionless countenance when his employer briskly entered at half-past nine in company with his young lady stenographer. With a snappy "Good-morning, Pitcher," Maxwell dashed at his desk as though he were intending to leap over it, and then plunged into the great heap of letters and telegrams waiting there for him.

The young lady had been Maxwell's stenographer for a year. She was beautiful in a way that was decidedly unstenographic. She forewent the pomp of the alluring pompadour. She wore no chains, bracelets, or lockets. She had not the air of being about to accept an invitation to luncheon. Her dress was gray and plain, but it fitted her figure with fidelity and discretion. In her neat black turban hat was the gold-green wing of a macaw. On this morning she was softly and shyly radiant. Her eyes were dreamily bright, her cheeks genuine peach-blow, her expression a happy one, tinged with reminiscence.

Pitcher, still mildly curious, noticed a difference

in her ways this morning. Instead of going straight into the adjoining room, where her desk was, she lingered, slightly irresolute, in the outer office. Once she moved over by Maxwell's desk, near enough for him to be aware of her presence.

The machine sitting at that desk was no longer a man; it was a busy New York broker, moved by buzzing wheels and uncoiling springs.

"Well—what is it? Anything?" asked Maxwell, sharply. His opened mail lay like a bank of stage snow on his crowded desk. His keen gray eye, impersonal and brusque, flashed upon her half impatiently.

"Nothing," answered the stenographer, moving away with a little smile.

"Mr. Pitcher," she said to the confidential clerk, "did Mr. Maxwell say anything yesterday about engaging another stenographer?"

"He did," answered Pitcher. "He told me to get another one. I notified the agency yesterday afternoon to send over a few samples this morning. It's 9.45 o'clock, and not a single picture hat or piece of pineapple chewing gum has showed up yet."

"I will do the work as usual, then," said the young lady, "until some one comes to fill the place." And she went to her desk at once and hung the black turban hat with the gold-green macaw wing in its accustomed place.

He who has been denied the spectacle of a busy Manhattan broker during a rush of business is handicapped for the profession of anthropology. The poet sings of the "crowded hour of glorious life." The broker's hour is not only crowded, but minutes and seconds are hanging to all the straps and packing both front and rear platforms.

And this day was Harvey Maxwell's busy day. The ticker began to reel out jerkily its fitful coils of tape, the desk telephone had a chronic attack of buzzing. Men began to throng into the office and call at him over the railing, jovially, sharply, viciously, excitedly. Messenger boys ran in and out with messages and telegrams. The clerks in the office jumped about like sailors during a storm. Even Pitcher's face relaxed into something resembling animation.

On the Exchange there were hurricanes and landslides and snowstorms and glaciers and volcanoes, and those elemental disturbances were reproduced in miniature in the broker's offices. Maxwell shoved his chair against the wall and transacted business after the manner of a toe dancer. He jumped from ticker to 'phone, from desk to door with the trained agility of a harlequin.

In the midst of this growing and important stress

the broker became suddenly aware of a high-rolled fringe of golden hair under a nodding canopy of velvet and ostrich tips, and imitation sealskin sacque and a string of beads as large as hickory nuts, ending near the floor with a silver heart. There was a self-possessed young lady connected with these accessories; and Pitcher was there to construe her.

"Lady from the Stenographer's Agency to see about the position," said Pitcher.

Maxwell turned half around, with his hands full of papers and ticker tape.

"What position?" he asked, with a frown.

"Position of stenographer," said Pitcher. "You told me yesterday to call them up and have one sent over this morning."

"You are losing your mind, Pitcher," said Maxwell. "Why should I have given you any such instructions? Miss Leslie has given perfect satisfaction during the year she has been here. The place is hers as long as she chooses to retain it. There's no place open here, madam. Countermand that order with the agency, Pitcher, and don't bring any more of 'em here."

The silver heart left the office, swinging and banging itself independently against the office furniture as it indignantly departed. Pitcher seized a moment to remark to the bookkeeper that the "old man" seemed to get more absentminded and forgetful every day of the world.

The rush and pace of business grew fiercer and faster. On the floor they were pounding half a dozen stocks in which Maxwell's customers were heavy investors. Orders to buy and sell were coming and going as swift as the flight of swallows. Some of his own holdings were imperilled, and the man was working like some high-geared, delicate, strong machine—strung to full tension, going at full speed, accurate, never hesitating, with the proper word and decision and act ready and prompt as clockwork. Stocks and bonds, loans and mortgages, margins and securities—here was a world of finance, and there was no room in it for the human world or the world of nature.

When the luncheon hour drew near there came a slight lull in the uproar.

Maxwell stood by his desk with his hands full of telegrams and memoranda, with a fountain pen over his right ear and his hair hanging in disorderly strings over his forehead. His window was open, for the beloved janitress, Spring had turned on a little warmth through the waking registers of the earth.

And through the window came a wandering—perhaps a lost—odor—a delicate, sweet odor of lilac that fixed the broker for a moment immovable. For this odor belonged to Miss Leslie; it was her own, and hers only.

The odor brought her vividly, almost tangibly before him. The world of finance dwindled suddenly to a speck. And she was in the next room—twenty steps away.

"By George, I'll do it now," said Maxwell, half aloud. "I'll ask her now, I wonder I didn't do it long ago."

He dashed into the inner office with the haste of a short trying to cover. He charged upon the desk of the stenographer.

She looked up at him with a smile. A soft pink crept over her cheek, and her eyes were kind and frank. Maxwell leaned one elbow on her desk. He still clutched fluttering papers with both hands and the pen was above his ear.

"Miss Leslie," he began, hurriedly, "I have but a moment to spare. I want to say something in that moment. Will you be my wife? I haven't had time to make love to you in the ordinary way, but I really do love you. Talk quick, please—those fellows are clubbing the stuffing out of Union Pacific."

"Oh, what are you talking about?" exclaimed the young lady. She rose to her feet and gazed upon him, round-eyed.

"Don't you understand?" said Maxwell, restively.

"I want you to marry me. I love you, Miss Leslie. I wanted to tell you, and I snatched a minute when things had slackened up a bit. They're calling me for the 'phone now. Tell 'em to wait a minute, Pitcher. Won't you, Miss Leslie?"

The stenographer acted very queerly. At first she seemed overcome with amazement; then tears flowed from her wondering eyes; and then she smiled sunnily through them, and one of her arms slid tenderly about the broker's neck.

"I know now," she said, softly. "It's this old business that has driven everything else out of your head for the time. I was frightened at first. Don't you remember, Harvey? We were married last evening at 8 o'clock in the Little Church around the Corner."

Lena Wrace

She arranged herself there, on that divan, and I knew she'd come to tell me all about it. It was wonderful, how, at forty-seven, she could still give that effect of triumph and excess, of something rich and ruinous and beautiful spread out on the brocades. The attitude showed me that her affair with Norman Hippisley was prospering; otherwise she couldn't have afforded the extravagance of it.

"I know what you want," I said. "You want me to congratulate you."

"Yes. I do."

"I congratulate you on your courage."

"Oh, you don't like him," she said placably.

"No, I don't like him at all."

"He likes you," she said. "He thinks no end of your painting."

"I'm not denying he's a judge of painting. I'm not even denying he can paint a little himself."

"Better than you, Roly."

"If you allow for the singular, obscene ugliness of his imagination, yes."

"It's beautiful enough when he gets it into paint," she said. "He makes beauty—his own beauty."

"Oh, very much his own."

"Well, *you* just go on imitating other people's—God's or somebody's."

She continued with her air of perfect reasonableness. "I know he isn't good looking. Not half so good looking as you are. But I like him. I like his slender little body and his clever, faded face. There's a quality about him, a distinction. And look at his eyes. *Your* mind doesn't come rushing and blazing out of your eyes, my dear."

"No. No. I'm afraid it doesn't rush. And for all the blaze——"

"Well, that's what I'm in love with, the rush, Roly, and the blaze. And I'm in love *for the first time*" (she underlined it) "with a man."

"Come," I said, "come!"

"Oh, *I* know. I know you're thinking of Lawson Young and Dicky Harper."

"I was."

"Well, but they don't count. I wasn't *in love* with Lawson. I was his career. If he hadn't been a Cabinet Minister; if he hadn't been so desperately gone on me; if he hadn't said it all depended on me——"

"Yes," I said. "I can see how it would go to your head."

"It didn't. It went to my heart." She was quite serious and solemn. "I held him in my hands, Roly. And he held England. I couldn't let him drop, could I? I had to think of England."

It was wonderful—Lena Wrace thinking that she thought of England.

I said: "Of course. But for your political foresight and your virtuous action we should never have had Tariff Reform."

"We should never have had anything," she said. "And look at him now. Look how he's crumpled up since he left me. It's pitiful."

"It is. I'm afraid Mrs. Withers doesn't care about Tariff Reform."

"Poor thing. No. Don't imagine I'm jealous of her, Roly. She hasn't got him. I mean she hasn't got what I had."

"All the same, he left you. And you weren't ecstatically happy with him the last year or two."

"I daresay I'd have done better to have married you, if that's what you mean."

It wasn't what I meant. But she'd always entertained the illusion that she could marry me any minute if she wanted to; and I hadn't the heart to take it from her since it seemed to console her for the way, the really very infamous way he had left her.

So I said: "Much better."

"It would have been so nice, so safe," she said. "But I never played for safety." Then she made one of her quick turns.

"Frances Archdale ought to marry you. Why doesn't she?"

"How should I know? Frances's reasons would be exquisite. I suppose I didn't appeal to her sense of fitness."

"Sense of fiddlesticks. She just hasn't got any temperament, that girl."

"Any temperament for me, you mean."

"I mean pure cussedness," said Lena.

"Perhaps. But, you see, if I were unfortunate enough she probably *would* marry me. If I lost my eyesight or a leg or an arm, if I couldn't sell any more pictures——"

"If you can understand Frances, you can understand me. That's how I felt about Dicky. I wasn't in love with him. I was sorry for him. I knew he'd go to pieces if I wasn't there to keep him together. Perhaps it's the maternal instinct."

"Perhaps," I said. Lena's reasons for her behaviour amused me; they were never exquisite, like Frances's, but she was anxious that you should think they were.

"So you see," she said, "they don't count, and Norry really *is* the first."

I reflected that he would be also, probably, the last. She had, no doubt, to make the most of him. But it was preposterous that she should waste so much good passion; preposterous that she should imagine for one moment she could keep the fellow. I had to warn her.

"Of course, if you care to take the risk of him——" I said. "He won't stick to you, Lena."

"Why shouldn't he?"

I couldn't tell her. I couldn't say: "Because you're thirteen years older than he is." That would have been cruel. And it would have been absurd, too, when she could so easily look not a year older than his desiccated thirty-four. It only took a little success like this, her actual triumph in securing him.

So I said: "Because it isn't in him. He's a bounder and a rotter." Which was true.

"Not a bounder, Roly, dear. His father's Sir Gilbert Hippisley. Hippisleys of Leicestershire."

"A moral bounder, Lena. A slimy eel. Slips and wriggles out of things. You'll never hold him. You're not his first affair, you know."

"I don't care," she said, "as long as I'm his last."

I could only stand and stare at that; her monstrous assumption of his fidelity. Why, he couldn't even be faithful to one art. He wrote as well as he painted, and he acted as well as he wrote, and he was never really happy with a talent till he had debauched it.

"The others," she said, "don't bother me a bit. He's slipped and wriggled out of their clutches, if you like ... Yet there was something about all of them. Distinguished. That's it. He's so awfully fine and fastidious about the women he takes up with. It flatters you, makes you feel so sure of yourself. You know he wouldn't take up with *you* if you weren't fine and fastidious, too—one of his great ladies ... You think I'm a snob, Roly?"

"I think you don't mind coming *after* Lady Willersey."

"Well," she said, "if you *have* to come after somebody——"

"True." I asked her if she was giving me her reasons.

"Yes, if you want them. *I* don't. I'm content to love out of all reason."

And she did. She loved extravagantly, unintelligibly, out of all reason; yet irrefutably—to the end. There's a sort of reason in that, isn't there? She had the sad logic of her passions.

She got up and gathered herself together in her sombre, violent beauty and in its glittering sheath, her red fox skins, all her savage splendour, leaving a scent of crushed orris root in the warmth of her lair.

Well, she managed to hold him, tight, for a year, fairly intact. I can't for the life of me imagine how she could have cared for the fellow, with his face all dried and frayed with make-up. There was something lithe and sinuous about him that may, of course, have appealed to her. And I understand his infatuation. He was decadent, exhausted; and there would be moments when he found her primitive violence stimulating before it wore him out.

They kept up the ménage for two astounding years.

Well, not so very astounding, if you come to think of it. There was Lena's money, left her by old Weinberger, her maternal uncle. You've got to reckon with Lena's money. Not that she, poor soul, ever reckoned with it; she was absolutely free from that taint, and she couldn't conceive other people reckoning. Only, instinctively, she knew. She knew how to hold Hippisley. She knew there were things he couldn't resist, things like wines and motor-cars he could be faithful to. From the very beginning she built for permanence, for eternity. She took a house in Avenue Road, with a studio for Hippisley in the garden; she bought a motor-car and engaged an inestimable cook. Lena's dinners, in those years, were exquisite affairs, and she took care to ask the right people, people who would be useful to

Hippisley; dealers whom old Weinberger had known, and journalists, and editors, and publishers. And all his friends and her own; even friends' friends. Her hospitality was boundless and eccentric, and Hippisley liked that sort of thing. He thrived in a liberal air, an air of gorgeous spending, though he sported a supercilious smile at the *fioritura*, the luscious excess of it. He had never had too much, poor devil, of his own. I've seen the little fellow swaggering about at her parties, with his sharp, frayed face, looking fine and fastidious, safeguarding himself with twinklings and gestures that gave the dear woman away. I've seen him, in goggles and a magnificent fur-lined coat, shouting to her chauffeur, giving counter-orders to her own, while she sat snuggling up in the corner of the car, smiling at his mastery.

It went on till poor Lena was forty-nine. Then, as she said, she began to "shake in her shoes." I told her it didn't matter so long as she didn't let him see her shaking. That depressed her, because she knew she couldn't hide it; there was nothing secret in her nature; she had always let "them" see. And they were bothering her—"the others"—more than "a bit." She was jealous of every one of them, of any woman he said more than five words to. Jealous of the models, first of all, before she found out that they didn't matter; he was so used to them. She would stick there, in his studio, while they sat, until one day he got furious and turned her out of it. But she'd seen enough to set her mind at rest. He was fine and fastidious, and the models were all "common."

"And their figures, Roly, you should have seen them when they were undressed. Of course, you *have* seen them. Well, there isn't—is there?"

And there wasn't. Hippisley had grown out of models just as he had grown out of cheap Burgundy. And he'd left the stage, because he was tired of it; so there was, mercifully, no danger from that quarter. What she dreaded was the moment when he'd "take" to writing again, for then he'd have to have a secretary. Also she was jealous of his writing, because it absorbed more of his attention than his painting, and exhausted him more, left her less of him.

And that year, their third year, he flung up his painting and was, as she expressed it, "at it" again. Worse than ever. And he wanted a secretary.

She took care to find him one. One who wouldn't be dangerous. "You should just see her, Roly." She brought her in to tea one day for me to look at and say whether she would "do."

I wasn't sure—what can you be sure of?—but I could see why Lena thought she would. She was a little unhealthy thing, dark and sallow and sulky, with thin lips that showed a lack of temperament, and she had just that touch of "commonness"—a stiffness and preciseness like a board-school teacher—which Lena relied on to put him off. She wore a shabby brown skirt and a yellowish blouse. Her name was Ethel Reeves.

Lena had secured safety, she said, in the house. But what was the good of that, when outside it he was going about everywhere with Sybil Fermor?

She came and told me all about it, with a sort of hope that I'd say something either consoling or revealing, something that she could go on.

"*You* know him, Roly," she said.

I reminded her that she hadn't always given me that credit.

"*I* know how he spends his time," she said.

"How do you know?"

"Well, for one thing, Ethel tells me."

"How does she know?"

"She—she posts the letters."

"Does she read them?"

"She needn't. He's too transparent."

"Lena, do you use her to spy on him?" I said.

"Well," she retorted, "if he uses her——"

I asked her if it hadn't struck her that Sybil Fermor might be using him.

"Do you mean—as a paravent? Or"—she revised it—"a parachute?"

"For Bertie Granville," I elucidated. "A parachute, by all means."

She considered it. "It won't work," she said. "If it's her reputation she's thinking of, wouldn't Norry be worse?"

I said that was the beauty of him, if Letty Granville's attention was to be diverted.

"Oh, Roly," she said, "do you really think it's that?"

I said I did, and she powdered her nose and said I was a dear, and I'd bucked her up no end, and went away quite happy.

Letty Granville's divorce suit proved to her that I was right.

The next time I saw her she told me she'd been mistaken about Sybil Fermor. It was Lady Hermione Nevin. Norry had been using Sybil as a "paravent" for *her*. I said she was wrong again. Didn't she know that Hermione was engaged to Billy Craven. They were head over ears in love with each other. I asked her what on earth had made her think of her? And she said Lady Hermione had paid him thirty guineas for a picture. That looked, she said, as if she was pretty far gone on him. (She tended to disparage Hippisley's talents. Jealousy again.)

I said it looked as if he had the iciest reasons for cultivating Lady Hermione. And again she told me I was a dear. "You don't know, Roly, what a comfort you are to me."

Then Barbara Vining turned up out of nowhere, and from the first minute Lena gave herself up for lost.

"I'm done for," she said. "I'd fight her if it was any good fighting. But what chance have I? At forty-nine against nineteen, and that face?"

The face was adorable, if you adore a child's face on a woman's body. Small and pink; a soft, innocent forehead, fawnskin hair, a fawn's nose, a fawn's mouth, a fawn's eyes. You saw her at Lena's garden parties staring at Hippisley over the rim of her plate while she browsed on Lena's cakes and ices, or bounding about Lena's tennis-court with the sash ribbons flying from her little butt end.

Oh, yes, she had her there. As much as he wanted. And there would be Ethel Reeves, in a new blouse, looking on from a back seat, subtle and sullen, or handing round cups and plates without speaking to anybody, like a servant. I used to think she spied on them for Lena. They were always mouching about the garden together or sitting secretly in corners; Lena even had her to stay with them; let him take her for long drives in her car. She knew when she was beaten.

I said: "Why do you let him do it, Lena? Why don't you turn them both neck and crop out of the house?"

"Because I want him in it. I want him at any cost. And I want him to have what he wants, too, even if it's Barbara. I want him to be happy . . . I'm making a virtue of necessity. It can be done, Roly, if you give up beautifully."

I put it to her it wasn't giving up beautifully to fret herself into an unbecoming illness, to carry her disaster on her face. She would come to me looking more ruined than ruinous, haggard and ashy, her eyes all shrunk and hot with crying, and stand before the glass, looking at herself and dabbing on powder in an utter abandonment to misery.

"I know," she moaned. "As if losing him wasn't enough, I must go and lose my looks. I know crying's simply suicidal at my age, yet I keep on at it. I'm doing for myself. I'm digging my own grave, Roly. A little deeper every day."

Then she said suddenly: "Do you know, you're the only man in London I could come to looking like this."

I said: "Isn't that a bit unkind of you? It sounds as though you thought I didn't matter."

133

She broke down on that. "Can't you see it's because I know *I* don't any more. Nobody cares whether my nose is red or not. But you're not a brute. You don't let me feel I don't matter. I know I never did matter to you, Roly, but the effect's soothing, all the same ... Ethel says if she were me she wouldn't stand it. To have it going on under my nose. Ethel is so high-minded. I suppose it's easy to be high-minded if you've always looked like that. And if you've never *had* anybody. She doesn't know what it is. I tell you, I'd rather have Norry there with Barbara than not have him at all."

I thought and said that would just about suit Hippisley's book. He'd rather be there than anywhere else, since he had to be somewhere. To be sure, she irritated him with her perpetual clinging, and wore him out. I've seen him wince at the sound of her voice in the room. He'd say things to her; not often, but just enough to see how far he could go. He was afraid of going too far. He wasn't prepared to give up the comfort of Lena's house, the opulence and peace. There wasn't one of Lena's wines he could have turned his back on. After all, when she worried him he could keep himself locked up in the studio away from her.

There was Ethel Reeves; but Lena didn't worry about his being locked up with *her*. She was very kind to Hippisley's secretary. Since she wasn't dangerous, she liked to see her there, well housed, eating rich food and getting stronger and stronger every day.

I must say my heart bled for Lena when I thought of young Barbara. It was still bleeding when one afternoon she walked in with her old triumphant look; she wore her hat with an *air crâne*, and the powder on her face was even and intact, like the first pure fall of snow. She looked ten years younger, and I judged that Hippisley's affair with Barbara was at an end.

Well—it had never had a beginning; nor the ghost of a beginning. It had never happened at all. She had come to tell me that; that there was nothing in it— nothing but her jealousy; the miserable, damnable jealousy that had made her think things. She said it would be a lesson to her to trust him in the future not to go falling in love. For, she argued, if he hadn't done it this time with Barbara, he'd never do it.

I asked her how she knew he hadn't this time, when appearances all pointed that way. And she said that Barbara had come and told her. Somebody, it seemed, had been telling Barbara it was known that she'd taken Hippisley from Lena, and that Lena was crying herself into a nervous breakdown. And the child had gone straight to Lena and told her it was a beastly lie. She hadn't taken Hippisley. She liked ragging with him and all that, and being seen about with him at parties, because he was a celebrity, and it made the other women, the women he wouldn't talk to, furious. But as for taking him, why, she wouldn't take him from anybody as a gift. She didn't want him, a scrubby old thing like that! She didn't *like* that dragged look about his mouth, and the way the skin wrinkled on his eyelids. There was a sincerity about Barbara that would have blasted Hippisley if he'd known.

Besides, she wouldn't have hurt Lena for the world. She wouldn't have spoken to Norry if she'd dreamed that Lena minded. But Lena had seemed so remarkably not to mind. When she came to that part of it she cried.

Lena said that was all very well, and it didn't matter whether Barbara was in love with Norry or not; but how did she know Norry wasn't in love with *her*? And Barbara replied amazingly that of course she knew. They'd been alone together.

When I remarked that it was precisely *that*, Lena said no. That was nothing in itself; but it would prove one way or another; and it seemed that when Norry found himself alone with Barbara, he used to yawn.

After that Lena settled down to a period of

felicity. She'd come to me, excited and exulting, bringing her poor little happiness with her like a new toy. She'd sit there looking at it, turning it over and over, and holding it up to me to show how beautiful it was.

She pointed out to me that I had been wrong and she right about him, from the beginning. She knew him.

"And to think what a fool, what a damned silly fool I was, with my jealousy. When all those years there was never anybody but me. Do you remember Sybil Fermor, and Lady Hermione—and Barbara? To think I should have so clean forgotten what he was like . . . Don't you think, Roly, there must be something in me, after all, to have kept him all these years?"

I said there must indeed have been, to have inspired so remarkable a passion. For Hippisley was making love to her all over again. Their happy relations were proclaimed, not only by her own engaging frankness, but still more by the marvellous renaissance of her beauty. She had given up her habit of jealousy as she had given up eating sweets, because both were murderous to her complexion. Not that Hippisley gave her any cause. He had ceased to cultivate the society of young and pretty ladies, and devoted himself with almost ostentatious fidelity to

Lena. Their affair had become irreproachable with time; it had the permanence of a successful marriage without the unflattering element of legal obligation. And he had kept his secretary. Lena had left off being afraid either that Ethel would leave or that Hippisley would put some dangerous woman in her place.

There was no change in Ethel, except that she looked rather more subtle and less sullen. Lena ignored her subtlety as she had ignored her sulks. She had no more use for her as a confidant and spy, and Ethel lived in a back den off Hippisley's study with her Remington, and displayed a convenient apathy in allowing herself to be ignored.

"Really," Lena would say in the unusual moments when she thought of her, "if it wasn't for the clicking, you wouldn't know she was there."

And as a secretary she maintained, up to the last, an admirable efficiency.

Up to the last.

It was Hippisley's death that ended it. You know how it happened—suddenly, of heart failure, in Paris. He'd gone there with Furnival to get material for that book they were doing together. Lena was literally "prostrated" with the shock; and Ethel Reeves had to go over to Paris to bring back his papers and his body.

It was the day after the funeral that it all came out. Lena and Ethel were sitting up together over the papers and the letters, turning out his bureau. I suppose that, in the grand immunity his death conferred on her, poor Lena had become provokingly possessive. I can hear her saying to Ethel that there had never been anybody but her, all those years. Praising his faithfulness; holding out her dead happiness, and apologizing to Ethel for talking about it when Ethel didn't understand, never having had any.

She must have said something like that, to bring it on herself, just then, of all moments.

And I can see Ethel Reeves, sitting at his table, stolidly sorting out his papers, wishing that Lena'd go away and leave her to her work. And her sullen eyes firing out questions, asking her what she wanted, what she had to do with Norman Hippisley's papers, what she was there for, fussing about, when it was all over?

What she wanted—what she had come for—was her letters. They were locked up in his bureau in the secret drawer.

She told me what had happened then. Ethel lifted her sullen, subtle eyes and said, "You think he kept them?"

She said she knew he'd kept them. They were in that drawer.

And Ethel said, "Well then, he didn't. They aren't. He burnt them. We burnt them . . . We could, at least, get rid of them!"

Then she threw it at her. She had been Hippisley's mistress for three years.

When Lena asked for proofs of the incredible assertion she had her letters to show.

Oh, it was her moment. She must have been looking out for it, saving up for it, all those years; gloating over her exquisite secret, her return for all the slighting and ignoring. That was what had made her poisonous, the fact that Lena hadn't reckoned with her, hadn't thought her dangerous, hadn't been afraid to leave Hippisley with her, the rich, arrogant contempt in her assumption that Ethel would "do" and her comfortable confidences. It made her amorous and malignant. It stimulated her to the attempt.

I think she must have hated Lena more vehemently than she loved Hippisley. She couldn't, then, have had much reliance on her power to capture; but her hatred was a perpetual suggestion.

Supposing—supposing she were to try and take him?

Then she had tried.

I daresay she hadn't much difficulty. Hippisley wasn't quite so fine and fastidious as Lena thought

him. I've no doubt he liked Ethel's unwholesome-
ness, just as he had liked the touch of morbidity in
Lena.

And the spying? That had been all part of the
game; his and Ethel's. *They* played for safety, if you
like. They had *had* to throw Lena off the scent. They
used Sybil Fermor and Lady Hermione and Barbara
Vining one after the other as their "paravents."
Finally they had used Lena. That was their cleverest
stroke. It brought them a permanent security. For,
you see, Hippisley wasn't going to give up his free
quarters, his studio, the dinners and the motor-car,
if he could help it—not for Ethel. And Ethel knew
it. They insured her, too.

Can't you see her, letting herself go in an ecstasy
of revenge, winding up with an hysterical youp?
"You? You thought it was you? It was me—*me*—
ME . . . You thought what we meant you to think."

Lena still comes and talks to me. To hear her you
would suppose that Lawson Young and Dicky
Harper never existed, that her passion for Norman
Hippisley was the unique, solitary manifestation of
her soul. It certainly burnt with the intensest flame.
It certainly consumed her. What's left of her's all
shrivelled, warped, as she writhed in her fire.

Yesterday she said to me: "Roly, I'm *glad* he's
dead. Safe from her clutches."

She'll cling for a little while to this last illusion: that he had been reluctant; but I doubt if she really believes it now.

For, you see, Ethel flourishes. In passion, you know, nothing succeeds like success; and her affair with Norman Hippisley advertised her, so that very soon it ranked as the first of a series of successes. She goes about dressed in stained glass Futurist muslins, and contrives provocative effects out of a tilted nose, and sulky eyes, and sallowness set off by a black velvet band on the forehead, and a black scarf of hair dragged tight from a raking backward peak.

I saw her the other night sketching a frivolous gesture——

The Fisherman of Pass Christian

The swift breezes on the beach at Pass Christian meet and conflict as though each strove for the mastery of the air. The land-breeze blows down through the pines, resinous, fragrant, cold, bringing breath-like memories of dim, dark woods shaded by myriad pine-needles. The breeze from the Gulf is warm and soft and languorous, blowing up from the south with its suggestion of tropical warmth and passion. It is strong and masterful, and tossed Annette's hair and whipped her skirts about her in bold disregard for the proprieties.

Arm in arm with Philip, she was strolling slowly down the great pier which extends from the Mexican Gulf Hotel into the waters of the Sound. There was no moon to-night, but the sky glittered and scintillated with myriad stars, brighter than you can ever see farther North, and the great waves that the Gulf breeze tossed up in restless profusion gleamed with the white fire of phosphorescent flame. The wet sands on the beach glowed white fire; the posts of the pier where the waves had leapt and left a laughing kiss, the sides of the little boats and fish-cars tugging at their ropes, alike showed white and flaming, as though the sea and all it touched were afire.

Annette and Philip paused midway the pier to watch two fishermen casting their nets. With heads bared to the breeze, they stood in clear silhouette against the white background of sea.

"See how he uses his teeth," almost whispered Annette.

Drawing himself up to his full height, with one end of the huge seine between his teeth, and the cord in his left hand, the taller fisherman of the two paused a half instant, his right arm extended, grasping the folds of the net. There was a swishing rush through the air, and it settled with a sort of sob as it cut the waters and struck a million sparkles of fire from the waves. Then, with backs bending under the strain, the two men swung on the cord, drawing in the net, laden with glittering restless fish, which were unceremoniously dumped on the boards to be put into the fish-car awaiting them.

Philip laughingly picked up a soft, gleaming jelly-fish, and threatened to put it on Annette's neck. She screamed, ran, slipped on the wet boards, and in another instant would have fallen over into the water below. The tall fisherman caught her in his arms and set her on her feet.

"Mademoiselle must be very careful," he said in

the softest and most correct French. "The tide is in and the water very rough. It would be very difficult to swim out there to-night."

Annette murmured confused thanks, which were supplemented by Philip's hearty tones. She was silent until they reached the pavilion at the end of the pier. The semi-darkness was unrelieved by lantern or light. The strong wind wafted the strains from a couple of mandolins, a guitar, and a tenor voice stationed in one corner to sundry engrossed couples in sundry other corners. Philip found an untenanted nook and they ensconced themselves therein.

"Do you know there's something mysterious about that fisherman?" said Annette, during a lull in the wind.

"Because he did not let you go over?" inquired Philip.

"No; he spoke correctly, and with the accent that goes only with an excellent education."

Philip shrugged his shoulders. "That's nothing remarkable. If you stay about Pass Christian for any length of time, you'll find more things than perfect French and courtly grace among fishermen to surprise you. These are a wonderful people who live across the Lake."

Annette was lolling in the hammock under the

big catalpa-tree some days later, when the gate opened, and Natalie's big sun-bonnet appeared. Natalie herself was discovered blushing in its dainty depths. She was only a little Creole seaside girl, you must know, and very shy of the city demoiselles. Natalie's patois was quite as different from Annette's French as it was from the postmaster's English.

"Mees Annette," she began, peonyhued all over at her own boldness, "we will have one lil' hay-ride this night, and a fish-fry at the end. Will you come?"

Annette sprang to her feet in delight. "Will I come? Certainly. How delightful! You are so good to ask me. What shall—what time—" But Natalie's pink bonnet had fled precipitately down the shaded walk. Annette laughed joyously as Philip lounged down the gallery.

"I frightened the child away," she told him.

You've never been for a hay-ride and fish-fry on the shores of the Mississippi Sound, have you? When the summer boarders and the Northern visitors undertake to give one, it is a comparatively staid affair, where due regard is had for one's wearing apparel, and where there are servants to do the hardest work. Then it isn't enjoyable at all. But when the natives, the boys and girls who live there, make up their minds to have fun, you may depend upon its being just the best kind.

This time there were twenty boys and girls, a mamma or so, several papas, and a grizzled fisherman to restrain the ardor of the amateurs. The cart was vast and solid, and two comfortable, sleepy-looking mules constituted the drawing power. There were also tin horns, some guitars, an accordeon, and a quartet of much praised voices. The hay in the bottom of the wagon was freely mixed with pine needles, whose prickiness through your hose was amply compensated for by its delicious fragrance.

After a triumphantly noisy passage down the beach one comes to the stretch of heavy sand that lies between Pass Christian proper and Henderson's Point. This is a hard pull for the mules, and the more ambitious riders get out and walk. Then, after a final strain through the shifting sands, bravo! the shell road is reached, and one goes cheering through the pine-trees to Henderson's Point.

If ever you go to Pass Christian, you must have a fish-fry at Henderson's Point. It is the pine-thicketed, white-beached peninsula jutting out from the land, with one side caressed by the waters of the Sound and the other purred over by the blue waves of the Bay of St. Louis. Here is the beginning of the great three-mile trestle bridge to the town of Bay St. Louis, and to-night from the beach could be seen the lights of the villas glittering across the Bay like myriads of unsleeping eyes.

Here upon a firm stretch of white sand camped the merry-makers. Soon a great fire of driftwood and pine cones tossed its flames defiantly at a radiant moon in the sky, and the fishers were casting their nets in the sea. The more daring of the girls waded barelegged in the water, holding pine-torches, spearing flounders and peering for soft-shell crabs.

Annette had wandered farther in the shallow water than the rest. Suddenly she stumbled against a stone, the torch dropped and spluttered at her feet. With a little helpless cry she looked at the stretch of unfamiliar beach and water to find herself all alone.

"Pardon me, mademoiselle," said a voice at her elbow; "you are in distress?"

It was her fisherman, and with a scarce conscious sigh of relief, Annette put her hand into the outstretched one at her side.

"I was looking for soft shells," she explained, "and lost the crowd, and now my torch is out."

"Where is the crowd?" There was some amusement in the tone, and Annette glanced up quickly, prepared to be thoroughly indignant at this fisherman who dared make fun at her; but there was such a kindly look about his mouth that she was reassured and said meekly,—

"At Henderson's Point."

"You have wandered a half-mile away," he mused, "and have nothing to show for your pains but very wet skirts. If mademoiselle will permit me, I will take her to her friends, but allow me to suggest that mademoiselle will leave the water and walk on the sands."

"But I am barefoot," wailed Annette, "and I am afraid of the fiddlers."

Fiddler crabs, you know, aren't pleasant things to be dangling around one's bare feet, and they are more numerous than sand fleas down at Henderson's Point.

"True," assented the fisherman; "then we shall have to wade back."

The fishing was over when they rounded the point and came in sight of the cheery bonfire with its Rembrandt-like group, and the air was savoury with the smell of frying fish and crabs. The fisherman was not to be tempted by appeals to stay, but smilingly disappeared down the sands, the red glare of his torch making a glowing track in the water.

"Ah, Mees Annette," whispered Natalie, between mouthfuls of a rich croaker, "you have found a beau in the water."

"And the fisherman of the Pass, too," laughed her cousin Ida.

Annette tossed her head, for Philip had growled audibly.

"Do you know, Philip," cried Annette a few days after, rudely shaking him from his siesta on the gallery,—"do you know that I have found my fisherman's hut?"

"Hum," was the only response.

"Yes, and it's the quaintest, most delightful spot imaginable. Philip, do come with me and see it."

"Hum."

"Oh, Philip, you are so lazy; do come with me."

"Yes, but, my dear Annette," protested Philip, "this is a warm day, and I am tired."

Still, his curiosity being aroused, he went grumbling. It was not a very long drive, back from the beach across the railroad and through the pine forest to the bank of a dark, slow-flowing bayou. The fisherman's hut was small, two-roomed, whitewashed, pine-boarded, with the traditional mud chimney acting as a sort of support to one of its uneven sides. Within was a weird assortment of curios from every uncivilized part of the globe. Also were there fishing-tackle and guns in reckless profusion. The fisherman, in the kitchen of the mud-chimney, was sardonically waging war with a basket of little bayou crabs.

"Entrez, mademoiselle et monsieur," he said pleasantly, grabbing a vicious crab by its flippers, and smiling at its wild attempts to bite. "You see I am busy, but make yourself at home."

"Well, how on earth—" began Philip.

"Sh—sh—" whispered Annette. "I was driving out in the woods this morning, and stumbled on the hut. He asked me in, but I came right over after you."

The fisherman, having succeeded in getting the last crab in the kettle of boiling water, came forward smiling and began to explain the curios.

"Then you have not always lived at Pass Christian," said Philip.

"Mais non, monsieur, I am spending a summer here."

"And he spends his winters, doubtless, selling fish in the French market," spitefully soliloquised Philip.

The fisherman was looking unutterable things into Annette's eyes, and, it seemed to Philip, taking an unconscionably long time explaining the use of an East Indian stiletto.

"Oh, wouldn't it be delightful!" came from Annette at last.

"What?" asked Philip.

"Why, Monsieur LeConte says he'll take six of us

out in his catboat tomorrow for a fishing-trip on the Gulf."

"Hum," drily.

"And I'll get Natalie and her cousins."

"Yes," still more drily.

Annette chattered on, entirely oblivious of the strainedness of the men's adieus, and still chattered as they drove through the pines.

"I did not know that you were going to take fishermen and marchands into the bosom of your social set when you came here," growled Philip, at last.

"But, Cousin Phil, can't you see he is a gentleman? The fact that he makes no excuses or protestations is a proof."

"You are a fool," was the polite response.

Still, at six o'clock next morning, there was a little crowd of seven upon the pier, laughing and chatting at the little "Virginie" dipping her bows in the water and flapping her sails in the brisk wind. Natalie's pink bonnet blushed in the early sunshine, and Natalie's mamma, comely and portly, did chaperonage duty. It was not long before the sails gave swell into the breeze and the little boat scurried to the Sound. Past the lighthouse on its gawky iron stalls, she flew, and now rounded the white sands of Cat Island.

"Bravo, the Gulf!" sang a voice on the lookout.

The little boat dipped, halted an instant, then rushed fast into the blue Gulf waters.

"We will anchor here," said the host, "have luncheon, and fish."

Philip could not exactly understand why the fisherman should sit so close to Annette and whisper so much into her ears. He chafed at her acting the part of hostess, and was possessed of a murderous desire to throw the pink sun-bonnet and its owner into the sea, when Natalie whispered audibly to one of her cousins that "Mees Annette act nice wit' her lovare."

The sun was banking up flaming pillars of rose and gold in the west when the little "Virginie" rounded Cat Island on her way home, and the quick Southern twilight was fast dying into darkness when she was tied up to the pier and the merry-makers sprang off with baskets of fish. Annette had distinguished herself by catching one small shark, and had immediately ceased to fish and devoted her attention to her fisherman and his line. Philip had angled fiercely, landing trout, croakers, sheepshead, snappers in bewildering luck. He had broken each hopeless captive's neck savagely, as though they were personal enemies. He did not look happy as they landed, though pæans of praise were being sung in his honour.

As the days passed on, "the fisherman of the

Pass" began to dance attendance on Annette. What had seemed a joke became serious. Aunt Nina, urged by Philip, remonstrated, and even the mamma of the pink sunbonnet began to look grave. It was all very well for a city demoiselle to talk with a fisherman and accept favours at his hands, provided that the city demoiselle understood that a vast and bridgeless gulf stretched between her and the fisherman. But when the demoiselle forgot the gulf and the fisherman refused to recognise it, why, it was time to take matters in hand.

To all of Aunt Nina's remonstrances, Philip's growlings, and the averted glances of her companions, Annette was deaf. "You are narrow-minded," she said laughingly. "I am interested in Monsieur LeConte simply as a study. He is entertaining; he talks well of his travels, and as for refusing to recognise the difference between us, why, he never dreamed of such a thing."

Suddenly a peremptory summons home from Annette's father put an end to the fears of Philip. Annette pouted, but papa must be obeyed. She blamed Philip and Aunt Nina for telling tales, but Aunt Nina was uncommunicative, and Philip too obviously cheerful to derive much satisfaction from.

That night she walked with the fisherman hand in hand on the sands. The wind from the pines bore the scarcely recognisable, subtle freshness of early autumn, and the waters had a hint of dying summer in their sob on the beach.

"You will remember," said the fisherman, "that I have told you nothing about myself."

"Yes," murmured Annette.

"And you will keep your promises to me?"

"Yes."

"Let me hear you repeat them again."

"I promise you that I will not forget you. I promise you that I will never speak of you to anyone until I see you again. I promise that I will then clasp your hand wherever you may be."

"And mademoiselle will not be discouraged, but will continue her studies?"

"Yes."

It was all very romantic, by the waves of the Sound, under a harvest moon, that seemed all sympathy for these two, despite the fact that it was probably looking down upon hundreds of other equally romantic couples. Annette went to bed with glowing cheeks, and a heart whose pulsations would have caused a physician to prescribe unlimited digitalis.

It was still hot in New Orleans when she returned home, and it seemed hard to go immediately to work. But if one is going to be an opera-singer some day and capture the world with one's voice, there is nothing to do but to study, study, sing, practise, even though one's throat be parched, one's head a great ache, and one's heart a nest of discouragement and sadness at what seems the uselessness of it all. Annette had now a new incentive to work; the fisherman had once praised her voice when she hummed a barcarole on the sands, and he had insisted that there was power in its rich notes. Though the fisherman had showed no cause why he should be accepted as a musical critic, Annette had somehow respected his judgment and been accordingly elated.

It was the night of the opening of the opera. There was the usual crush, the glitter and confusing radiance of the brilliant audience. Annette, with papa, Aunt Nina, and Philip, was late reaching her box. The curtain was up, and "La Juive" was pouring forth defiance at her angry persecutors. Annette listened breathlessly. In fancy, she too was ringing her voice out to an applauding house. Her head unconsciously beat time to the music, and one hand half held her cloak from her bare shoulders.

Then Eleazar appeared, and the house rose at the end of his song. Encores it gave, and bravos and cheers. He bowed calmly, swept his eyes over the tiers until they found Annette, where they rested in a half-smile of recognition.

"Philip," gasped Annette, nervously raising her glasses, "my fisherman!"

"Yes, an opera-singer is better than a marchand," drawled Philip.

The curtain fell on the first act. The house was won by the new tenor; it called and recalled him before the curtain. Clearly he had sung his way into the hearts of his audience at once.

"Papa, Aunt Nina," said Annette, "you must come behind the scenes with me. I want you to meet him. He is delightful. You must come."

Philip was bending ostentatiously over the girl in the next box. Papa and Aunt Nina consented to be dragged behind the scenes. Annette was well known, for, in hopes of some day being an occupant of one of the dressing-rooms, she had made friends with everyone connected with the opera.

Eleazar received them, still wearing his brown garb and patriarchal beard.

"How you deceived me!" she laughed, when the greetings and introductions were over.

"I came to America early," he smiled back at her, "and thought I'd try a little incognito at the Pass. I was not well, you see. It has been of great benefit to me."

"I kept my promise," she said in a lower tone.

"Thank you; that also has helped me."

Annette's teacher began to note a wonderful improvement in his pupil's voice. Never did a girl study so hard or practise so faithfully. It was truly wonderful. Now and then Annette would say to papa as if to reassure herself,—

"And when Monsieur Cherbart says I am ready to go to Paris, I may go, papa?"

And papa would say a "Certainly" that would send her back to the piano with renewed ardour.

As for Monsieur LeConte, he was the idol of New Orleans. Seldom had there been a tenor who had sung himself so completely into the very hearts of a populace. When he was billed, the opera displayed "Standing Room" signs, no matter what the other attractions in the city might be. Sometimes Monsieur LeConte delighted small audiences in Annette's parlour, when the hostess was in a perfect flutter of happiness. Not often, you know, for the leading tenor was in great demand at the homes of society queens.

"Do you know," said Annette, petulantly, one evening, "I wish for the old days at Pass Christian."

"So do I," he answered tenderly; "will you repeat them with me next summer?"

"If I only could!" she gasped.

Still she might have been happy, had it not been for Madame Dubeau,—Madame Dubeau, the flute-voiced leading soprano, who wore the single dainty curl on her forehead, and thrilled her audiences often-times more completely than the fisherman. Madame Dubeau was La Juive to his Eleazar, Leonore to his Manfred, Elsa to his Lohengrin, Aida to his Rhad-ames, Marguerite to his Faust; in brief, Madame Dubeau was his opposite. She caressed him as Mignon, pleaded with him as Michaela, died for him in "Les Huguenots," broke her heart for love of him in "La Favorite." How could he help but love her, Annette asked herself, how could he? Madame Dubeau was beautiful and gifted and charming.

Once she whispered her fears to him when there was the meagrest bit of an opportunity. He laughed. "You don't understand, little one," he said tenderly; "the relations of professional people to each other are peculiar. After you go to Paris, you will know."

Still, New Orleans had built up its romance, and gossiped accordingly.

"Have you heard the news?" whispered Lola to Annette, leaning from her box at the opera one night. The curtain had just gone up on "Herodias," and for some reason or other, the audience applauded with more warmth than usual. There was a noticeable number of good-humoured, benignant smiles on the faces of the applauders.

"No," answered Annette, breathlessly,—"no, indeed, Lola; I am going to Paris next week. I am so delighted I can't stop to think."

"Yes, that is excellent," said Lola, "but all New Orleans is smiling at the romance. Monsieur LeConte and Madame Dubeau were quietly married last night, but it leaked out this afternoon. See all the applause she's receiving!"

Annette leaned back in her chair, very white and still. Her box was empty after the first act, and a quiet little tired voice that was almost too faint to be heard in the carriage on the way home, said—

"Papa, I don't think I care to go to Paris, after all."

H. G. WELLS

In the Modern Vein
An Unsympathetic Love Story

Of course the cultivated reader has heard of Aubrey Vair. He has published on three several occasions volumes of delicate verses,—some, indeed, border on indelicacy,—and his column "Of Things Literary" in the *Climax* is well known. His Byronic visage and an interview have appeared in the *Perfect Lady*. It was Aubrey Vair, I believe, who demonstrated that the humour of Dickens was worse than his sentiment, and who detected "a subtle bourgeois flavour" in Shakespeare. However, it is not generally known that Aubrey Vair has had erotic experiences as well as erotic inspirations. He adopted Goethe some little time since as his literary prototype, and that may have had something to do with his temporary lapse from sexual integrity.

For it is one of the commonest things that undermine literary men, giving us landslips and picturesque effects along the otherwise even cliff of their respectable life, ranking next to avarice, and certainly above drink, this instability called genius, or, more fully, the consciousness of genius, such as

Aubrey Vair possessed. Since Shelley set the fashion, your man of gifts has been assured that his duty to himself and his duty to his wife are incompatible, and his renunciation of the Philistine has been marked by such infidelity as his means and courage warranted. Most virtue is lack of imagination. At any rate, a minor genius without his affections twisted into an inextricable muddle, and who did not occasionally shed sonnets over his troubles, I have never met.

Even Aubrey Vair did this, weeping the sonnets overnight into his blotting-book, and pretending to write literary *causerie* when his wife came down in her bath slippers to see what kept him up. She did not understand him, of course. He did this even before the other woman appeared, so ingrained is conjugal treachery in the talented mind. Indeed, he wrote more sonnets before the other woman came than after that event, because thereafter he spent much of his leisure in cutting down the old productions, retrimming them, and generally altering this readymade clothing of his passion to suit her particular height and complexion.

Aubrey Vair lived in a little red villa with a lawn at the back and a view of the Downs behind Reigate. He lived upon discreet investment eked out by literary work. His wife was handsome, sweet, and gentle, and—such is the tender humility of good married women—she found her life's happiness in seeing that little Aubrey Vair had well-cooked variety for dinner, and that their house was the neatest and brightest of all the houses they entered.

Aubrey Vair enjoyed the dinners, and was proud of the house, yet nevertheless he mourned because his genius dwindled. Moreover, he grew plump, and corpulence threatened him.

We learn in suffering what we teach in song, and Aubrey Vair knew certainly that his soul could give no creditable crops unless his affections were harrowed. And how to harrow them was the trouble, for Reigate is a moral neighbourhood.

So Aubrey Vair's romantic longings blew loose for a time, much as a seedling creeper might, planted in the midst of a flower-bed. But at last, in the fulness of time, the other woman came to the embrace of Aubrey Vair's yearning heart-tendrils, and his romantic episode proceeded as is here faithfully written down.

The other woman was really a girl, and Aubrey Vair met her first at a tennis party at Redhill. Aubrey Vair did not play tennis after the accident to Miss Morton's eye, and because latterly it made him pant and get warmer and moister than even a poet should be; and this young lady had only recently arrived in

England, and could not play. So they gravitated into the two vacant basket chairs beside Mrs. Bayne's deaf aunt, in front of the hollyhocks, and were presently talking at their ease together.

The other woman's name was unpropitious,— Miss Smith,—but you would never have suspected it from her face and costume. Her parentage was promising, she was an orphan, her mother was a Hindoo, and her father an Indian civil servant; and Aubrey Vair—himself a happy mixture of Kelt and Teuton, as, indeed, all literary men have to be nowadays—naturally believed in the literary consequences of a mixture of races. She was dressed in white. She had finely moulded pale features, great depth of expression, and a cloud of delicately *frisé* black hair over her dark eyes, and she looked at Aubrey Vair with a look half curious and half shy, that contrasted admirably with the stereotyped frankness of your common Reigate girl.

"This is a splendid lawn—the best in Redhill," said Aubrey Vair in the course of the conversation; "and I like it all the better because the daisies are spared." He indicated the daisies with a graceful sweep of his rather elegant hand.

"They are sweet little flowers," said the lady in white, "and I have always associated them with England, chiefly, perhaps, through a picture I saw 'over there' when I was very little, of children making daisy chains. I promised myself that pleasure when I came home. But, alas! I feel now rather too large for such delights."

"I do not see why we should not be able to enjoy these simple pleasures as we grow older—why our growth should have in it so much forgetting. For my own part"—

"Has your wife got Jane's recipe for stuffing trout?" asked Mrs. Bayne's deaf aunt abruptly.

"I really don't know," said Aubrey Vair.

"That's all right," said Mrs. Bayne's deaf aunt. "It ought to please even you."

"Anything will please me," said Aubrey Vair; "I care very little"—

"Oh, it's a lovely dish," said Mrs. Bayne's deaf aunt, and relapsed into contemplation.

"I was saying," said Aubrey Vair, "that I think I still find my keenest pleasures in childish pastimes. I have a little nephew that I see a great deal of, and when we fly kites together, I am sure it would be hard to tell which of us is the happier. By the bye, you should get at your daisy chains in that way. Beguile some little girl."

"But I did. I took that Morton mite for a walk in the meadows, and timidly broached the subject. And she reproached me for suggesting 'frivolous pursuits.' It was a horrible disappointment."

"The governess here," said Aubrey Vair, "is robbing that child of its youth in a terrible way. What will a life be that has no childhood at the beginning?"

"Some human beings are never young," he continued, "and they never grow up. They lead absolutely colourless lives. They are—they are etiolated. They never love, and never feel the loss of it. They are—for the moment I can think of no better image—they are human flower-pots, in which no soul has been planted. But a human soul properly growing must begin in a fresh childishness."

"Yes," said the dark lady thoughtfully, "a careless childhood, running wild almost. That should be the beginning."

"Then we pass through the wonder and diffidence of youth."

"To strength and action," said the dark lady. Her dreamy eyes were fixed on the Downs, and her fingers tightened on her knees as she spoke. "Ah, it is a grand thing to live—as a man does—self-reliant and free."

"And so at last," said Aubrey Vair, "come to the culmination and crown of life." He paused and glanced hastily at her. Then he dropped his voice almost to a whisper—"And the culmination of life is love."

Their eyes met for a moment, but she looked away at once. Aubrey Vair felt a peculiar thrill and a catching in his breath, but his emotions were too complex for analysis. He had a certain sense of surprise, also, at the way his conversation had developed.

Mrs. Bayne's deaf aunt suddenly dug him in the chest with her ear-trumpet, and someone at tennis bawled, "Love all!"

"Did I tell you Jane's girls have had scarlet fever?" asked Mrs. Bayne's deaf aunt.

"No," said Aubrey Vair.

"Yes; and they are peeling now," said Mrs. Bayne's deaf aunt, shutting her lips tightly, and nodding in a slow, significant manner at both of them.

There was a pause. All three seemed lost in thought, too deep for words.

"Love," began Aubrey Vair presently, in a severely philosophical tone, leaning back in his chair, holding his hands like a praying saint's in front of him, and staring at the toe of his shoe,—"love is, I believe, the one true and real thing in life. It rises above reason, interest, or explanation. Yet I never read of an age when it was so much forgotten as it is now. Never was love expected to run so much in appointed channels, never was it so despised, checked, ordered, and obstructed. Policemen say, 'This way, Eros!' As a result, we relieve our emotional possibilities in the hunt for gold and notoriety. And after all, with the best fortune in these, we only hold up the gilded images of our success, and are weary slaves, with unsatisfied hearts, in the pageant of life."

Aubrey Vair sighed, and there was a pause. The girl looked at him out of the mysterious darkness of her eyes. She had read many books, but Aubrey Vair was her first literary man, and she took this kind of thing for genius—as girls have done before.

"We are," continued Aubrey Vair, conscious of a favourable impression,—"we are like fireworks, mere dead, inert things until the appointed spark comes; and then—if it is not damp—the dormant soul blazes forth in all its warmth and beauty. That is living. I sometimes think, do you know, that we should be happier if we could die soon after that golden time, like the Ephemerides. There is a decay sets in."

"Eigh?" said Mrs. Bayne's deaf aunt startlingly. "I didn't hear you."

"I was on the point of remarking," shouted Aubrey Vair, wheeling the array of his thoughts,—"I was on the point of remarking that few people in

Redhill could match Mrs. Morton's fine broad green."

"Others have noticed it," Mrs. Bayne's deaf aunt shouted back. "It is since she has had in her new false teeth."

This interruption dislocated the conversation a little. However—

"I must thank you, Mr. Vair," said the dark girl, when they parted that afternoon, "for having given me very much to think about."

And from her manner, Aubrey Vair perceived clearly he had not wasted his time.

It would require a subtler pen than mine to tell how from that day a passion for Miss Smith grew like Jonah's gourd in the heart of Aubrey Vair. He became pensive, and in the prolonged absence of Miss Smith, irritable. Mrs. Aubrey Vair felt the change in him, and put it down to a vitriolic Saturday Reviewer. Indisputably the *Saturday* does at times go a little far. He re-read *Elective Affinities*, and lent it to Miss Smith. Incredible as it may appear to members of the Areopagus Club, where we know Aubrey Vair, he did also beyond all question inspire a sort of passion in that sombre-eyed, rather clever, and really very beautiful girl.

He talked to her a lot about love and destiny, and

all that bric-à-brac of the minor poet. And they talked together about his genius. He elaborately, though discreetly, sought her society, and presented and read to her the milder of his unpublished sonnets. We consider his Byronic features pasty, but the feminine mind has its own laws. I suppose, also where a girl is not a fool, a literary man has an enormous advantage over anyone but a preacher, in the show he can make of his heart's wares.

At last a day in that summer came when he met her alone, possibly by chance, in a quiet lane towards Horley. There were ample hedges on either side, rich with honeysuckle, vetch, and mullein.

They conversed intimately of his poetic ambitions, and then he read her those verses of his subsequently published in *Hobson's Magazine*: "Tenderly ever, since I have met thee." He had written these the day before; and though I think the sentiment is uncommonly trite, there is a redeeming note of sincerity about the lines not conspicuous in all Aubrey Vair's poetry.

He read rather well, and a swell of genuine emotion crept into his voice as he read, with one white hand thrown out to point the rhythm of the lines. "Ever, my sweet, for thee," he concluded, looking up into her face.

Before he looked up, he had been thinking chiefly

of his poem and its effect. Straightway he forgot it. Her arms hung limply before her, and her hands were clasped together. Her eyes were very tender.

"Your verses go to the heart," she said softly.

Her mobile features were capable of wonderful shades of expression. He suddenly forgot his wife and his position as a minor poet as he looked at her. It is possible that his classical features may themselves have undergone a certain transfiguration. For one brief moment—and it was always to linger in his memory—destiny lifted him out of his vain little self to a nobler level of simplicity. The copy of "Tenderly ever" fluttered from his hand. Considerations vanished. Only one thing seemed of importance.

"I love you," he said abruptly.

An expression of fear came into her eyes. The grip of her hands upon one another tightened convulsively. She became very pale.

Then she moved her lips as if to speak, bringing her face slightly nearer to his. There was nothing in the world at that moment for either of them but one another. They were both trembling exceedingly. In a whisper she said, "You love me?"

Aubrey Vair stood quivering and speechless, looking into her eyes. He had never seen such a light as he saw there before. He was in a wild tumult of emotion. He was dreadfully scared at what he had done. He could not say another word. He nodded.

"And this has come to me?" she said presently, in the same awe-stricken whisper, and then, "Oh, my love, my love!"

And thereupon Aubrey Vair had her clasped to himself, her cheek upon his shoulder and his lips to hers.

Thus it was that Aubrey Vair came by the cardinal memory of his life. To this day it recurs in his works.

A little boy clambering in the hedge some way down the lane saw this group with surprise, and then with scorn and contempt. Recking nothing of his destiny, he turned away, feeling that he at least could never come to the unspeakable unmanliness of hugging girls. Unhappily for Reigate scandal, his shame for his sex was altogether too deep for words.

An hour after, Aubrey Vair returned home in a hushed mood. There were muffins after his own heart for his tea—Mrs. Aubrey Vair had had hers. And there were chrysanthemums, chiefly white ones,—flowers he loved,—set out in the china bowl he was wont to praise. And his wife came behind him to kiss him as he sat eating.

"De lill Jummuns," she remarked, kissing him under the ear.

Then it came into the mind of Aubrey Vair with startling clearness, while his ear was being kissed, and with his mouth full of muffin, that life is a singularly complex thing.

The summer passed at last into the harvest-time, and the leaves began falling. It was evening, the warm sunset light still touched the Downs, but up the valley a blue haze was creeping. One or two lamps in Reigate were already alight.

About half-way up the slanting road that scales the Downs, there is a wooden seat where one may obtain a fine view of the red villas scattered below, and of the succession of blue hills beyond. Here the girl with the shadowy face was sitting.

She had a book on her knees, but it lay neglected. She was leaning forward, her chin resting upon her hand. She was looking across the valley into the darkening sky, with troubled eyes.

Aubrey Vair appeared through the hazel-bushes, and sat down beside her. He held half a dozen dead leaves in his hand.

She did not alter her attitude. "Well?" she said.

"Is it to be flight?" he asked.

Aubrey Vair was rather pale. He had been having

bad nights latterly, with dreams of the Continental Express, Mrs. Aubrey Vair possibly even in pursuit,—he always fancied her making the tragedy ridiculous by tearfully bringing additional pairs of socks, and any such trifles he had forgotten, with her,—all Reigate and Redhill in commotion. He had never eloped before, and he had visions of difficulties with hotel proprietors. Mrs. Aubrey Vair might telegraph ahead. Even he had had a prophetic vision of a headline in a halfpenny evening newspaper: "Young Lady abducts a Minor Poet." So there was a quaver in his voice as he asked, "Is it to be flight?"

"As you will," she answered, still not looking at him.

"I want you to consider particularly how this will affect you. A man," said Aubrey Vair, slowly, and staring hard at the leaves in his hand, "even gains a certain éclat in these affairs. But to a woman it is ruin—social, moral."

"This is not love," said the girl in white.

"Ah, my dearest! Think of yourself."

"Stupid!" she said, under her breath.

"You spoke?"

"Nothing."

"But cannot we go on, meeting one another, loving one another, without any great scandal or misery? Could we not"—

174

"That," interrupted Miss Smith, "would be unspeakably horrible."

"This is a dreadful conversation to me. Life is so intricate, such a web of subtle strands binds us this way and that. I cannot tell what is right. You must consider"—

"A man would break such strands."

"There is no manliness," said Aubrey Vair, with a sudden glow of moral exaltation, "in doing wrong. My love"—

"We could at least die together, dearest," she said.

"Good Lord!" said Aubrey Vair. "I mean—consider my wife."

"You have not considered her hitherto."

"There is a flavour—of cowardice, of desertion, about suicide," said Aubrey Vair. "Frankly, I have the English prejudice, and do not like any kind of running away."

Miss Smith smiled very faintly. "I see clearly now what I did not see. My love and yours are very different things."

"Possibly it is a sexual difference," said Aubrey Vair; and then, feeling the remark inadequate, he relapsed into silence.

They sat for some time without a word. The two lights in Reigate below multiplied to a score of bright points, and, above, one star had become visible. She began laughing, an almost noiseless, hysterical laugh that jarred unaccountably upon Aubrey Vair.

Presently she stood up. "They will wonder where I am," she said. "I think I must be going."

He followed her to the road. "Then this is the end?" he said, with a curious mixture of relief and poignant regret.

"Yes, this is the end," she answered, and turned away.

There straightway dropped into the soul of Aubrey Vair a sense of infinite loss. It was an altogether new sensation. She was perhaps twenty yards away, when he groaned aloud with the weight of it, and suddenly began running after her with his arms extended.

"Annie," he cried,—"Annie! I have been talking *rot*. Annie, now I know I love you! I cannot spare you. This must not be. I did not understand."

The weight was horrible.

"Oh, stop, Annie!" he cried, with a breaking voice, and there were tears on his face.

She turned upon him suddenly, and his arms fell by his side. His expression changed at the sight of her pale face.

"You do not understand," she said. "I have said good-bye."

She looked at him; he was evidently greatly distressed, a little out of breath, and he had just stopped blubbering. His contemptible quality reached the pathetic. She came up close to him, and, taking his damp Byronic visage between her hands, she kissed him again and again. "Good-bye, little man that I loved," she said; "and good-bye to this folly of love."

Then, with something that may have been a laugh or a sob,—she herself, when she came to write it all in her novel, did not know which,—she turned and hurried away again, and went out of the path that Aubrey Vair must pursue, at the cross-roads.

Aubrey Vair stood, where she had kissed him, with a mind as inactive as his body, until her white dress had disappeared. Then he gave an involuntary sigh, a large exhaustive expiration, and so awoke himself, and began walking, pensively dragging his feet through the dead leaves, home. Emotions are terrible things.

"Do you like the potatoes, dear?" asked Mrs. Aubrey Vair at dinner. "I cooked them myself."

Aubrey Vair descended slowly from cloudy, impalpable meditations to the level of fried potatoes. "These potatoes"—he remarked, after a pause during which he was struggling with recollection.

"Yes. These potatoes have exactly the tints of the dead leaves of the hazel."

"What a fanciful poet it is!" said Mrs. Aubrey Vair. "Taste them. They are very nice potatoes indeed."

Lilacs

Mme. Adrienne Farival never announced her coming; but the good nuns knew very well when to look for her. When the scent of the lilac blossoms began to permeate the air, Sister Agathe would turn many times during the day to the window; upon her face the happy, beatific expression with which pure and simple souls watch for the coming of those they love.

But it was not Sister Agathe; it was Sister Marceline who first espied her crossing the beautiful lawn that sloped up to the convent. Her arms were filled with great bunches of lilacs which she had gathered along her path. She was clad all in brown; like one of the birds that come with the spring, the nuns used to say. Her figure was rounded and graceful, and she walked with a happy, buoyant step. The cabriolet which had conveyed her to the convent moved slowly up the gravel drive that led to the imposing entrance. Beside the driver was her modest little black trunk, with her name and address printed in white letters upon it: "Mme. A. Farival, Paris." It was the crunching of the gravel which had attracted

Sister Marceline's attention. And then the commotion began.

White-capped heads appeared suddenly at the windows; she waved her parasol and her bunch of lilacs at them. Sister Marceline and Sister Marie Anne appeared, fluttered and expectant at the doorway. But Sister Agathe, more daring and impulsive than all, descended the steps and flew across the grass to meet her. What embraces, in which the lilacs were crushed between them! What ardent kisses! What pink flushes of happiness mounting the cheeks of the two women!

Once within the convent Adrienne's soft brown eyes moistened with tenderness as they dwelt caressingly upon the familiar objects about her, and noted the most trifling details. The white, bare boards of the floor had lost nothing of their luster. The stiff, wooden chairs, standing in rows against the walls of hall and parlor, seemed to have taken on an extra polish since she had seen them, last lilac time. And there was a new picture of the Sacré-Coeur hanging over the hall table. What had they done with Ste. Catherine de Sienne, who had occupied that position of honor for so many years? In the chapel—it was no use trying to deceive her—she saw at a glance that St. Joseph's mantle had been embellished with a new coat of blue, and the aureole about his head freshly gilded. And the Blessed Virgin there neglected! Still wearing her garb of last spring, which looked almost dingy by contrast. It was not just—such partiality! The Holy Mother had reason to be jealous and to complain.

But Adrienne did not delay to pay her respects to the Mother Superior, whose dignity would not permit her to so much as step outside the door of her private apartments to welcome this old pupil. Indeed, she was dignity in person; large, uncompromising, unbending. She kissed Adrienne without warmth, and discussed conventional themes learnedly and prosaically during the quarter of an hour which the young woman remained in her company.

It was then that Adrienne's latest gift was brought in for inspection. For Adrienne always brought a handsome present for the chapel in her little black trunk. Last year it was a necklace of gems for the Blessed Virgin, which the Good Mother was only permitted to wear on extra occasions, such as great feast days of obligation. The year before it had been a precious crucifix—an ivory figure of Christ suspended from an ebony cross, whose extremities were tipped with wrought silver. This time it was a linen embroidered altar cloth of such rare and delicate workmanship that the Mother Superior, who knew the value of such things, chided Adrienne for the extravagance.

"But, dear Mother, you know it is the greatest pleasure I have in life—to be with you all once a year, and to bring some such trifling token of my regard."

The Mother Superior dismissed her with the rejoinder: "Make yourself at home, my child. Sister Thérèse will see to your wants. You will occupy Sister Marceline's bed in the end room, over the chapel. You will share the room with Sister Agathe."

There was always one of the nuns detailed to keep Adrienne company during her fortnight's stay at the convent. This had become almost a fixed regulation. It was only during the hours of recreation that she found herself with them all together. Those were hours of much harmless merry-making under the trees or in the nuns' refectory.

This time it was Sister Agathe who waited for her outside of the Mother Superior's door. She was taller and slenderer than Adrienne, and perhaps ten years older. Her fair blonde face flushed and paled with every passing emotion that visited her soul. The two women linked arms and went together out into the open air.

There was so much which Sister Agathe felt that Adrienne must see. To begin with, the enlarged poultry yard, with its dozens upon dozens of new inmates. It took now all the time of one of the lay sisters to attend to them. There had been no change made in the vegetable garden, but—yes there had; Adrienne's quick eye at once detected it. Last year old Philippe had planted his cabbages in a large square to the right. This year they were set out in an oblong bed to the left. How it made Sister Agathe laugh to think Adrienne should have noticed such a trifle! And old Philippe, who was nailing a broken trellis not far off, was called forward to be told about it.

He never failed to tell Adrienne how well she looked, and how she was growing younger each year. And it was his delight to recall certain of her youthful and mischievous escapades. Never would he forget that day she disappeared; and the whole convent in a hubbub about it! And how at last it was he who discovered her perched among the tallest branches of the highest tree on the grounds, where she had climbed to see if she could get a glimpse of Paris! And her punishment afterwards!—half of the Gospel of Palm Sunday to learn by heart!

"We may laugh over it, my good Philippe, but we must remember that Madame is older and wiser now."

"I know well, Sister Agathe, that one ceases to

commit follies after the first days of youth." And Adrienne seemed greatly impressed by the wisdom of Sister Agathe and old Philippe, the convent gardener.

A little later when they sat upon a rustic bench which overlooked the smiling landscape about them, Adrienne was saying to Sister Agathe, who held her hand and stroked it fondly:

"Do you remember my first visit, four years ago, Sister Agathe? and what a surprise it was to you all!"

"As if I could forget it, dear child!"

"And I! Always shall I remember that morning as I walked along the boulevard with a heaviness of heart—oh, a heaviness which I hate to recall. Suddenly there was wafted to me the sweet odor of lilac blossoms. A young girl had passed me by, carrying a great bunch of them. Did you ever know, Sister Agathe, that there is nothing which so keenly revives a memory as a perfume—an odor?"

"I believe you are right, Adrienne. For now that you speak of it, I can feel how the odor of fresh bread—when Sister Jeanne bakes—always makes me think of the great kitchen of ma tante de Sierge, and crippled Julie, who sat always knitting at the sunny window. And I never smell the sweet scented honeysuckle without living again through the blessed day of my first communion."

"Well, that is how it was with me, Sister Agathe, when the scent of the lilacs at once changed the whole current of my thoughts and my despondency. The boulevard, its noises, its passing throng, vanished from before my senses as completely as if they had been spirited away. I was standing here with my feet sunk in the green sward as they are now. I could see the sunlight glancing from that old white stone wall, could hear the notes of birds, just as we hear them now, and the humming of insects in the air. And through all I could see and could smell the lilac blossoms, nodding invitingly to me from their thick-leaved branches. It seems to me they are richer than ever this year, Sister Agathe. And do you know, I became like an *enragée*; nothing could have kept me back. I do not remember now where I was going; but I turned and retraced my steps homeward in a perfect fever of agitation: 'Sophie! my little trunk—quick—the black one! A mere handful of clothes! I am going away. Don't ask me any questions. I shall be back in a fortnight.' And every year since then it is the same. At the very first whiff of a lilac blossom, I am gone! There is no holding me back."

"And how I wait for you, and watch those lilac bushes, Adrienne! If you should once fail to come, it would be like the spring coming without the sunshine or the song of birds.

"But do you know, dear child, I have sometimes feared that in moments of despondency such as you have just described, I fear that you do not turn as you might to our Blessed Mother in heaven, who is ever ready to comfort and solace an afflicted heart with the precious balm of her sympathy and love."

"Perhaps I do not, dear Sister Agathe. But you cannot picture the annoyances which I am constantly submitted to. That Sophie alone, with her detestable ways! I assure you she of herself is enough to drive me to St. Lazare."

"Indeed, I do understand that the trials of one living in the world must be very great, Adrienne; particularly for you, my poor child, who have to bear them alone, since Almighty God was pleased to call to himself your dear husband. But on the other hand, to live one's life along the lines which our dear Lord traces for each one of us, must bring with it resignation and even a certain comfort. You have your household duties, Adrienne, and your music, to which, you say, you continue to devote yourself. And then, there are always good works—the poor—who are always with us—to be relieved; the afflicted to be comforted."

"But, Sister Agathe! Will you listen! Is it not La Rose that I hear moving down there at the edge of the pasture? I fancy she is reproaching me with being an ingrate, not to have pressed a kiss yet on that white forehead of hers. Come, let us go."

The two women arose and walked again, hand in hand this time, over the tufted grass down the gentle decline where it sloped toward the broad, flat meadow, and the limpid stream that flowed cool and fresh from the woods. Sister Agathe walked with her composed, nunlike tread; Adrienne with a balancing motion, a bounding step, as though the earth responded to her light footfall with some subtle impulse all its own.

They lingered long upon the foot-bridge that spanned the narrow stream which divided the convent grounds from the meadow beyond. It was to Adrienne indescribably sweet to rest there in soft, low converse with this gentle-faced nun, watching the approach of evening. The gurgle of the running water beneath them; the lowing of cattle approaching in the distance, were the only sounds that broke upon the stillness, until the clear tones of the angelus bell pealed out from the convent tower. At the sound both women instinctively sank to their knees, signing themselves with the sign of the cross. And Sister Agathe repeated the customary invocation, Adrienne responding in musical tones:

"The Angel of the Lord declared unto Mary,
And she conceived by the Holy Ghost—"

and so forth, to the end of the brief prayer, after which they arose and retraced their steps toward the convent.

It was with subtle and naive pleasure that Adrienne prepared herself that night for bed. The room which she shared with Sister Agathe was immaculately white. The walls were a dead white, relieved only by one florid print depicting Jacob's dream at the foot of the ladder, upon which angels mounted and descended. The bare floors, a soft yellow-white, with two little patches of gray carpet beside each spotless bed. At the head of the white-draped beds were two bénitiers containing holy water absorbed in sponges.

Sister Agathe disrobed noiselessly behind her curtains and glided into bed without having revealed, in the faint candlelight, as much as a shadow of herself. Adrienne pattered about the room, shook and folded her garments with great care, placing them on the back of a chair as she had been taught to do when a child at the convent. It secretly pleased Sister Agathe to feel that her dear Adrienne clung to the habits acquired in her youth.

But Adrienne could not sleep. She did not greatly desire to do so. These hours seemed too precious to be cast into the oblivion of slumber.

"Are you not asleep, Adrienne?"

"No, Sister Agathe. You know it is always so the first night. The excitement of my arrival—I don't know what—keeps me awake."

"Say your 'Hail, Mary,' dear child, over and over."

"I have done so, Sister Agathe; it does not help."

"Then lie quite still on your side and think of nothing but your own respiration. I have heard that such inducement to sleep seldom fails."

"I will try. Good night, Sister Agathe.

"Good night, dear child. May the Holy Virgin guard you."

An hour later Adrienne was still lying with wide, wakeful eyes, listening to the regular breathing of Sister Agathe. The trailing of the passing wind through the treetops, the ceaseless babble of the rivulet were some of the sounds that came to her faintly through the night.

The days of the fortnight which followed were in character much like the first peaceful, uneventful day of her arrival, with the exception only that she devoutly heard mass every morning at an early hour in the convent chapel, and on Sundays sang in the choir in her agreeable, cultivated voice, which was heard with delight and the warmest appreciation.

When the day of her departure came, Sister

Agathe was not satisfied to say good-bye at the portal as the others did. She walked down the drive beside the creeping old cabriolet, chattering her pleasant last words. And then she stood—it was as far as she might go—at the edge of the road, waving good-bye in response to the fluttering of Adrienne's handkerchief. Four hours later Sister Agathe, who was instructing a class of little girls for their first communion, looked up at the classroom clock and murmured: "Adrienne is at home now."

Yes, Adrienne was at home. Paris had engulfed her.

At the very hour when Sister Agathe looked up at the clock, Adrienne, clad in a charming negligee, was reclining indolently in the depths of a luxurious armchair. The bright room was in its accustomed state of picturesque disorder. Musical scores were scattered upon the open piano. Thrown carelessly over the backs of chairs were puzzling and astonishing-looking garments.

In a large gilded cage near the window perched a clumsy green parrot. He blinked stupidly at a young girl in street dress who was exerting herself to make him talk.

In the center of the room stood Sophie, that thorn in her mistress's side. With hands plunged in the deep pockets of her apron, her white starched cap quivering with each emphatic motion of her grizzled head, she was holding forth, to the evident ennui of the two young women. She was saying:

"Heaven knows I have stood enough in the six years I have been with Mademoiselle; but never such indignities as I have had to endure in the past two weeks at the hands of that man who calls himself a manager! The very first day—and I, good enough to notify him at once of Mademoiselle's flight—he arrives like a lion; I tell you, like a lion. He insists upon knowing Mademoiselle's whereabouts. How can I tell him any more than the statue out there in the square? He calls me a liar! Me, me—a liar! He declares he is ruined. The public will not stand La Petite Gilberta in the role which Mademoiselle has made so famous—La Petite Gilberta, who dances like a jointed wooden figure and sings like a *traînée* of a *café chantant*. If I were to tell La Gilberta that, as I easily might, I guarantee it would not be well for the few straggling hairs which he has left on that miserable head of his!

"What could he do? He was obliged to inform the public that Mademoiselle was ill; and then began my real torment! Answering this one and that one with their cards, their flowers, their dainties in covered dishes! which, I must admit, saved Florine and me much cooking. And all the while having to tell them that the physician had advised for Mademoiselle a rest of two weeks at some watering-place, the name of which I had forgotten!"

Adrienne had been contemplating old Sophie with quizzical, half-closed eyes, and pelting her with hot-house roses which lay in her lap, and which she nipped off short from their graceful stems for that purpose. Each rose struck Sophie full in the face; but they did not disconcert her or once stem the torrent of her talk.

"Oh, Adrienne!" entreated the young girl at the parrot's cage. "Make her hush; please do something. How can you ever expect Zozo to talk? A dozen times he has been on the point of saying something! I tell you, she stupefies him with her chatter."

"My good Sophie," remarked Adrienne, not changing her attitude, "you see the roses are all used up. But I assure you, anything at hand goes," carelessly picking up a book from the table beside her. "What is this? Mons. Zola! Now I warn you, Sophie, the weightiness, the heaviness of Mons. Zola are such that they cannot fail to prostrate you; thankful you may be if they leave you with energy to regain your feet."

"Mademoiselle's pleasantries are all very well; but if I am to be shown the door for it—if I am to be crippled for it—I shall say that I think Mademoiselle is a woman without conscience and without heart. To torture a man as she does! A man? No, an angel!

"Each day he has come with sad visage and drooping mien. No news, Sophie?'

"'None, Monsieur Henri.' 'Have you no idea where she has gone?' 'Not any more than the statue in the square, Monsieur.' 'Is it perhaps possible that she may not return at all?' with his face blanching like that curtain.

"I assure him you will be back at the end of the fortnight. I entreat him to have patience. He drags himself, *désolé*, about the room, picking up Mademoiselle's fan, her gloves, her music, and turning them over and over in his hands. Mademoiselle's slipper, which she took off to throw at me in the impatience of her departure, and which I purposely left lying where it fell on the chiffonier—he kissed it—I saw him do it—and thrust it into his pocket, thinking himself unobserved.

"The same song each day. I beg him to eat a little good soup which I have prepared. 'I cannot eat, my dear Sophie.' The other night he came and stood long gazing out of the window at the stars. When he turned he was wiping his eyes; they were red. He said he had been riding in the dust, which had inflamed them. But I knew better; he had been crying.

"*Ma foi!* in his place I would snap my finger at

such cruelty. I would go out and amuse myself. What is the use of being young!"

Adrienne arose with a laugh. She went and seizing old Sophie by the shoulders shook her till the white cap wobbled on her head.

"What is the use of all this litany, my good Sophie? Year after year the same! Have you forgotten that I have come a long, dusty journey by rail, and that I am perishing of hunger and thirst? Bring us a bottle of Château Yquem and a biscuit and my box of cigarettes." Sophie had freed herself, and was retreating toward the door. "And, Sophie! If Monsieur Henri is still waiting, tell him to come up."

It was precisely a year later. The spring had come again, and Paris was intoxicated.

Old Sophie sat in her kitchen discoursing to a neighbor who had come in to borrow some trifling kitchen utensil from the old *bonne*.

"You know, Rosalie, I begin to believe it is an attack of lunacy which seizes her once a year. I wouldn't say it to everyone, but with you I know it will go no further. She ought to be treated for it; a physician should be consulted; it is not well to neglect such things and let them run on.

"It came this morning like a thunder clap. As I am sitting here, there had been no thought or mention of a journey. The baker had come into the kitchen—you know what a gallant he is—with always a girl in his eye. He laid the bread down upon the table and beside it a bunch of lilacs. I didn't know they had bloomed yet. 'For Mam'selle Florine, with my regards,' he said with his foolish simper.

"Now, you know I was not going to call Florine from her work in order to present her the baker's flowers. All the same, it would not do to let them wither. I went with them in my hand into the dining room to get a majolica pitcher which I had put away in the closet there, on an upper shelf, because the handle was broken. Mademoiselle, who rises early, had just come from her bath, and was crossing the hall that opens into the dining room. Just as she was, in her white *peignoir*, she thrust her head into the dining room, snuffling the air and exclaiming, 'What do I smell?'

"She espied the flowers in my hand and pounced upon them like a cat upon a mouse. She held them up to her, burying her face in them for the longest time, only uttering a long 'Ah!'

"'Sophie, I am going away. Get out the little black trunk; a few of the plainest garments I have; my brown dress that I have not yet worn.'

"'But, Mademoiselle,' I protested, 'you forget that you have ordered a breakfast of a hundred francs for tomorrow.'

"'Shut up!' she cried, stamping her foot.

"'You forget how the manager will rave,' I persisted, 'and vilify me. And you will go like that without a word of adieu to Monsieur Paul, who is an angel if ever one trod the earth.'

"I tell you, Rosalie, her eyes flamed.

"'Do as I tell you this instant,' she exclaimed, 'or I will strangle you—with your Monsieur Paul and your manager and your hundred francs!'"

"Yes," affirmed Rosalie, "it is insanity. I had a cousin seized in the same way one morning, when she smelled calf's liver frying with onions. Before night it took two men to hold her."

"I could well see it was insanity, my dear Rosalie, and I uttered not another word as I feared for my life. I simply obeyed her every command in silence. And now—whiff, she is gone! God knows where. But between us, Rosalie—I wouldn't say it to Florine—but I believe it is for no good. I, in Monsieur Paul's place, should have her watched. I would put a detective upon her track.

"Now I am going to close up; barricade the entire establishment. Monsieur Paul, the manager, visitors, all—all may ring and knock and shout themselves hoarse. I am tired of it all. To be vilified and called a liar—at my age, Rosalie!"

★

Adrienne left her trunk at the small railway station, as the old cabriolet was not at the moment available; and she gladly walked the mile or two of pleasant roadway which led to the convent. How infinitely calm, peaceful, penetrating was the charm of the verdant, undulating country spreading out on all sides of her! She walked along the clear smooth road, twirling her parasol; humming a gay tune; nipping here and there a bud or a waxlike leaf from the hedges along the way; and all the while drinking deep draughts of complacency and content.

She stopped, as she had always done, to pluck lilacs in her path.

As she approached the convent she fancied that a white-capped face had glanced fleetingly from a window; but she must have been mistaken. Evidently she had not been seen, and this time would take them by surprise. She smiled to think how Sister Agathe would utter a little joyous cry of amazement, and in fancy she already felt the warmth and tenderness of the nun's embrace. And how Sister Marceline and the others would laugh, and make game of her puffed sleeves! For puffed sleeves had come into fashion since last year; and the vagaries of fashion always afforded infinite merriment to the nuns. No, they surely had not seen her.

She ascended lightly the stone steps and rang the

bell. She could hear the sharp metallic sound reverberate through the halls. Before its last note had died away the door was opened very slightly, very cautiously by a lay sister who stood there with downcast eyes and flaming cheeks. Through the narrow opening she thrust forward toward Adrienne a package and a letter, saying, in confused tones: "By order of our Mother Superior." After which she closed the door hastily and turned the heavy key in the great lock.

Adrienne remained stunned. She could not gather her faculties to grasp the meaning of this singular reception. The lilacs fell from her arms to the stone portico on which she was standing. She turned the note and the parcel stupidly over in her hands, instinctively dreading what their contents might disclose.

The outlines of the crucifix were plainly to be felt through the wrapper of the bundle, and she guessed, without having courage to assure herself, that the jeweled necklace and the altar cloth accompanied it.

Leaning against the heavy oaken door for support, Adrienne opened the letter. She did not seem to read the few bitter reproachful lines word by word—the lines that banished her forever from this haven of peace, where her soul was wont to come and refresh itself. They imprinted themselves as a

whole upon her brain, in all their seeming cruelty—
she did not dare to say injustice.

There was no anger in her heart; that would
doubtless possess her later, when her nimble intelli-
gence would begin to seek out the origin of this
treacherous turn. Now, there was only room for
tears. She leaned her forehead against the heavy
oaken panel of the door and wept with the abandonment of a little child.

She descended the steps with a nerveless and
dragging tread. Once as she was walking away, she
turned to look back at the imposing façade of the
convent, hoping to see a familiar face, or a hand,
even, giving a faint token that she was still cherished
by some one faithful heart. But she saw only the
polished windows looking down at her like so many
cold and glittering and reproachful eyes.

In the little white room above the chapel, a
woman knelt beside the bed on which Adrienne had
slept. Her face was pressed deep in the pillow in her
efforts to smother the sobs that convulsed her frame.
It was Sister Agathe.

After a short while, a lay sister came out of the
door with a broom, and swept away the lilac blossoms which Adrienne had let fall upon the portico.

FYODOR DOSTOEVSKY

A Little Hero
A story

At that time I was nearly eleven, I had been sent in
July to spend the holiday in a village near Moscow
with a relation of mine called T., whose house was
full of guests, fifty, or perhaps more ... I don't
remember, I didn't count. The house was full of
noise and gaiety. It seemed as though it were a continual holiday, which would never end. It seemed as
though our host had taken a vow to squander all his
vast fortune as rapidly as possible, and he did indeed
succeed, not long ago, in justifying this surmise, that
is, in making a clean sweep of it all to the last stick.

Fresh visitors used to drive up every minute.
Moscow was close by, in sight, so that those who
drove away only made room for others, and the
everlasting holiday went on its course. Festivities
succeeded one another, and there was no end in
sight to the entertainments. There were riding parties about the environs; excursions to the forest or
the river; picnics, dinners in the open air; suppers on
the great terrace of the house, bordered with three
rows of gorgeous flowers that flooded with their

fragrance the fresh night air, and illuminated the brilliant lights which made our ladies, who were almost every one of them pretty at all times, seem still more charming, with their faces excited by the impressions of the day, with their sparkling eyes, with their interchange of spritely conversation, their peals of ringing laughter; dancing, music, singing; if the sky were overcast tableaux vivants, charades, proverbs were arranged, private theatricals were got up. There were good talkers, story-tellers, wits.

Certain persons were prominent in the foreground. Of course backbiting and slander ran their course, as without them the world could not get on, and millions of persons would perish of boredom, like flies. But as I was at that time eleven I was absorbed by very different interests, and either failed to observe these people, or if I noticed anything, did not see it all. It was only afterwards that some things came back to my mind. My childish eyes could only see the brilliant side of the picture, and the general animation, splendour, and bustle—all that, seen and heard for the first time, made such an impression upon me that for the first few days, I was completely bewildered and my little head was in a whirl.

I keep speaking of my age, and of course I was a child, nothing more than a child. Many of these lovely ladies petted me without dreaming of considering my age. But strange to say, a sensation which I did not myself understand already had possession of me; something was already whispering in my heart, of which till then it had had no knowledge, no conception, and for some reason it began all at once to burn and throb, and often my face glowed with a sudden flush. At times I felt as it were abashed, and even resentful of the various privileges of my childish years. At other times a sort of wonder overwhelmed me, and I would go off into some corner where I could sit unseen, as though to take breath and remember something—something which it seemed to me I had remembered perfectly till then, and now had suddenly forgotten, something without which I could not show myself anywhere, and could not exist at all.

At last it seemed to me as though I were hiding something from every one. But nothing would have induced me to speak of it to any one, because, small boy that I was, I was ready to weep with shame. Soon in the midst of the vortex around me I was conscious of a certain loneliness. There were other children, but all were either much older or younger than I; besides, I was in no mood for them. Of course nothing would have happened to me if I had not been in an exceptional position. In the eyes of those charming ladies I was still the little unformed creature whom they at once liked to pet, and with whom they could play as though he were a little doll. One of them particularly, a fascinating, fair woman, with very thick luxuriant hair, such as I had never seen before and probably shall never see again, seemed to have taken a vow never to leave me in peace. I was confused, while she was amused by the laughter which she continually provoked from all around us by her wild, giddy pranks with me, and this apparently gave her immense enjoyment. At school among her schoolfellows she was probably nicknamed the Tease. She was wonderfully good-looking, and there was something in her beauty which drew one's eyes from the first moment. And certainly she had nothing in common with the ordinary modest little fair girls, white as down and soft as white mice, or pastors' daughters. She was not very tall, and was rather plump, but had soft, delicate, exquisitely cut features. There was something quick as lightning in her face, and indeed she was like fire all over, light, swift, alive. Her big open eyes seemed to flash sparks; they glittered like diamonds, and I would never exchange such blue sparkling eyes for any black ones, were they blacker than any Andalusian orb. And, indeed, my blonde was fully a match for the famous brunette whose praises were sung by a great and well-known poet, who, in a superb poem, vowed by all Castille that he was ready to break his bones to be permitted only to touch the mantle of his divinity with the tip of his finger. Add to that, that *my* charmer was the merriest in the world, the wildest giggler, playful as a child, although she had been married for the last five years. There was a continual laugh upon her lips, fresh as the morning rose that, with the first ray of sunshine, opens its fragrant crimson bud with the cool dewdrops still hanging heavy upon it.

I remember that the day after my arrival private theatricals were being got up. The drawing-room was, as they say, packed to overflowing; there was not a seat empty, and as I was somehow late I had to enjoy the performance standing. But the amusing play attracted me to move forwarder and forwarder, and unconsciously I made my way to the first row, where I stood at last leaning my elbows on the back of an armchair, in which a lady was sitting. It was my blonde divinity, but we had not yet made acquaintance. And I gazed, as it happened, at her marvellous, fascinating shoulders, plump and white as milk, though it did not matter to me in the least whether I stared at a woman's exquisite shoulders or at the cap with flaming ribbons that covered the grey locks of a venerable lady in the front row. Near my blonde divinity sat a spinster lady not in her first youth, one of those who, as I chanced to observe later, always take refuge in the immediate neighbourhood of young and pretty women, selecting such as are not fond of cold-shouldering young men. But that is not the point, only this lady, noting my fixed gaze, bent down to her neighbour and with a simper whispered something in her ear. The blonde lady turned at once, and I remember that her glowing eyes so flashed upon me in the half dark, that, not prepared to meet them, I started as though I were scalded. The beauty smiled.

"Do you like what they are acting?" she asked, looking into my face with a shy and mocking expression.

"Yes," I answered, still gazing at her with a sort of wonder that evidently pleased her.

"But why are you standing? You'll get tired. Can't you find a seat?"

"That's just it, I can't," I answered, more occupied with my grievance than with the beauty's sparkling eyes, and rejoicing in earnest at having found a kind heart to whom I could confide my troubles. "I have looked everywhere, but all the chairs are taken," I added, as though complaining to her that all the chairs were taken.

"Come here," she said briskly, quick to act on every decision, and, indeed, on every mad idea that flashed on her giddy brain, "come here, and sit on my knee."

"On your knee," I repeated, taken aback. I have mentioned already that I had begun to resent the privileges of childhood and to be ashamed of them in earnest. This lady, as though in derision, had gone ever so much further than the others. Moreover, I had always been a shy and bashful boy, and of late had begun to be particularly shy with women.

"Why yes, on my knee. Why don't you want to sit on my knee?" she persisted, beginning to laugh more and more, so that at last she was simply giggling, goodness knows at what, perhaps at her freak, or perhaps at my confusion. But that was just what she wanted.

I flushed, and in my confusion looked round trying to find where to escape; but seeing my intention she managed to catch hold of my hand to prevent me from going away, and pulling it towards her, suddenly, quite unexpectedly, to my intense astonishment, squeezed it in her mischievous warm fingers, and began to pinch my fingers till they hurt so much that I had to do my very utmost not to cry out, and in my effort to control myself made the most absurd grimaces. I was, besides, moved to the greatest amazement, perplexity, and even horror, at the discovery that there were ladies so absurd and spiteful as to talk nonsense to boys, and even pinch their fingers, for no earthly reason and before everybody. Probably my unhappy face reflected my bewilderment, for the mischievous creature laughed in my face, as though she were crazy, and meantime she was pinching my fingers more and more vigorously. She was highly delighted in playing such a mischievous prank and completely mystifying and embarrassing a poor boy. My position was desperate. In the first place I was hot with shame, because almost every one near had turned round to look at us, some in wonder, others with laughter, grasping at once that the beauty was up to some mischief. I dreadfully wanted to scream, too, for she was wringing my fingers with positive fury just because I didn't scream; while I, like a Spartan, made up my mind to endure the agony, afraid by crying out of causing a general fuss, which was more than I could face. In utter despair I began at last struggling with her, trying with all my might to pull away my hand, but my persecutor was much stronger than I was. At last I could bear it no longer, and uttered a shriek— that was all she was waiting for! Instantly she let me go, and turned away as though nothing had happened, as though it was not she who had played the trick but some one else, exactly like some schoolboy who, as soon as the master's back is turned, plays some trick on some one near him, pinches some small weak boy, gives him a flip, a kick, or a nudge with his elbows, and instantly turns again, buries himself in his book and begins repeating his lesson, and so makes a fool of the infuriated teacher who flies down like a hawk at the noise.

But luckily for me the general attention was distracted at the moment by the masterly acting of our host, who was playing the chief part in the performance, some comedy of Scribe's. Every one began to applaud; under cover of the noise I stole away and hurried to the furthest end of the room, from which, concealed behind a column, I looked with horror towards the place where the treacherous beauty was sitting. She was still laughing, holding her handkerchief to her lips. And for a long time she was continually turning round, looking for me in every direction, probably regretting that our silly tussle was so soon over, and hatching some other trick to play on me.

That was the beginning of our acquaintance, and from that evening she would never let me alone. She persecuted me without consideration or conscience, she became my tyrant and tormentor. The whole absurdity of her jokes with me lay in the fact that she pretended to be head over ears in love with me, and teased me before every one. Of course for a wild creature as I was all this was so tiresome and vexatious that it almost reduced me to tears, and I was sometimes put in such a difficult position that I was on the point of fighting with my treacherous admirer. My naïve confusion, my desperate distress, seemed to egg her on to persecute me more; she knew no mercy, while I did not know how to get away from her. The laughter which always accompanied us, and which she knew so well how to excite, roused her to fresh pranks. But at last people began to think that she went a little too far in her jests. And, indeed, as I remember now, she did take outrageous liberties with a child such as I was.

But that was her character; she was a spoilt child in every respect. I heard afterwards that her husband, a very short, very fat, and very red-faced man, very rich and apparently very much occupied with business, spoilt her more than any one. Always busy and flying round, he could not stay two hours in one place. Every day he drove into Moscow, sometimes twice in the day, and always, as he declared himself, on business. It would be hard to find a livelier and more good-natured face than his facetious but always well-bred countenance. He not only loved his wife to the point of weakness, softness: he simply worshipped her like an idol.

He did not restrain her in anything. She had

masses of friends, male and female. In the first place, almost everybody liked her; and secondly, the feather-headed creature was not herself over particular in the choice of her friends, though there was a much more serious foundation to her character than might be supposed from what I have just said about her. But of all her friends she liked best of all one young lady, a distant relation, who was also of our party now. There existed between them a tender and subtle affection, one of those attachments which sometimes spring up at the meeting of two dispositions often the very opposite of each other, of which one is deeper, purer and more austere, while the other, with lofty humility, and generous self-criticism, lovingly gives way to the other, conscious of the friend's superiority and cherishing the friendship as a happiness. Then begins that tender and noble subtlety in the relations of such characters, love and infinite indulgence on the one side, on the other love and respect—a respect approaching awe, approaching anxiety as to the impression made on the friend so highly prized, and an eager, jealous desire to get closer and closer to that friend's heart in every step in life.

These two friends were of the same age, but there was an immense difference between them in everything—in looks, to begin with. Madame M.

was also very handsome, but there was something special in her beauty that strikingly distinguished her from the crowd of pretty women; there was something in her face that at once drew the affection of all to her, or rather, which aroused a generous and lofty feeling of kindliness in every one who met her. There are such happy faces. At her side everyone grew as it were better, freer, more cordial; and yet her big mournful eyes, full of fire and vigour, had a timid and anxious look, as though every minute dreading something antagonistic and menacing, and this strange timidity at times cast so mournful a shade over her mild, gentle features which recalled the serene faces of Italian Madonnas, that looking at her one soon became oneself sad, as though for some trouble of one's own. The pale, thin face, in which, through the irreproachable beauty of the pure, regular lines and the mournful severity of some mute hidden grief, there often flitted the clear looks of early childhood, telling of trustful years and perhaps simple-hearted happiness in the recent past, the gentle but diffident, hesitating smile, all aroused such unaccountable sympathy for her that every heart was unconsciously stirred with a sweet and warm anxiety that powerfully interceded on her behalf even at a distance, and made even strangers feel akin to her. But the lovely creature seemed silent and reserved, though no one could have been more attentive and loving if any one needed sympathy. There are women who are like sisters of mercy in life. Nothing can be hidden from them, nothing, at least, that is a sore or wound of the heart. Any one who is suffering may go boldly and hopefully to them without fear of being a burden, for few men know the infinite patience of love, compassion and forgiveness that may be found in some women's hearts. Perfect treasures of sympathy, consolation and hope are laid up in these pure hearts, so often full of suffering of their own—for a heart which loves much grieves much—though their wounds are carefully hidden from the curious eye, for deep sadness is most often mute and concealed. They are not dismayed by the depth of the wound, nor by its foulness and its stench; any one who comes to them is deserving of help; they are, as it were, born for heroism . . . Mme. M. was tall, supple and graceful, but rather thin. All her movements seemed somehow irregular, at times slow, smooth, and even dignified, at times childishly hasty; and yet, at the same time, there was a sort of timid humility in her gestures, something tremulous and defenceless, though it neither desired nor asked for protection.

I have mentioned already that the outrageous teasing of the treacherous fair lady abashed me, flabbergasted me, and wounded me to the quick. But there was for that another secret, strange and foolish reason, which I concealed, at which I shuddered as at a skeleton. At the very thought of it, brooding, utterly alone and overwhelmed, in some dark mysterious corner to which the inquisitorial mocking eye of the blue-eyed rogue could not penetrate, I almost gasped with confusion, shame and fear—in short, I was in love; that perhaps is nonsense, that could hardly have been. But why was it, of all the faces surrounding me, only her face caught my attention? Why was it that it was only she whom I cared to follow with my eyes, though I certainly had no inclination in those days to watch ladies and seek their acquaintance? This happened most frequently on the evenings when we were all kept indoors by bad weather, and when, lonely, hiding in some corner of the big drawing-room, I stared about me aimlessly, unable to find anything to do, for except my teasing ladies, few people ever addressed me, and I was insufferably bored on such evenings. Then I stared at the people round me, listened to the conversation, of which I often did not understand one word, and at that time the mild eyes, the gentle smile and lovely face of Mme. M. (for she was the object of my passion) for some reason caught my fascinated attention; and the strange vague, but unutterably sweet impression remained with me. Often for hours together I could not tear myself away from her; I studied every gesture, every move- ment she made, listened to every vibration of her rich, silvery, but rather muffled voice; but strange to say, as the result of all my observations, I felt, mixed with a sweet and timid impression, a feeling of intense curiosity. It seemed as though I were on the verge of some mystery.

Nothing distressed me so much as being mocked at in the presence of Mme. M. This mockery and humorous persecution, as I thought, humiliated me. And when there was a general burst of laughter at my expense, in which Mme. M. sometimes could not help joining, in despair, beside myself with misery, I used to tear myself from my tormentor and run away upstairs, where I remained in solitude the rest of the day, not daring to show my face in the drawing-room. I did not yet, however, understand my shame nor my agitation; the whole process went on in me unconsciously. I had hardly said two words to Mme. M., and indeed I should not have dared to. But one evening after an unbearable day I turned back from an expedition with the rest of the com- pany. I was horribly tired and made my way home across the garden. On a seat in a secluded avenue I saw Mme. M. She was sitting quite alone, as though she had purposely chosen this solitary spot, her head was drooping and she was mechanically twisting her handkerchief. She was so lost in thought that she did not hear me till I reached her.

Noticing me, she got up quickly from her seat, turned round, and I saw her hurriedly wipe her eyes with her handkerchief. She was crying. Drying her eyes, she smiled to me and walked back with me to the house. I don't remember what we talked about; but she frequently sent me off on one pretext or another, to pick a flower, or to see who was riding in the next avenue. And when I walked away from her, she at once put her handkerchief to her eyes again and wiped away rebellious tears, which would persist in rising again and again from her heart and dropping from her poor eyes. I realized that I was very much in her way when she sent me off so often, and, indeed, she saw herself that I noticed it all, but yet could not control herself, and that made my heart ache more and more for her. I raged at myself at that moment and was almost in despair; cursed myself for my awkwardness and lack of resource, and at the same time did not know how to leave her tactfully, without betraying that I had noticed her distress, but walked beside her in mournful bewilderment, almost in alarm, utterly at a loss and unable to find a single word to keep up our scanty conversation.

This meeting made such an impression on me that I stealthily watched Mme. M. the whole evening with eager curiosity, and never took my eyes off her. But it happened that she twice caught me unawares watching her, and on the second occasion, noticing me, she gave me a smile. It was the only time she smiled that evening. The look of sadness had not left her face, which was now very pale. She spent the whole evening talking to an ill-natured and quarrelsome old lady, whom nobody liked owing to her spying and backbiting habits, but of whom every one was afraid, and consequently every one felt obliged to be polite to her . . .

At ten o'clock Mme. M.'s husband arrived. Till that moment I watched her very attentively, never taking my eyes off her mournful face; now at the unexpected entrance of her husband I saw her start, and her pale face turned suddenly as white as a handkerchief. It was so noticeable that other people observed it. I overheard a fragmentary conversation from which I guessed that Mme. M. was not quite happy; they said her husband was as jealous as an Arab, not from love, but from vanity. He was before all things a European, a modern man, who sampled the newest ideas and prided himself upon them. In appearance he was a tall, dark-haired, particularly thick-set man, with European whiskers, with a self-satisfied, red face, with teeth white as sugar, and with an irreproachably gentlemanly deportment. He was called a *clever man*. Such is the name given in certain circles to a peculiar species of mankind which grows fat at other people's expense, which does absolutely nothing and has no desire to do anything, and whose heart has turned into a lump of fat from everlasting slothfulness and idleness. You continually hear from such men that there is nothing they can do owing to certain very complicated and hostile circumstances, which "thwart their genius," and that it was "sad to see the waste of their talents." This is a fine phrase of theirs, their *mot d'ordre*, their watchword, a phrase which these well-fed, fat friends of ours bring out at every minute, so that it has long ago bored us as an arrant Tartuffism, an empty form of words. Some, however, of these amusing creatures, who cannot succeed in finding anything to do—though, indeed, they never seek it—try to make every one believe that they have not a lump of fat for a heart, but on the contrary, something *very deep*, though what precisely the greatest surgeon would hardly venture to decide—from civility, of course. These gentlemen make their way in the world through the fact that all their instincts are bent in the direction of coarse sneering, short-sighted censure and immense conceit. Since they have nothing else to do but note and emphasize the mistakes and weaknesses of others, and as they have precisely as much good feeling as an oyster, it is not difficult for them with such powers of self-preservation to get on with people fairly successfully. They pride themselves extremely upon that. They are, for instance, as good as persuaded that almost the whole world owes them something; that it is theirs, like an oyster which they keep in reserve; that all are fools except themselves; that every one is like an orange or a sponge, which they will squeeze as soon as they want the juice; that they are the masters everywhere, and that all this acceptable state of affairs is solely due to the fact that they are people of so much intellect and character. In their measure-less conceit they do not admit any defects in themselves, they are like that species of practical rogues, innate Tartuffes and Falstaffs, who are such thorough rogues that at last they have come to believe that that is as it should be, that is, that they should spend their lives in knavishness; they have so often assured every one that they are honest men, that they have come to believe that they are honest men, and that their roguery is honesty. They are never capable of inner judgment before their conscience, of generous self-criticism; for some things they are too fat. Their own priceless personality, their Baal and Moloch, their magnificent *ego* is always in their foreground everywhere. All nature, the whole world for them is no more than a splendid mirror created for the little god to admire himself continually in it, and to see no one and nothing behind himself; so it is not strange that he sees everything in the world in such a hideous light. He has a phrase in readiness for everything and—the acme of ingenuity on his part—the most fashionable phrase. It is just these people, indeed, who help to make the fashion, proclaiming at every cross-road an idea in which they scent success. A fine nose is just what they have for sniffing a fashionable phrase and making it their own before other people get hold of it, so that it seems to have originated with them. They have a particular store of phrases for proclaiming their profound sympathy for humanity, for defining what is the most correct and rational form of philanthropy, and continually attacking romanticism, in other words, everything fine and true, each atom of which is more precious than all their mollusc tribe. But they are too coarse to recognize the truth in an indirect, roundabout and unfinished form, and they reject everything that is immature, still fermenting and unstable. The well-nourished man has spent all his life in merry-making, with everything provided, has done nothing himself and does not know how hard every sort of work is, and so woe betide you if you jar upon his fat feelings by any sort of roughness; he'll never forgive you for that, he will always remember it and will gladly avenge it. The long and short of it is, that my hero is neither more nor less than a gigantic, incredibly swollen bag, full of sentences, fashionable phrases, and labels of all sorts and kinds.

M. M., however, had a speciality and was a very remarkable man; he was a wit, good talker and story-teller, and there was always a circle round him in every drawing-room. That evening he was particularly successful in making an impression. He took possession of the conversation; he was in his best form, gay, pleased at something, and he compelled the attention of all; but Mme. M. looked all the time as though she were ill; her face was so sad that I fancied every minute that tears would begin quivering on her long eyelashes. All this, as I have said, impressed me extremely and made me wonder. I went away with a feeling of strange curiosity, and dreamed all night of M. M., though till then I had rarely had dreams.

Next day, early in the morning, I was summoned to a rehearsal of some tableaux vivants in which I had to take part. The tableaux vivants, theatricals, and afterwards a dance were all fixed for the same evening, five days later—the birthday of our host's younger daughter. To this entertainment, which was almost improvised, another hundred guests were invited from Moscow and from surrounding villas, so that there was a great deal of fuss, bustle and commotion. The rehearsal, or rather review of the costumes, was fixed so early in the morning because our manager, a well-known artist, a friend of our host's, who had consented through affection for him to undertake the arrangement of the tableaux and the training of us for them, was in haste now to get to Moscow to purchase properties and to make final preparations for the fête, as there was no time to lose. I took part in one tableau with Mme. M. It was a scene from mediæval life and was called "The Lady of the Castle and Her Page."

I felt unutterably confused on meeting Mme. M. at the rehearsal. I kept feeling that she would at once read in my eyes all the reflections, the doubts, the surmises, that had arisen in my mind since the previous day. I fancied, too, that I was, as it were, to blame in regard to her, for having come upon her tears the day before and hindered her grieving, so that she could hardly help looking at me askance, as an unpleasant witness and unforgiven sharer of her secret. But, thank goodness, it went off without any great trouble; I was simply not noticed. I think she had no thoughts to spare for me or for the rehearsal; she was absent-minded, sad and gloomily thoughtful; it was evident that she was worried by some great anxiety. As soon as my part was over I ran away to change my clothes, and ten minutes later came out on the verandah into the garden. Almost at the same time Mme. M. came out by another door, and immediately afterwards coming towards us appeared her self-satisfied husband, who was returning from the garden, after just escorting into it quite a crowd of ladies and there handing them over to a competent *cavaliere servente*. The meeting of the husband and wife was evidently unexpected. Mme. M., I don't know why, grew suddenly confused, and a faint trace of vexation was betrayed in her impatient movement. The husband, who had been carelessly whistling an air and with an air of profundity stroking his whiskers, now, on meeting his wife, frowned and scrutinized her, as I remember now, with a markedly inquisitorial stare.

"You are going into the garden?" he asked, noticing the parasol and book in her hand.

"No, into the copse," she said, with a slight flush.

"Alone?"

"With him," said Mme. M., pointing to me. "I

always go a walk alone in the morning," she added, speaking in an uncertain, hesitating voice, as people do when they tell their first lie.

"H'm ... and I have just taken the whole party there. They have all met there together in the flower arbour to see N. off. He is going away, you know ... Something has gone wrong in Odessa. Your cousin" (he meant the fair beauty) "is laughing and crying at the same time; there is no making her out. She says, though, that you are angry with N. about something and so wouldn't go and see him off. Nonsense, of course?"

"She's laughing," said Mme. M., coming down the verandah steps.

"So this is your daily *cavaliere servente*," added M. M., with a wry smile, turning his lorgnette upon me.

"Page!" I cried, angered by the lorgnette and the jeer; and laughing straight in his face I jumped down the three steps of the verandah at one bound.

"A pleasant walk," muttered M. M., and went on his way.

Of course, I immediately joined Mme. M. as soon as she indicated me to her husband, and looked as though she had invited me to do so an hour before, and as though I had been accompanying her on her walks every morning for the last month. But I could not make out why she was so confused, so embarrassed, and what was in her mind when she brought herself to have recourse to her little lie? Why had she not simply said that she was going alone? I did not know how to look at her, but overwhelmed with wonder I began by degrees very naïvely peeping into her face; but just as an hour before at the rehearsal she did not notice either my looks or my mute question. The same anxiety, only more intense and more distinct, was apparent in her face, in her agitation, in her walk. She was in haste, and walked more and more quickly and kept looking uneasily down every avenue, down every path in the wood that led in the direction of the garden. And I, too, was expecting something. Suddenly there was the sound of horses' hoofs behind us. It was the whole party of ladies and gentlemen on horseback escorting N., the gentleman who was so suddenly deserting us.

Among the ladies was my fair tormentor, of whom M. M. had told us that she was in tears. But characteristically she was laughing like a child, and was galloping briskly on a splendid bay horse. On reaching us N. took off his hat, but did not stop, nor say one word to Mme. M. Soon all the cavalcade disappeared from our sight. I glanced at Mme. M. and almost cried out in wonder; she was standing as white as a handkerchief and big tears were gushing from her eyes. By chance our eyes met: Mme. M. suddenly flushed and turned away for an instant, and a distinct look of uneasiness and vexation flitted across her face. I was in the way, worse even than last time, that was clearer than day, but how was I to get away?

And, as though guessing my difficulty, Mme. M. opened the book which she had in her hand, and colouring and evidently trying not to look at me she said, as though she had only suddenly realized it—

"Ah! It is the second part. I've made a mistake; please bring me the first."

I could not but understand. My part was over, and I could not have been more directly dismissed.

I ran off with her book and did not come back. The first part lay undisturbed on the table that morning . . .

But I was not myself; in my heart there was a sort of haunting terror. I did my utmost not to meet Mme. M. But I looked with wild curiosity at the self-satisfied person of M. M., as though there must be something special about him now. I don't understand what was the meaning of my absurd curiosity. I only remember that I was strangely perplexed by all that I had chanced to see that morning. But the day was only just beginning and it was fruitful in events for me.

Dinner was very early that day. An expedition to a neighbouring hamlet to see a village festival that was taking place there had been fixed for the evening, and so it was necessary to be in time to get ready. I had been dreaming for the last three days of this excursion, anticipating all sorts of delights. Almost all the company gathered together on the verandah for coffee. I cautiously followed the others and concealed myself behind the third row of chairs. I was attracted by curiosity, and yet I was very anxious not to be seen by Mme. M. But as luck would have it I was not far from my fair tormentor. Something miraculous and incredible was happening to her that day; she looked twice as handsome. I don't know how and why this happens, but such miracles are by no means rare with women. There was with us at this moment a new guest, a tall, pale-faced young man, the official admirer of our fair beauty, who had just arrived from Moscow as though on purpose to replace N., of whom rumour said that he was desperately in love with the same lady. As for the newly arrived guest, he had for a long time past been on the same terms as Benedick with Beatrice, in Shakespeare's *Much Ado about Nothing*. In short, the fair beauty was in her very best form that day. Her

chatter and her jests were so full of grace, so trust-
fully naïve, so innocently careless, she was persuaded
of the general enthusiasm with such graceful self-
confidence that she really was all the time the centre
of peculiar adoration. A throng of surprised and
admiring listeners was continually round her, and
she had never been so fascinating. Every word she
uttered was marvellous and seductive, was caught
up and handed round in the circle, and not one
word, one jest, one sally was lost. I fancy no one had
expected from her such taste, such brilliance, such
wit. Her best qualities were, as a rule, buried under
the most harum-scarum wilfulness, the most school-
boyish pranks, almost verging on buffoonery; they
were rarely noticed, and, when they were, were
hardly believed in, so that now her extraordinary
brilliancy was accompanied by an eager whisper of
amazement among all. There was, however, one
peculiar and rather delicate circumstance, judging at
least by the part in it played by Mme. M.'s husband,
which contributed to her success. The madcap
ventured—and I must add to the satisfaction of
almost every one or, at any rate, to the satisfaction
of all the young people—to make a furious attack
upon him, owing to many causes, probably of great
consequence in her eyes. She carried on with him a
regular cross-fire of witticisms, of mocking and

sarcastic sallies, of that most illusive and treacherous kind that, smoothly wrapped up on the surface, hit the mark without giving the victim anything to lay hold of, and exhaust him in fruitless efforts to repel the attack, reducing him to fury and comic despair.

I don't know for certain, but I fancy the whole proceeding was not improvised but premeditated. This desperate duel had begun earlier, at dinner. I call it desperate because M. M. was not quick to surrender. He had to call upon all his presence of mind, all his sharp wit and rare resourcefulness not to be completely covered with ignominy. The conflict was accompanied by the continual and irrepressible laughter of all who witnessed and took part in it. That day was for him very different from the day before. It was noticeable that Mme. M. several times did her utmost to stop her indiscreet friend, who was certainly trying to depict the jealous husband in the most grotesque and absurd guise, in the guise of "a bluebeard" it must be supposed, judging from all probabilities, from what has remained in my memory and finally from the part which I myself was destined to play in the affair.

I was drawn into it in a most absurd manner, quite unexpectedly. And as ill-luck would have it at that moment I was standing where I could be seen, suspecting no evil and actually forgetting the precautions I had so long practised. Suddenly I was brought into the foreground as a sworn foe and natural rival of M. M., as desperately in love with his wife, of which my persecutress vowed and swore that she had proofs, saying that only that morning she had seen in the copse . . .

But before she had time to finish I broke in at the most desperate minute. That minute was so diabolically calculated, was so treacherously prepared to lead up to its finale, its ludicrous *dénouement*, and was brought out with such killing humour that a perfect outburst of irrepressible mirth saluted this last sally. And though even at the time I guessed that mine was not the most unpleasant part in the performance, yet I was so confused, so irritated and alarmed that, full of misery and despair, gasping with shame and tears, I dashed through two rows of chairs, stepped forward, and addressing my tormentor, cried, in a voice broken with tears and indignation:

"Aren't you ashamed . . . aloud . . . before all the ladies . . . to tell such a wicked . . . lie? . . . Like a small child . . . before all these men . . . What will they say? . . . A big girl like you . . . and married! . . ."

But I could not go on, there was a deafening roar of applause. My outburst created a perfect furore.

My naïve gesture, my tears, and especially the fact that I seemed to be defending M. M., all this provoked such fiendish laughter, that even now I cannot help laughing at the mere recollection of it. I was overcome with confusion, senseless with horror and, burning with shame, hiding my face in my hands rushed away, knocked a tray out of the hands of a footman who was coming in at the door, and flew upstairs to my own room. I pulled out the key, which was on the outside of the door, and locked myself in. I did well, for there was a hue and cry after me. Before a minute had passed my door was besieged by a mob of the prettiest ladies. I heard their ringing laughter, their incessant chatter, their trilling voices; they were all twittering at once, like swallows. All of them, every one of them, begged and besought me to open the door, if only for a moment; swore that no harm should come to me, only that they wanted to smother me with kisses. But ... what could be more horrible than this novel threat? I simply burned with shame the other side of the door, hiding my face in the pillows and did not open, did not even respond. The ladies kept up their knocking for a long time, but I was deaf and obdurate as only a boy of eleven could be.

But what could I do now? Everything was laid bare, everything had been exposed, everything I had so jealously guarded and concealed! . . . Everlasting disgrace and shame had fallen on me! But it is true that I could not myself have said why I was frightened and what I wanted to hide; yet I was frightened of something and had trembled like a leaf at the thought of *that something's* being discovered. Only till that minute I had not known what it was: whether it was good or bad, splendid or shameful, praiseworthy or reprehensible? Now in my distress, in the misery that had been forced upon me, I learned that it was *absurd* and *shameful*. Instinctively I felt at the same time that this verdict was false, inhuman, and coarse; but I was crushed, annihilated; consciousness seemed checked in me and thrown into confusion; I could not stand up against that verdict, nor criticize it properly. I was befogged; I only felt that my heart had been inhumanly and shamelessly wounded, and was brimming over with impotent tears. I was irritated; but I was boiling with indignation and hate such as I had never felt before, for it was the first time in my life that I had known real sorrow, insult, and injury—and it was truly that, without any exaggeration. The first untried, unformed feeling had been so coarsely handled in me, a child. The first fragrant, virginal modesty had been so soon exposed and insulted, and the first and perhaps very real and æsthetic impression had been so outraged. Of course there was much my persecutors did not know and did not divine in my sufferings. One circumstance, which I had not succeeded in analysing till then, of which I had been as it were afraid, partly entered into it. I went on lying on my bed in despair and misery, hiding my face in my pillow, and I was alternately feverish and shivery. I was tormented by two questions: first, what had the wretched fair beauty seen, and, in fact, what could she have seen that morning in the copse between Mme. M. and me? And secondly, how could I now look Mme. M. in the face without dying on the spot of shame and despair?

An extraordinary noise in the yard roused me at last from the state of semi-consciousness into which I had fallen. I got up and went to the window. The whole yard was packed with carriages, saddle-horses, and bustling servants. It seemed that they were all setting off; some of the gentlemen had already mounted their horses, others were taking their places in the carriages . . . Then I remembered the expedition to the village fête, and little by little an uneasiness came over me; I began anxiously looking for my pony in the yard; but there was no pony there, so they must have forgotten me. I could not restrain myself, and rushed headlong downstairs, thinking no more of unpleasant meetings or my recent ignominy . . .

Terrible news awaited me. There was neither a horse nor seat in any of the carriages to spare for me; everything had been arranged, all the seats were taken, and I was forced to give place to others. Overwhelmed by this fresh blow, I stood on the steps and looked mournfully at the long rows of coaches, carriages, and chaises, in which there was not the tiniest corner left for me, and at the smartly dressed ladies, whose horses were restlessly curvetting.

One of the gentlemen was late. They were only waiting for his arrival to set off. His horse was standing at the door, champing the bit, pawing the earth with his hoofs, and at every moment starting and rearing. Two stable-boys were carefully holding him by the bridle, and every one else apprehensively stood at a respectful distance from him.

A most vexatious circumstance had occurred, which prevented my going. In addition to the fact that new visitors had arrived, filling up all the seats, two of the horses had fallen ill, one of them being my pony. But I was not the only person to suffer: it appeared that there was no horse for our new visitor, the pale-faced young man of whom I have spoken already. To get over this difficulty our host had been obliged to have recourse to the extreme step of offering his fiery unbroken stallion, adding, to satisfy his conscience, that it was impossible to ride him, and that they had long intended to sell the beast for its vicious character, if only a purchaser could be found.

But, in spite of his warning, the visitor declared that he was a good horseman, and in any case ready to mount anything rather than not go. Our host said no more, but now I fancied that a sly and ambiguous smile was straying on his lips. He waited for the gentleman who had spoken so well of his own horsemanship, and stood, without mounting his horse, impatiently rubbing his hands and continually glancing towards the door; some similar feeling seemed shared by the two stable-boys, who were holding the stallion, almost breathless with pride at seeing themselves before the whole company in charge of a horse which might any minute kill a man for no reason whatever. Something akin to their master's sly smile gleamed, too, in their eyes, which were round with expectation, and fixed upon the door from which the bold visitor was to appear. The horse himself, too, behaved as though he were in league with our host and the stable-boys. He bore himself proudly and haughtily, as though he felt that he were being watched by several dozen curious eyes and were glorying in his evil reputation exactly as some incorrigible rogue might glory in his criminal exploits. He seemed to be defying the bold man who would venture to curb his independence.

That bold man did at last make his appearance. Conscience-stricken at having kept every one waiting, hurriedly drawing on his gloves, he came forward without looking at anything, ran down the steps, and only raised his eyes as he stretched out his hand to seize the mane of the waiting horse. But he was at once disconcerted by his frantic rearing and a warning scream from the frightened spectators. The young man stepped back and looked in perplexity at the vicious horse, which was quivering all over, snorting with anger, and rolling his bloodshot eyes ferociously, continually rearing on his hind legs and flinging up his fore legs as though he meant to bolt into the air and carry the two stable-boys with him. For a minute the young man stood completely nonplussed; then, flushing slightly with some embarrassment, he raised his eyes and looked at the frightened ladies.

"A very fine horse!" he said, as though to himself, "and to my thinking it ought to be a great pleasure to ride him; but . . . but do you know, I think I won't go?" he concluded, turning to our host with the broad, good-natured smile which so suited his kind and clever face.

"Yet I consider you are an excellent horseman, I assure you," answered the owner of the unapproachable horse, delighted, and he warmly and even gratefully pressed the young man's hand, "just because from the first moment you saw the sort of brute you had to deal with," he added with dignity. "Would you believe me, though I have served twenty-three years in the hussars, yet I've had the pleasure of being laid on the ground three times, thanks to that beast, that is, as often as I mounted the useless animal. Tancred, my boy, there's no one here fit for you! Your rider, it seems, must be some Ilya Muromets, and he must be sitting quiet now in the village of Kapatcharovo, waiting for your teeth to fall out. Come, take him away, he has frightened people enough. It was waste of time to bring him out," he cried, rubbing his hands complacently.

It must be observed that Tancred was no sort of use to his master and simply ate corn for nothing; moreover, the old hussar had lost his reputation for a knowledge of horseflesh by paying a fabulous sum for the worthless beast, which he had purchased only for his beauty . . . yet he was delighted now that Tancred had kept up his reputation, had disposed of another rider, and so had drawn closer on himself fresh senseless laurels.

"So you are not going?" cried the blonde beauty,

who was particularly anxious that her *cavaliere servente* should be in attendance on this occasion. "Surely you are not frightened?"

"Upon my word I am," answered the young man.

"Are you in earnest?"

"Why, do you want me to break my neck?"

"Then make haste and get on my horse; don't be afraid, it is very quiet. We won't delay them, they can change the saddles in a minute! I'll try to take yours. Surely Tancred can't always be so unruly."

No sooner said than done, the madcap leaped out of the saddle and was standing before us as she finished the last sentence.

"You don't know Tancred, if you think he will allow your wretched side-saddle to be put on him! Besides, I would not let you break your neck, it would be a pity!" said our host, at that moment of inward gratification affecting, as his habit was, a studied brusqueness and even coarseness of speech which he thought in keeping with a jolly good fellow and an old soldier, and which he imagined to be particularly attractive to the ladies. This was one of his favourite fancies, his favourite whim, with which we were all familiar.

"Well, cry-baby, wouldn't you like to have a try? You wanted so much to go?" said the valiant horsewoman, noticing me and pointing tauntingly at

Tancred, because I had been so imprudent as to catch her eye, and she would not let me go without a biting word, that she might not have dismounted from her horse absolutely for nothing.

"I expect you are not such a——We all know you are a hero and would be ashamed to be afraid; especially when you will be looked at, you fine page," she added, with a fleeting glance at Mme. M., whose carriage was the nearest to the entrance.

A rush of hatred and vengeance had flooded my heart, when the fair Amazon had approached us with the intention of mounting Tancred ... But I cannot describe what I felt at this unexpected challenge from the madcap. Everything was dark before my eyes when I saw her glance at Mme. M. For an instant an idea flashed through my mind ... but it was only a moment, less than a moment, like a flash of gunpowder; perhaps it was the last straw, and I suddenly now was moved to rage as my spirit rose, so that I longed to put all my enemies to utter confusion, and to revenge myself on all of them and before everyone, by showing the sort of person I was. Or whether by some miracle, some prompting from mediæval history, of which I had known nothing till then, sent whirling through my giddy brain, images of tournaments, paladins, heroes, lovely ladies, the clash of swords, shouts and the applause of the crowd, and amidst those shouts the timid cry of a frightened heart, which moves the proud soul more sweetly than victory and fame—I don't know whether all this romantic nonsense was in my head at the time, or whether, more likely, only the first dawning of the inevitable nonsense that was in store for me in the future, anyway, I felt that my hour had come. My heart leaped and shuddered, and I don't remember how, at one bound, I was down the steps and beside Tancred.

"You think I am afraid?" I cried, boldly and proudly, in such a fever that I could hardly see, breathless with excitement, and flushing till the tears scalded my cheeks. "Well, you shall see!" And clutching at Tancred's mane I put my foot in the stirrup before they had time to make a movement to stop me; but at that instant Tancred reared, jerked his head, and with a mighty bound forward wrenched himself out of the hands of the petrified stable-boys, and dashed off like a hurricane, while every one cried out in horror.

Goodness knows how I got my other leg over the horse while it was in full gallop; I can't imagine, either, how I did not lose hold of the reins. Tancred bore me beyond the trellis gate, turned sharply to the right and flew along beside the fence regardless of the road. Only at that moment I heard behind me a shout from fifty voices, and that shout was echoed in my swooning heart with such a feeling of pride and pleasure that I shall never forget that mad moment of my boyhood. All the blood rushed to my head, bewildering me and overpowering my fears. I was beside myself. There certainly was, as I remember it now, something of the knight-errant about the exploit.

My knightly exploits, however, were all over in an instant or it would have gone badly with the knight. And, indeed, I do not know how I escaped as it was. I did know how to ride, I had been taught. But my pony was more like a sheep than a riding horse. No doubt I should have been thrown off Tancred if he had had time to throw me, but after galloping fifty paces he suddenly took fright at a huge stone which lay across the road and bolted back. He turned sharply, galloping at full speed, so that it is a puzzle to me even now that I was not sent spinning out of the saddle and flying like a ball for twenty feet, that I was not dashed to pieces, and that Tancred did not dislocate his leg by such a sudden turn. He rushed back to the gate, tossing his head furiously, bounding from side to side as though drunk with rage, flinging his legs at random in the air, and at every leap trying to shake me off his back as though a tiger had leaped on him and were thrusting its teeth and claws into his back.

In another instant I should have flown off; I was falling; but several gentlemen flew to my rescue. Two of them intercepted the way into the open country, two others galloped up, closing in upon Tancred so that their horses' sides almost crushed my legs, and both of them caught him by the bridle. A few seconds later we were back at the steps.

They lifted me down from the horse, pale and scarcely breathing. I was shaking like a blade of grass in the wind; it was the same with Tancred, who was standing, his hoofs as it were thrust into the earth and his whole body thrown back, puffing his fiery breath from red and streaming nostrils, twitching and quivering all over, seeming overwhelmed with wounded pride and anger at a child's being so bold with impunity. All around me I heard cried of bewilderment, surprise, and alarm.

At that moment my straying eyes caught those of Mme. M., who looked pale and agitated, and—I can never forget that moment—in one instant my face was flooded with colour, glowed and burned like fire; I don't know what happened to me, but confused and frightened by my own feelings I timidly dropped my eyes to the ground. But my glance was noticed, it was caught, it was stolen from me. All eyes turned on Mme. M., and finding herself unawares the centre of attention, she, too, flushed like a child from some naïve and involuntary feeling and made an unsuccessful effort to cover her confusion by laughing . . .

All this, of course, was very absurd-looking from outside, but at that moment an extremely naïve and unexpected circumstance saved me from being laughed at by every one, and gave a special colour to the whole adventure. The lovely persecutor who was the instigator of the whole escapade, and who till then had been my irreconcileable foe, suddenly rushed up to embrace and kiss me. She had hardly been able to believe her eyes when she saw me dare to accept her challenge, and pick up the gauntlet she had flung at me by glancing at Mme. M. She had almost died of terror and self-reproach when I had flown off on Tancred; now, when it was all over, and particularly when she caught the glance at Mme. M., my confusion and my sudden flush of colour, when the romantic strain in her frivolous little head had given a new secret, unspoken significance to the moment—she was moved to such enthusiasm over my "knightliness," that touched, joyful and proud of me, she rushed up and pressed me to her bosom. She lifted the most naïve, stern-looking little face, on which there quivered and gleamed two little crystal tears, and gazing at the crowd that thronged about her said in a grave, earnest voice, such as they had never heard her use before, pointing to me: "Mais c'est très sérieux, messieurs, ne riez pas!" She did not notice that all were standing, as though fascinated, admiring her bright enthusiasm. Her swift, unexpected action, her earnest little face, the simple-hearted naïveté, the unexpected feeling betrayed by the tears that welled in her invariably laughter-loving eyes, were such a surprise that every one stood before her as though electrified by her expression, her rapid, fiery words and gestures. It seemed as though no one could take his eyes off her for fear of missing that rare moment in her enthusiastic face. Even our host flushed crimson as a tulip, and people declared that they heard him confess afterwards that "to his shame" he had been in love for a whole minute with his charming guest. Well, of course, after this I was a knight, a hero.

"De Lorge! Toggenburg!" was heard in the crowd.

There was a sound of applause.

"Hurrah for the rising generation!" added the host.

"But he is coming with us, he certainly must come with us," said the beauty; "we will find him a place, we must find him a place. He shall sit beside me, on my knee ... but no, no! That's a mistake! ..." she corrected herself, laughing, unable to restrain her mirth at our first encounter. But as she laughed she stroked my hand tenderly, doing all she could to soften me, that I might not be offended.

"Of course, of course," several voices chimed in; "he must go, he has won his place."

The matter was settled in a trice. The same old maid who had brought about my acquaintance with the blonde beauty was at once besieged with entreaties from all the younger people to remain at home and let me have her seat. She was forced to consent, to her intense vexation, with a smile and a stealthy hiss of anger. Her protectress, who was her usual refuge, my former foe and new friend, called to her as she galloped off on her spirited horse, laughing like a child, that she envied her and would have been glad to stay at home herself, for it was just going to rain and we should all get soaked.

And she was right in predicting rain. A regular downpour came on within an hour and the expedition was done for. We had to take shelter for some hours in the huts of the village, and had to return home between nine and ten in the evening in the damp mist that followed the rain. I began to be a little feverish. At the minute when I was starting, Mme. M. came up to me and expressed surprise that my neck was uncovered and that I had nothing on over my jacket. I answered that I had not had time to get my coat. She took out a pin and pinned up the turned down collar of my shirt, took off her own neck a crimson gauze kerchief, and put it round my neck that I might not get a sore throat. She did this so hurriedly that I had not time even to thank her.

But when we got home I found her in the little drawing-room with the blonde beauty and the pale-faced young man who had gained glory for horsemanship that day by refusing to ride Tancred. I went up to thank her and give back the scarf. But now, after all my adventures, I felt somehow ashamed. I wanted to make haste and get upstairs, there at my leisure to reflect and consider. I was brimming over with impressions. As I gave back the kerchief I blushed up to my ears, as usual.

"I bet he would like to keep the kerchief," said the young man laughing. "One can see that he is sorry to part with your scarf."

"That's it, that's it!" the fair lady put in. "What a boy! Oh!" she said, shaking her head with obvious vexation, but she stopped in time at a grave glance from Mme. M., who did not want to carry the jest too far.

I made haste to get away.

"Well, you are a boy," said the madcap, overtaking me in the next room and affectionately taking me by both hands, "why, you should have simply not returned the kerchief if you wanted so much to have it. You should have said you put it down somewhere, and that would have been the end of it. What a simpleton! Couldn't even do that! What a funny boy!"

And she tapped me on the chin with her finger, laughing at my having flushed as red as a poppy.

"I am your friend now, you know; am I not? Our enmity is over, isn't it? Yes or no?"

I laughed and pressed her fingers without a word.

"Oh, why are you so . . . why are you so pale and shivering? Have you caught a chill?"

"Yes, I don't feel well."

"Ah, poor fellow! That's the result of over-excitement. Do you know what? You had better go to bed without sitting up for supper, and you will be all right in the morning. Come along."

She took me upstairs, and there was no end to the care she lavished on me. Leaving me to undress she ran downstairs, got me some tea, and brought it up herself when I was in bed. She brought me up a warm quilt as well. I was much impressed and touched by all the care and attention lavished on me; or perhaps I was affected by the whole day, the expedition and feverishness. As I said good-night to her I hugged her warmly, as though she were my dearest and nearest friend, and in my exhausted state all the emotions of the day came back to me in a rush; I almost shed tears as I nestled to her bosom. She noticed my overwrought condition, and I believe my madcap herself was a little touched.

"You are a very good boy," she said, looking at me with gentle eyes, "please don't be angry with me. You won't, will you?"

In fact, we became the warmest and truest of friends.

It was rather early when I woke up, but the sun was already flooding the whole room with brilliant light. I jumped out of bed feeling perfectly well and strong, as though I had had no fever the day before; indeed, I felt now unutterably joyful. I recalled the previous day and felt that I would have given any happiness if I could at that minute have embraced my new friend, the fair-haired beauty, again, as I had the night before; but it was very early and every one was still asleep. Hurriedly dressing I went out into the garden and from there into the copse. I made my way where the leaves were thickest, where the fragrance of the trees was more resinous, and where the sun peeped in most gaily, rejoicing that it could penetrate the dense darkness of the foliage. It was a lovely morning.

Going on further and further, before I was aware of it I had reached the further end of the copse and came out on the river Moskva. It flowed at the bottom of the hill two hundred paces below. On the opposite bank of the river they were mowing. I watched whole rows of sharp scythes gleam all together in the sunlight at every swing of the mower and then vanish again like little fiery snakes going into hiding; I watched the cut grass flying on one side in dense rich swathes and being laid in long straight lines. I don't know how long I spent in contemplation. At last I was roused from my reverie by hearing a horse snorting and impatiently pawing the ground twenty paces from me, in the track which ran from the high road to the manor house. I don't know whether I heard this horse as soon as the rider rode up and stopped there, or whether the sound had long been in my ears without rousing me from my dreaming. Moved by curiosity I went into the copse, and before I had gone many steps I caught the sound of voices speaking rapidly, though in subdued tones. I went up closer, carefully parting the branches of the bushes that edged the path, and at once sprang back in amazement. I caught a glimpse of a familiar white dress and a soft feminine voice resounded like music in my heart. It was Mme. M. She was standing beside a man on horseback who, stooping down from the saddle, was hurriedly talking to her, and to my amazement I recognized him as N., the young man who had gone away the morning before and over whose departure M. M. had been so busy. But people had said at the time that he was going far away to somewhere in the South of Russia, and so I was very much surprised at seeing him with us again so early, and alone with Mme. M.

She was moved and agitated as I had never seen her before, and tears were glistening on her cheeks. The young man was holding her hand and stooping down to kiss it. I had come upon them at the moment of parting. They seemed to be in haste. At last he took out of his pocket a sealed envelope, gave it to Mme. M., put one arm round her, still not dismounting, and gave her a long, fervent kiss. A minute later he lashed his horse and flew past me like an arrow. Mme. M. looked after him for some moments, then pensively and disconsolately turned homewards. But after going a few steps along the track she seemed suddenly to recollect herself, hurriedly parted the bushes and walked on through the copse.

I followed her, surprised and perplexed by all

that I had seen. My heart was beating violently, as
though from terror. I was, as it were, benumbed and
befogged; my ideas were shattered and turned
upside down; but I remember I was, for some
reason, very sad. I got glimpses from time to time
through the green foliage of her white dress before
me: I followed her mechanically, never losing sight
of her, though I trembled at the thought that she
might notice me. At last she came out on the little
path that led to the house. After waiting half a
minute I, too, emerged from the bushes; but what
was my amazement when I saw lying on the red
sand of the path a sealed packet, which I recognized,
from the first glance, as the one that had been given
to Mme. M. ten minutes before.

I picked it up. On both sides the paper was blank,
there was no address on it. The envelope was not
large, but it was fat and heavy, as though there were
three or more sheets of notepaper in it.

What was the meaning of this envelope? No
doubt it would explain the whole mystery. Perhaps
in it there was said all that N. had scarcely hoped to
express in their brief, hurried interview. He had not
even dismounted ... Whether he had been in haste
or whether he had been afraid of being false to himself at the hour of parting—God only knows ...

I stopped, without coming out on the path, threw

the envelope in the most conspicuous place on it, and kept my eyes upon it, supposing that Mme. M. would notice the loss and come back and look for it. But after waiting four minutes I could stand it no longer, I picked up my find again, put it in my pocket, and set off to overtake Mme. M. I came upon her in the big avenue in the garden. She was walking straight towards the house with a swift and hurried step, though she was lost in thought, and her eyes were on the ground. I did not know what to do. Go up to her, give it her? That would be as good as saying that I knew everything, that I had seen it all. I should betray myself at the first word. And how should I look, at her? How would she look at me. I kept expecting that she would discover her loss and return on her tracks. Then I could, unnoticed, have flung the envelope on the path and she would have found it. But no! We were approaching the house; she had already been noticed . . .

As ill-luck would have it every one had got up very early that day, because, after the unsuccessful expedition of the evening before, they had arranged something new, of which I had heard nothing. All were preparing to set off, and were having breakfast in the verandah. I waited for ten minutes, that I might not be seen with Mme. M., and making a circuit of the garden approached the house from the other side a long time after her. She was walking up and down the verandah with her arms folded, looking pale and agitated, and was obviously trying her utmost to suppress the agonizing, despairing misery which could be plainly discerned in her eyes, her walk, her every movement. Sometimes she went down the verandah steps and walked a few paces among the flower-beds in the direction of the garden; her eyes were impatiently, greedily, even incautiously, seeking something on the sand of the path and on the floor of the verandah. There could be no doubt she had discovered her loss and imagined she had dropped the letter somewhere here, near the house—yes, that must be so, she was convinced of it.

Some one noticed that she was pale and agitated, and others made the same remark. She was besieged with questions about her health and condolences. She had to laugh, to jest, to appear lively. From time to time she looked at her husband, who was standing at the end of the terrace talking to two ladies, and the poor woman was overcome by the same shudder, the same embarrassment, as on the day of his first arrival. Thrusting my hand into my pocket and holding the letter tight in it, I stood at a little distance from them all, praying to fate that Mme. M. should notice me. I longed to cheer her up, to relieve her anxiety if only by a glance; to say a word to her on the sly. But when she did chance to look at me I dropped my eyes.

I saw her distress and I was not mistaken. To this day I don't know her secret. I know nothing but what I saw and what I have just described. The intrgiue was not such, perhaps, as one might suppose at the first glance. Perhaps that kiss was the kiss of farewell, perhaps it was the last slight reward for the sacrifice made to her peace and honour. N. was going away, he was leaving her, perhaps for ever. Even that letter I was holding in my hand—who can tell what it contained! How can one judge? and who can condemn? And yet there is no doubt that the sudden discovery of her secret would have been terrible—would have been a fatal blow for her. I still remember her face at that minute, it could not have shown more suffering. To feel, to know, to be convinced, to expect, as though it were one's execution, that in a quarter of an hour, in a minute perhaps, all might be discovered, the letter might be found by some one, picked up; there was no address on it, it might be opened, and then ... What then? What torture could be worse than what was awaiting her? She moved about among those who would be her judges. In another minute their smiling, flattering faces would be menacing and merciless. She would read mockery, malice and icy contempt on those faces, and then her life would be plunged in everlasting darkness, with no dawn to follow ... Yes, I did not understand it then as I understand it now. I could only have vague suspicions and misgivings, and a heartache at the thought of her danger, which I could not fully understand. But whatever lay hidden in her secret, much was expiated, if expiation were needed, by those moments of anguish of which I was witness and which I shall never forget.

But then came a cheerful summons to set off; immediately every one was bustling about gaily; laughter and lively chatter were heard on all sides. Within two minutes the verandah was deserted. Mme. M. declined to join the party, acknowledging at last that she was not well. But, thank God, all the others set off, every one was in haste, and there was no time to worry her with commiseration, inquiries, and advice. A few remained at home. Her husband said a few words to her; she answered that she would be all right directly, that he need not be uneasy, that there was no occasion for her to lie down, that she would go into the garden, alone ... with me ... here she glanced at me. Nothing could be more fortunate! I flushed with pleasure, with delight; a minute later we were on the way.

She walked along the same avenues and paths by

which she had returned from the copse, instinctively remembering the way she had come, gazing before her with her eyes fixed on the ground, looking about intently without answering me, possibly forgetting that I was walking beside her.

But when we had already reached the place where I had picked up the letter, and the path ended, Mme. M. suddenly stopped, and in a voice faint and weak with misery said that she felt worse, and that she would go home. But when she reached the garden fence she stopped again and thought a minute; a smile of despair came on her lips, and utterly worn out and exhausted, resigned, and making up her mind to the worst, she turned without a word and retraced her steps, even forgetting to tell me of her intention.

My heart was torn with sympathy, and I did not know what to do.

We went, or rather I led her, to the place from which an hour before I had heard the tramp of a horse and their conversation. Here, close to a shady elm tree, was a seat hewn out of one huge stone, about which grew ivy, wild jasmine, and dog-rose; the whole wood was dotted with little bridges, arbours, grottoes, and similar surprises. Mme. M. sat down on the bench and glanced unconsciously at the marvellous view that lay open before us. A minute later she opened her book, and fixed her eyes upon it without reading, without turning the pages, almost unconscious of what she was doing. It was about half-past nine. The sun was already high and was floating gloriously in the deep, dark blue sky, as though melting away in its own light. The mowers were by now far away; they were scarcely visible from our side of the river; endless ridges of mown grass crept after them in unbroken succession, and from time to time the faintly stirring breeze wafted their fragrance to us. The never ceasing concert of those who "sow not, neither do they reap" and are free as the air they cleave with their sportive wings was all about us. It seemed as though at that moment every flower, every blade of grass was exhaling the aroma of sacrifice, was saying to its Creator, "Father, I am blessed and happy."

I glanced at the poor woman, who alone was like one dead amidst all this joyous life; two big tears hung motionless on her lashes, wrung from her heart by bitter grief. It was in my power to relieve and console this poor, fainting heart, only I did not know how to approach the subject, how to take the first step. I was in agonies. A hundred times I was on the point of going up to her, but every time my face glowed like fire.

Suddenly a bright idea dawned upon me. I had found a way of doing it; I revived.

"Would you like me to pick you a nosegay?" I said, in such a joyful voice that Mme M. immediately raised her head and looked at me intently.

"Yes, do," she said at last in a weak voice, with a faint smile, at once dropping her eyes on the book again.

"Or soon they will be mowing the grass here and there will be no flowers," I cried, eagerly setting to work.

I had soon picked my nosegay, a poor, simple one, I should have been ashamed to take it indoors; but how light my heart was as I picked the flowers and tied them up! The dog-rose and the wild jasmine I picked closer to the seat, I knew that not far off there was a field of rye, not yet ripe. I ran there for cornflowers; I mixed them with tall ears of rye, picking out the finest and most golden. Close by I came upon a perfect nest of forget-me-nots, and my nosegay was almost complete. Farther away in the meadow there were dark-blue campanulas and wild pinks, and I ran down to the very edge of the river to get yellow water-lilies. At last, making my way back, and going for an instant into the wood to get some bright green fan-shaped leaves of the maple to put round the nosegay, I happened to come across a whole family of pansies, close to which, luckily for me, the fragrant scent of violets betrayed the little flower hiding in the thick lush grass and still glistening with drops of dew. The nosegay was complete. I bound it round with fine long grass which twisted into a rope, and I carefully lay the letter in the centre, hiding it with the flowers, but in such a way that it could be very easily noticed if the slightest attention were bestowed upon my nosegay.

I carried it to Mme. M.

On the way it seemed to me that the letter was lying too much in view: I hid it a little more. As I got nearer I thrust it still further in the flowers; and finally, when I was on the spot, I suddenly poked it so deeply into the centre of the nosegay that it could not be noticed at all from outside. My cheeks were positively flaming. I wanted to hide my face in my hands and run away at once, but she glanced at my flowers as though she had completely forgotten that I had gathered them. Mechanically, almost without looking, she held out her hand and took my present; but at once laid it on the seat as though I had handed it to her for that purpose and dropped her eyes to her book again, seeming lost in thought. I was ready to cry at this mischance. "If only my nosegay were close to her," I thought; "if only she had not forgotten it!" I lay down on the grass not far off, put my right arm under my head, and closed my eyes as though I were overcome by drowsiness. But I waited, keeping my eyes fixed on her.

Ten minutes passed, it seemed to me that she was getting paler and paler ... fortunately a blessed chance came to my aid.

This was a big, golden bee, brought by a kindly breeze, luckily for me. It first buzzed over my head, and then flew up to Mme. M. She waved it off once or twice, but the bee grew more and more persistent. At last Mme. M. snatched up my nosegay and waved it before my face. At that instant the letter dropped out from among the flowers and fell straight upon the open book. I started. For some time Mme. M., mute with amazement, stared first at the letter and then at the flowers which she was holding in her hands, and she seemed unable to believe her eyes. All at once she flushed, started, and glanced at me. But I caught her movement and I shut my eyes tight, pretending to be asleep. Nothing would have induced me to look her straight in the face at that moment. My heart was throbbing and leaping like a bird in the grasp of some village boy. I don't remember how long I lay with my eyes shut, two or three minutes. At last I ventured to open them. Mme. M. was greedily reading the letter, and from her glowing cheeks, her sparkling, tearful eyes, her bright face, every feature of which was quivering with joyful emotion, I guessed that there was happiness in the letter and all her misery was dispersed like smoke. An agonizing, sweet feeling gnawed at my heart, it was hard for me to go on pretending . . .

I shall never forget that minute!

Suddenly, a long way off, we heard voices—

"Mme. M.! Natalie! Natalie!"

Mme. M. did not answer, but she got up quickly from the seat, came up to me and bent over me. I felt that she was looking straight into my face. My eyelashes quivered, but I controlled myself and did not open my eyes. I tried to breathe more evenly and quietly, but my heart smothered me with its violent throbbing. Her burning breath scorched my cheeks; she bent close down to my face as though trying to make sure. At last a kiss and tears fell on my hand, the one which was lying on my breast.

"Natalie! Natalie! where are you," we heard again, this time quite close.

"Coming," said Mme. M., in her mellow, silvery voice, which was so choked and quivering with tears and so subdued that no one but I could hear that, "Coming!"

But at that instant my heart at last betrayed me and seemed to send all my blood rushing to my face.

At that instant a swift, burning kiss scalded my lips.
I uttered a faint cry. I opened my eyes, but at once
the same gauze kerchief fell upon them, as though
she meant to screen me from the sun. An instant
later she was gone. I heard nothing but the sound of
rapidly retreating steps. I was alone ...

I pulled off her kerchief and kissed it, beside
myself with rapture; for some moments I was almost
frantic ... Hardly able to breathe, leaning on my
elbow on the grass, I stared unconsciously before me
at the surrounding slopes, streaked with cornfields,
at the river that flowed twisting and winding
far away, as far as the eye could see, between fresh
hills and villages that gleamed like dots all over the
sunlit distance—at the dark-blue, hardly visible for-
ests, which seemed as though smoking at the edge
of the burning sky, and a sweet stillness inspired by
the triumphant peacefulness of the picture gradually
brought calm to my troubled heart. I felt more at
ease and breathed more freely, but my whole soul
was full of a dumb, sweet yearning, as though a veil
had been drawn from my eyes as though at a fore-
taste of something. My frightened heart, faintly
quivering with expectation, was groping timidly and
joyfully towards some conjecture ... and all at once
my bosom heaved, began aching as though something had pierced it, and tears, sweet tears, gushed

from my eyes. I hid my face in my hands, and quivering like a blade of grass, gave myself up to the first consciousness and revelation of my heart, the first vague glimpse of my nature. My childhood was over from that moment.

When two hours later I returned home I did not find Mme. M. Through some sudden chance she had gone back to Moscow with her husband. I never saw her again.

The Gilded Six-Bits

It was a Negro yard around a Negro house in a Negro settlement that looked to the payroll of the G and G Fertilizer works for its support.

But there was something happy about the place. The front yard was parted in the middle by a sidewalk from gate to door-step, a sidewalk edged on either side by quart bottles driven neck down into the ground on a slant. A mess of homey flowers planted without a plan but blooming cheerily from their helter-skelter places. The fence and house were whitewashed. The porch and steps scrubbed white.

The front door stood open to the sunshine so that the floor of the front room could finish drying after its weekly scouring. It was Saturday. Everything clean from the front gate to the privy house. Yard raked so that the strokes of the rake would make a pattern. Fresh newspaper cut in fancy edge on the kitchen shelves.

Missie May was bathing herself in the galvanized washtub in the bedroom. Her dark-brown skin glistened under the soapsuds that skittered down from her wash rag. Her stiff young breasts thrust forward aggressively like broad-based cones with the tips lacquered in black.

She heard men's voices in the distance and glanced at the dollar clock on the dresser.

"Humph! Ah'm way behind time t'day! Joe gointer be heah 'fore Ah git mah clothes on if Ah don't make haste."

She grabbed the clean meal sack at hand and dried herself hurriedly and began to dress. But before she could tie her slippers, there came the ring of singing metal on wood. Nine times.

Missie May grinned with delight. She had not seen the big tall man come stealing in the gate and creep up the walk grinning happily at the joyful mischief he was about to commit. But she knew that it was her husband throwing silver dollars in the door for her to pick up and pile beside her plate at dinner. It was this way every Saturday afternoon. The nine dollars hurled into the open door, he scurried to a hiding place behind the cape jasmine bush and waited.

Missie May promptly appeared at the door in mock alarm.

"Who dat chunkin' money in mah do'way?" she demanded. No answer from the yard. She leaped off the porch and began to search the shrubbery. She peeped under the porch and hung over the gate to look up and down the road. While she did this, the man behind the jasmine darted to the china berry tree. She spied him and gave chase.

"Nobody ain't gointer be chunkin' money at me and Ah not do 'em nothin'," she shouted in mock anger. He ran around the house with Missie May at his heels. She overtook him at the kitchen door. He ran inside but could not close it after him before she crowded in and locked with him in a rough and tumble. For several minutes the two were a furious mass of male and female energy. Shouting, laughing, twisting, turning, tussling, tickling each other in the ribs; Missie May clutching onto Joe and Joe trying, but not too hard, to get away.

"Missie May, take yo' hand out mah pocket!" Joe shouted out between laughs.

"Ah ain't, Joe, not lessen you gwine gimme whateve' it is good you got in yo' pocket. Turn it go, Joe, do Ah'll tear yo' clothes."

"Go on tear 'em. You de one dat pushes de needles round heah. Move yo' hand Missie May."

"Lemme git dat paper sack out yo' pocket. Ah bet its candy kisses."

"Tain't. Move yo' hand. Woman ain't got no business in a man's clothes nohow. Go way."

Missie May gouged way down and gave an upward jerk and triumphed.

"Unhhunh! Ah got it. It 'tis so candy kisses. Ah knowed you had somethin' for me in yo' clothes. Now Ah got to see whut's in every pocket you got."

Joe smiled indulgently and let his wife go through all of his pockets and take out the things that he had hidden there for her to find. She bore off the chewing gum, the cake of sweet soap, the pocket handkerchief as if she had wrested them from him, as if they had not been bought for the sake of this friendly battle.

"Whew! dat play-fight done got me all warmed up," Joe exclaimed. "Got me some water in de kittle?"

"Yo' water is on de fire and yo' clean things is cross de bed. Hurry up and wash yo'self and git changed so we kin eat. Ah'm hongry." As Missie said this, she bore the steaming kettle into the bedroom.

"You ain't hongry, sugar," Joe contradicted her. "Youse jes' a little empty. Ah'm de one whut's hongry. Ah could eat up camp meetin', back off 'ssociation, and drink Jurdan dry. Have it on de table when Ah git out de tub."

"Don't you mess wid mah business, man. You git in yo' clothes. Ah'm a real wife, not no dress and breath. Ah might not look lak one, but if you burn me, you won't git a thing but wife ashes."

Joe splashed in the bedroom and Missie May fanned around in the kitchen. A fresh red and white checked cloth on the table. Big pitcher of buttermilk beaded with pale drops of butter from the churn. Hot fried mullet, crackling bread, ham hock atop a mound of string beans and new potatoes, and perched on the window-sill a pone of spicy potato pudding.

Very little talk during the meal but that little consisted of banter that pretended to deny affection but in reality flaunted it. Like when Missie May reached for a second helping of the tater pone. Joe snatched it out of her reach.

After Missie May had made two or three unsuccessful grabs at the pan, she begged, "Aw, Joe gimme some mo' dat tater pone."

"Nope, sweetenin' is for us men-folks. Y'all pritty lil frail eels don't need nothin' lak dis. You too sweet already."

"Please, Joe."

"Naw, naw. Ah don't want you to git no sweeter than whut you is already. We goin' down de road a lil piece t'night so you go put on yo' Sunday-go-to-meetin' things."

Missie May looked at her husband to see if he was playing some prank. "Sho nuff, Joe?"

"Yeah. We goin' to de ice cream parlor."

"Where de ice cream parlor at, Joe?"

"A new man done come heah from Chicago and he done got a place and took and opened it up for a ice cream parlor, and bein' as it's real swell, Ah wants you to be one de first ladies to walk in dere and have some set down."

"Do Jesus, Ah ain't knowed nothin' 'bout it. Who de man done it?"

"Mister Otis D. Slemmons, of spots and places—Memphis, Chicago, Jacksonville, Philadelphia and so on."

"Dat heavy-set man wid his mouth full of gold teethes?"

"Yeah. Where did you see 'im at?"

"Ah went down to de sto' tuh git a box of lye and Ah seen 'im standin' on de corner talkin' to some of de mens, and Ah come on back and went to scrubbin' de floor, and he passed and tipped his hat whilst Ah was scourin' de steps. Ah thought Ah never seen *him* befo'."

Joe smiled pleasantly. "Yeah, he's up to date. He got de finest clothes Ah ever seen on a colored man's back."

"Aw, he don't look no better in his clothes than you do in yourn. He got a puzzlegut on 'im and he so chuckle-headed, he got a pone behind his neck."

Joe looked down at his own abdomen and said

wistfully, "Wisht Ah had a build on me lak he got. He ain't puzzle-gutted, honey. He jes' got a corperation. Dat make 'm look lak a rich white man. All rich mens is got some belly on 'em."

"Ah seen de pitchers of Henry Ford and he's a spare-built man and Rockefeller look lak he ain't got but one gut. But Ford and Rockefeller and dis Slemmons and all de rest kin be as many-gutted as dey please, Ah'm satisfied wid you jes' lak you is, baby. God took pattern after a pine tree and built you noble. Youse a pritty man, and if Ah knowed any way to make you mo' pritty still Ah'd take and do it."

Joe reached over gently and toyed with Missie May's ear. "You jes' say dat cause you love me, but Ah know Ah can't hold no light to Otis D. Slemmons. Ah ain't never been nowhere and Ah ain't got nothin' but you."

Missie May got on his lap and kissed him and he kissed back in kind. Then he went on. "All de womens is crazy 'bout 'im everywhere he go."

"How you know dat, Joe?"

"He tole us so hisself."

"Dat don't make it so. His mouf is cut crossways, ain't it? Well, he kin lie jes' lak anybody else."

"Good Lawd, Missie! You womens sho is hard to sense into things. He's got a five-dollar gold piece for a stick-pin and he got a ten-dollar gold piece on his watch chain and his mouf is jes' crammed full of gold teethes. Sho wisht it wuz mine. And whut make it so cool, he got money 'cumulated. And womens give it all to 'im."

"Ah don't see whut de womens see on 'im. Ah wouldn't give 'im a wink if de sheriff wuz after 'im."

"Well, he tole us how de white womens in Chicago give 'im all dat gold money. So he don't 'low nobody to touch it at all. Not even put dey finger on it. Dey tole 'im not to. You kin make 'miration at it, but don't tetch it."

"Whyn't he stay up dere where dey so crazy 'bout 'im?"

"Ah reckon dey done made 'im vast-rich and he wants to travel some. He say dey wouldn't leave 'im hit a lick of work. He got mo' lady people crazy 'bout him than he kin shake a stick at."

"Joe, Ah hates to see you so dumb. Dat stray nigger jes' tell y'all anything and y'all b'lieve it."

"Go 'head on now, honey and put on yo' clothes. He talkin' 'bout his pritty womens—Ah want 'im to see *mine*."

Missie May went off to dress and Joe spent the time trying to make his stomach punch out like Slemmons' middle. He tried the rolling swagger of the stranger, but found that his tall bone-and-muscle stride fitted ill with it. He just had time to drop back into his seat before Missie May came in dressed to go.

On the way home that night Joe was exultant. "Didn't Ah say ole Otis was swell? Can't he talk Chicago talk? Wuzn't dat funny whut he said when great big fat ole Ida Armstrong come in? He asted me, 'Who is dat broad wid de forte shake?' Dat's a new word. Us always thought forty was a set of figgers but he showed us where it means a whole heap of things. Sometimes he don't say forty, he jes' say thirty-eight and two and dat mean de same thing. Know whut he tole me when Ah wuz payin' for our ice cream? He say, 'Ah have to hand it to you, Joe. Dat wife of yours is jes' thirty-eight and two. Yessuh, she's forte!' Ain't he killin'?"

"He'll do in case of a rush. But he sho is got uh heap uh gold on 'im. Dat's de first time Ah ever seed gold money. It lookted good on him sho nuff, but it'd look a whole heap better on you."

"Who, me? Missie May youse crazy! Where would a po' man lak me git gold money from?"

Missie May was silent for a minute, then she said, "Us might find some goin' long de road some time. Us could."

"Who would be losin' gold money round heah? We ain't even seen none dese white folks wearin' no gold money on dey watch chain. You must be figgerin' Mister Packard or Mister Cadillac goin' pass through heah."

"You don't know whut been lost 'round heah. Maybe somebody way back in memorial times lost they gold money and went on off and it ain't never been found. And then if we wuz to find it, you could wear some 'thout havin' no gang of womens lak dat Slemmons say he got."

Joe laughed and hugged her. "Don't be so wishful 'bout me. Ah'm satisfied de way Ah is. So long as Ah be yo' husband, Ah don't keer 'bout nothin' else. Ah'd ruther all de other womens in de world to be dead than for you to have de toothache. Less we go to bed and git our night rest."

It was Saturday night once more before Joe could parade his wife in Slemmons' ice cream parlor again. He worked the night shift and Saturday was his only night off. Every other evening around six o'clock he left home, and dying dawn saw him hustling home around the lake where the challenging sun flung a flaming sword from east to west across the trembling water.

That was the best part of life—going home to Missie May. Their whitewashed house, the mock battle on Saturday, the dinner and ice cream parlor afterwards, church on Sunday nights when Missie out-dressed any woman in town—all, everything was right.

One night around eleven the acid ran out at the G. and G. The foreman knocked off the crew and let the steam die down. As Joe rounded the lake on his way home, a lean moon rode the lake in a silver boat. If anybody had asked Joe about the moon on the lake, he would have said he hadn't paid it any attention. But he saw it with his feelings. It made him yearn painfully for Missie. Creation obsessed him. He thought about children. They had been married more than a year now. They had money put away. They ought to be making little feet for shoes. A little boy child would be about right.

He saw a dim light in the bedroom and decided to come in through the kitchen door. He could wash the fertilizer dust off himself before presenting himself to Missie May. It would be nice for her not to know that he was there until he slipped into his place in bed and hugged her back. She always liked that.

He eased the kitchen door open slowly and silently, but when he went to set his dinner bucket on the table he bumped it into a pile of dishes, and something crashed to the floor. He heard his wife gasp in fright and hurried to reassure her.

"Iss me, honey. Don't git skeered."

There was a quick, large movement in the bed-room. A rustle, a thud, and a stealthy silence. The light went out.

What? Robbers? Murderers? Some varmint attacking his helpless wife, perhaps. He struck a match, threw himself on guard and stepped over the door-sill into the bedroom.

The great belt on the wheel of Time slipped and eternity stood still. By the match light he could see the man's legs fighting with his breeches in his frantic desire to get them on. He had both chance and time to kill the intruder in his helpless condition—half in and half out of his pants—but he was too weak to take action. The shapeless enemies of humanity that live in the hours of Time had waylaid Joe. He was assaulted in his weakness. Like Samson awakening after his haircut. So he just opened his mouth and laughed.

The match went out and he struck another and lit the lamp. A howling wind raced across his heart, but underneath its fury he heard his wife sobbing and Slemmons pleading for his life. Offering to buy it with all that he had. "Please, suh, don't kill me. Sixty-two dollars at de sto'. Gold money."

Joe just stood. Slemmons looked at the window, but it was screened. Joe stood out like a rough-backed mountain between him and the door. Barring him from escape, from sunrise, from life.

He considered a surprise attack upon the big clown that stood there laughing like a chessy cat. But before his fist could travel an inch, Joe's own rushed out to crush him like a battering ram. Then Joe stood over him.

"Git into yo' damn rags, Slemmons, and dat quick."

Slemmons scrambled to his feet and into his vest and coat. As he grabbed his hat, Joe's fury overrode his intentions and he grabbed at Slemmons with his left hand and struck at him with his right. The right landed. The left grazed the front of his vest. Slemmons was knocked a somersault into the kitchen and fled through the open door. Joe found himself alone with Missie May, with the golden watch charm clutched in his left fist. A short bit of broken chain dangled between his fingers.

Missie May was sobbing. Wails of weeping without words. Joe stood, and after awhile he found out that he had something in his hand. And then he stood and felt without thinking and without seeing with his natural eyes. Missie May kept on crying and Joe kept on feeling so much and not knowing what to do with all his feelings, he put Slemmons' watch charm in his pants pocket and took a good laugh and went to bed.

"Missie May, whut you cryin' for?"

"Cause Ah love you so hard and Ah know you don't love *me* no mo'."

Joe sank his face into the pillow for a spell then he said huskily, "You don't know de feelings of dat yet, Missie May."

"Oh Joe, honey, he said he wuz gointer give me dat gold money and he jes' kept on after me——"

Joe was very still and silent for a long time. Then he said, "Well, don't cry no mo', Missie May. Ah got yo' gold piece for you."

The hours went past on their rusty ankles. Joe still and quiet on one bed-rail and Missie May wrung dry of sobs on the other. Finally the sun's tide crept upon the shore of night and drowned all its hours. Missie May with her face stiff and streaked towards the window saw the dawn come into her yard. It was day. Nothing more. Joe wouldn't be coming home as usual. No need to fling open the front door and sweep off the porch, making it nice for Joe. Never no more breakfast to cook; no more washing and starching of Joe's jumper-jackets and pants. No more nothing. So why get up?

With this strange man in her bed, she felt embarrassed to get up and dress. She decided to wait till he had dressed and gone. Then she would get up, dress quickly and be gone forever beyond reach of

Joe's looks and laughs. But he never moved. Red light turned to yellow, then white.

From beyond the no-man's land between them came a voice. A strange voice that yesterday had been Joe's.

"Missie May, ain't you gonna fix me no breakfus'?"

She sprang out of bed. "Yeah, Joe. Ah didn't reckon you wuz hongry."

No need to die today. Joe needed her for a few more minutes anyhow.

Soon there was a roaring fire in the cook stove. Water bucket full and two chickens killed. Joe loved fried chicken and rice. She didn't deserve a thing and good Joe was letting her cook him some breakfast. She rushed hot biscuits to the table as Joe took his seat.

He ate with his eyes in his plate. No laughter, no banter.

"Missie May, you ain't eatin' yo' breakfus'."

"Ah don't choose none, Ah thank yuh."

His coffee cup was empty. She sprang to refill it. When she turned from the stove and bent to set the cup beside Joe's plate, she saw the yellow coin on the table between them.

She slumped into her seat and wept into her arms.

Presently Joe said calmly, "Missie May, you cry too much. Don't look back lak Lot's wife and turn to salt."

The sun, the hero of every day, the impersonal old man that beams as brightly on death as on birth, came up every morning and raced across the blue dome and dipped into the sea of fire every evening. Water ran down hill and birds nested.

Missie knew why she didn't leave Joe. She couldn't. She loved him too much, but she could not understand why Joe didn't leave her. He was polite, even kind at times, but aloof.

There were no more Saturday romps. No ringing silver dollars to stack beside her plate. No pockets to rifle. In fact the yellow coin in his trousers was like a monster hiding in the cave of his pockets to destroy her.

She often wondered if he still had it, but nothing could have induced her to ask nor yet to explore his pockets to see for herself. Its shadow was in the house whether or no.

One night Joe came home around midnight and complained of pains in the back. He asked Missie to rub him down with liniment. It had been three months since Missie had touched his body and it all seemed strange. But she rubbed him. Grateful for the chance. Before morning, youth triumphed and

Missie exulted. But the next day, as she joyfully made up their bed, beneath her pillow she found the piece of money with the bit of chain attached.

Alone to herself, she looked at the thing with loathing, but look she must. She took it into her hands with trembling and saw first thing that it was no gold piece. It was a gilded half dollar. Then she knew why Slemmons had forbidden anyone to touch his gold. He trusted village eyes at a distance not to recognize his stick-pin as a gilded quarter, and his watch charm as a four-bit piece.

She was glad at first that Joe had left it there. Perhaps he was through with her punishment. They were man and wife again. Then another thought came clawing at her. He had come home to buy from her as if she were any woman in the long house. Fifty cents for her love. As if to say that he could pay as well as Slemmons. She slid the coin into his Sunday pants pocket and dressed herself and left his house.

Half way between her house and the quarters she met her husband's mother, and after a short talk she turned and went back home. Never would she admit defeat to that woman who prayed for it nightly. If she had not the substance of marriage she had the outside show. Joe must leave *her*. She let him see she didn't want his gold four-bits too.

She saw no more of the coin for some time though she knew that Joe could not help finding it in his pocket. But his health kept poor, and he came home at least every ten days to be rubbed.

The sun swept around the horizon, trailing its robes of weeks and days. One morning as Joe came in from work, he found Missie May chopping wood. Without a word he took the ax and chopped a huge pile before he stopped.

"You ain't got no business choppin' wood, and you know it."

"How come? Ah been choppin' it for de last longest."

"Ah ain't blind. You makin' feet for shoes."

"Won't you be glad to have a lil baby chile, Joe?"

"You know dat 'thout astin' me."

"Iss gointer be a boy chile and de very spit of you."

"You reckon, Missie May?"

"Who else could it look lak?"

Joe said nothing, but he thrust his hand deep into his pocket and fingered something there.

It was almost six months later Missie May took to bed and Joe went and got his mother to come wait on the house.

Missie May was delivered of a fine boy. Her travail was over when Joe came in from work one morning. His mother and the old women were drinking great bowls of coffee around the fire in the kitchen.

The minute Joe came into the room his mother called him aside.

"How did Missie May make out?" he asked quickly.

"Who, dat gal? She strong as a ox. She gointer have plenty mo'. We done fixed her wid de sugar and lard to sweeten her for de nex' one."

Joe stood silent awhile.

"You ain't ast 'bout de baby, Joe. You oughter be mighty proud cause he sho is de spittin' image of yuh, son. Dat's yourn all right, if you never git another one, dat un is yourn. And you know Ah'm mighty proud too, son, cause Ah never thought well of you marryin' Missie May cause her ma used tuh fan her foot round right smart and Ah been mighty skeered dat Missie May wuz gointer git misput on her road."

Joe said nothing. He fooled around the house till late in the day then just before he went to work, he went and stood at the foot of the bed and asked his wife how she felt. He did this every day during the week.

On Saturday he went to Orlando to make his market. It had been a long time since he had done that.

Meat and lard, meal and flour, soap and starch. Cans of corn and tomatoes. All the staples. He fooled around town for awhile and bought bananas and apples. Way after while he went around to the candy store.

"Hello, Joe," the clerk greeted him. "Ain't seen you in a long time."

"Nope, Ah ain't been heah. Been round in spots and places."

"Want some of them molasses kisses you always buy?"

"Yessuh." He threw the gilded half dollar on the counter. "Will dat spend?"

"Whut is it, Joe? Well, I'll be doggone! A gold-plated four-bit piece. Where'd you git it, Joe?"

"Offen a stray nigger dat come through Eatonville. He had it on his watch chain for a charm—goin' round making out iss gold money. Ha ha! He had a quarter on his tie pin and it wuz all golded up too. Tryin' to fool people. Makin' out he so rich and everything. Ha! Ha! Tryin' to tole off folkses wives from home."

"How did you git it, Joe? Did he fool you, too?"

"Who, me? Naw suh! He ain't fooled me none. Know whut Ah done? He come round me wid his smart talk. Ah hauled off and knocked 'im down and took his old four-bits way from 'im. Gointer buy my

284

wife some good ole lasses kisses wid it. Gimme fifty cents worth of dem candy kisses."

"Fifty cents buys a mighty lot of candy kisses, Joe. Why don't you split it up and take some chocolate bars, too. They eat good, too."

"Yessuh, dey do, but Ah wants all dat in kisses. Ah got a lil boy chile home now. Tain't a week old yet, but he kin suck a sugar tit and maybe eat one them kisses hisself."

Joe got his candy and left the store. The clerk turned to the next customer. "Wisht I could be like these darkies. Laughin' all the time. Nothin' worries 'em."

Back in Eatonville, Joe reached his own front door. There was the ring of singing metal on wood. Fifteen times. Missie May couldn't run to the door, but she crept there as quickly as she could.

"Joe Banks, Ah hear you chunkin' money in mah do'way. You wait till Ah got mah strength back and Ah'm gointer fix you for dat."

D. H. LAWRENCE

The Horse Dealer's Daughter

"Well, Mabel, and what are you going to do with yourself?" asked Joe, with foolish flippancy. He felt quite safe himself. Without listening for an answer, he turned aside, worked a grain of tobacco to the tip of his tongue, and spat it out. He did not care about anything, since he felt safe himself.

The three brothers and the sister sat round the desolate breakfast table, attempting some sort of desultory consultation. The morning's post had given the final tap to the family fortunes, and all was over. The dreary dining-room itself, with its heavy mahogany furniture, looked as if it were waiting to be done away with.

But the consultation amounted to nothing. There was a strange air of ineffectuality about the three men, as they sprawled at table, smoking and reflecting vaguely on their own condition. The girl was alone, a rather short, sullen-looking young woman of twenty-seven. She did not share the same life as her brothers. She would have been good-looking, save for the impassive fixity of her face, "bull-dog," as her brothers called it.

There was a confused tramping of horses' feet outside. The three men all sprawled round in their chairs to watch. Beyond the dark holly-bushes that separated the strip of lawn from the highroad, they could see a cavalcade of shire horses swinging out of their own yard, being taken for exercise. This was the last time. These were the last horses that would go through their hands. The young men watched with critical, callous look. They were all frightened at the collapse of their lives, and the sense of disaster in which they were involved left them no inner freedom.

Yet they were three fine, well-set fellows enough. Joe, the eldest, was a man of thirty-three, broad and handsome in a hot, flushed way. His face was red, he twisted his black moustache over a thick finger, his eyes were shallow and restless. He had a sensual way of uncovering his teeth when he laughed, and his bearing was stupid. Now he watched the horses with a glazed look of helplessness in his eyes, a certain stupor of downfall.

The great draught-horses swung past. They were tied head to tail, four of them, and they heaved along to where a lane branched off from the highroad, planting their great hoofs floutingly in the fine black mud, swinging their great rounded haunches sumptuously, and trotting a few sudden steps as they were led into the lane, round the corner. Every movement showed a massive, slumbrous strength, and a stupidity which held them in subjection. The groom at the head looked back, jerking the leading rope. And the cavalcade moved out of sight up the lane, the tail of the last horse, bobbed up tight and stiff, held out taut from the swinging great haunches as they rocked behind the hedges in a motion-like sleep.

Joe watched with glazed hopeless eyes. The horses were almost like his own body to him. He felt he was done for now. Luckily he was engaged to a woman as old as himself, and therefore her father, who was steward of a neighbouring estate, would provide him with a job. He would marry and go into harness. His life was over, he would be a subject animal now.

He turned uneasily aside, the retreating steps of the horses echoing in his ears. Then, with foolish restlessness, he reached for the scraps of bacon-rind from the plates, and making a faint whistling sound, flung them to the terrier that lay against the fender. He watched the dog swallow them, and waited till the creature looked into his eyes. Then a faint grin came on his face, and in a high, foolish voice he said:

"You won't get much more bacon, shall you, you little b——?"

The dog faintly and dismally wagged its tail, then

lowered its haunches, circled round, and lay down again.

There was another helpless silence at the table. Joe sprawled uneasily in his seat, not willing to go till the family conclave was dissolved. Fred Henry, the second brother, was erect, clean-limbed, alert. He had watched the passing of the horses with more *sang-froid*. If he was an animal, like Joe, he was an animal which controls, not one which is controlled. He was master of any horse, and he carried himself with a well-tempered air of mastery. But he was not master of the situations of life. He pushed his coarse brown moustache upwards, off his lip, and glanced irritably at his sister, who sat impassive and inscrutable.

"You'll go and stop with Lucy for a bit, shan't you?" he asked. The girl did not answer.

"I don't see what else you can do," persisted Fred Henry.

"Go as a skivvy," Joe interpolated laconically.

The girl did not move a muscle.

"If I was her, I should go in for training for a nurse," said Malcolm, the youngest of them all. He was the baby of the family, a young man of twenty-two, with a fresh, jaunty *museau*.

But Mabel did not take any notice of him. They

had talked at her and round her for so many years, that she hardly heard them at all.

The marble clock on the mantel-piece softly chimed the half-hour, the dog rose uneasily from the hearthrug and looked at the party at the breakfast table. But still they sat on in ineffectual conclave.

"Oh, all right," said Joe suddenly, *à propos* of nothing. "I'll get a move on."

He pushed back his chair, straddled his knees with a downward jerk, to get them free, in horsey fashion, and went to the fire. Still he did not go out of the room; he was curious to know what the others would do or say. He began to charge his pipe, looking down at the dog and saying, in a high, affected voice:

"Going wi' me? Going wi' me are ter? Tha'rt goin' further than tha counts on just now, dost hear?"

The dog faintly wagged its tail, the man stuck out his jaw and covered his pipe with his hands, and puffed intently, losing himself in the tobacco, looking down all the while at the dog with an absent brown eye. The dog looked up at him in mournful distrust. Joe stood with his knees stuck out, in real horsey fashion.

"Have you had a letter from Lucy?" Fred Henry asked of his sister.

"Last week," came the neutral reply.

"And what does she say?"

There was no answer.

"Does she *ask* you to go and stop there?" persisted Fred Henry.

"She says I can if I like."

"Well, then, you'd better. Tell her you'll come on Monday."

This was received in silence.

"That's what you'll do then, is it?" said Fred Henry, in some exasperation.

But she made no answer. There was a silence of futility and irritation in the room. Malcolm grinned fatuously.

"You'll have to make up your mind between now and next Wednesday," said Joe loudly, "or else find yourself lodgings on the kerbstone."

The face of the young woman darkened, but she sat on immutable.

"Here's Jack Fergusson!" exclaimed Malcolm, who was looking aimlessly out of the window.

"Where?" exclaimed Joe, loudly.

"Just gone past."

"Coming in?"

Malcolm craned his neck to see the gate.

"Yes," he said.

There was a silence. Mabel sat on like one

condemned, at the head of the table. Then a whistle was heard from the kitchen. The dog got up and barked sharply. Joe opened the door and shouted:

"Come on."

After a moment a young man entered. He was muffled up in overcoat and a purple woollen scarf, and his tweed cap, which he did not remove, was pulled down on his head. He was of medium height, his face was rather long and pale, his eyes looked tired.

"Hello, Jack! Well, Jack!" exclaimed Malcolm and Joe. Fred Henry merely said, "Jack."

"What's doing?" asked the newcomer, evidently addressing Fred Henry.

"Same. We've got to be out by Wednesday.—Got a cold?"

"I have—got it bad, too."

"Why don't you stop in?"

"*Me* stop in? When I can't stand on my legs, perhaps I shall have a chance." The young man spoke huskily. He had a slight Scotch accent.

"It's a knock-out, isn't it," said Joe, boisterously, "if a doctor goes round croaking with a cold. Looks bad for the patients, doesn't it?"

The young doctor looked at him slowly.

"Anything the matter with *you*, then?" he asked sarcastically.

"Not as I know of. Damn your eyes, I hope not. Why?"

"I thought you were very concerned about the patients, wondered if you might be one yourself."

"Damn it, no, I've never been patient to no flaming doctor, and hope I never shall be," returned Joe.

At this point Mabel rose from the table, and they all seemed to become aware of her existence. She began putting the dishes together. The young doctor looked at her, but did not address her. He had not greeted her. She went out of the room with the tray, her face impassive and unchanged.

"When are you off then, all of you?" asked the doctor.

"I'm catching the eleven-forty," replied Malcolm. "Are you goin' down wi' th' trap, Joe?"

"Yes, I've told you I'm going down wi' th' trap, haven't I?"

"We'd better be getting her in then.—So long, Jack, if I don't see you before I go," said Malcolm, shaking hands.

He went out, followed by Joe, who seemed to have his tail between his legs.

"Well, this is the devil's own," exclaimed the doctor, when he was left alone with Fred Henry. "Going before Wednesday, are you?"

"That's the orders," replied the other.

"Where, to Northampton?"

"That's it."

"The devil!" exclaimed Fergusson, with quiet chagrin.

And there was silence between the two.

"All settled up, are you?" asked Fergusson.

"About."

There was another pause.

"Well, I shall miss yer, Freddy, boy," said the young doctor.

"And I shall miss thee, Jack," returned the other.

"Miss you like hell," mused the doctor.

Fred Henry turned aside. There was nothing to say. Mabel came in again, to finish clearing the table.

"What are *you* going to do, then, Miss Pervin?" asked Fergusson. "Going to your sister's, are you?"

Mabel looked at him with her steady, dangerous eyes, that always made him uncomfortable, unsettling his superficial ease.

"No," she said.

"Well, what in the name of fortune *are* you going to do? Say what you mean to do," cried Fred Henry, with futile intensity.

But she only averted her head, and continued her work. She folded the white table-cloth, and put on the chenille cloth.

"The sulkiest bitch that ever trod!" muttered her brother.

But she finished her task with perfectly impassive face, the young doctor watching her interestedly all the while. Then she went out.

Fred Henry stared after her, clenching his lips, his blue eyes fixing in sharp antagonism, as he made a grimace of sour exasperation.

"You could bray her into bits, and that's all you'd get out of her," he said, in a small, narrowed tone.

The doctor smiled faintly.

"What's she *going* to do, then?" he asked.

"Strike me if *I* know!" returned the other.

There was a pause. Then the doctor stirred.

"I'll be seeing you to-night, shall I?" he said to his friend.

"Ay—where's it to be? Are we going over to Jessdale?"

"I don't know. I've got such a cold on me. I'll come round to the Moon and Stars, anyway."

"Let Lizzie and May miss their night for once, eh?"

"That's it—if I feel as I do now."

"All's one—"

The two young men went through the passage and down to the back door together. The house was large, but it was servantless now, and desolate. At the back was a small bricked house-yard, and beyond that a big square, gravelled fine and red, and having stables on two sides. Sloping, dank, winter-dark fields stretched away on the open sides.

But the stables were empty. Joseph Pervin, the father of the family, had been a man of no educa-tion, who had become a fairly large horse dealer. The stables had been full of horses, there was a great turmoil and come-and-go of horses and of dealers and grooms. Then the kitchen was full of servants. But of late things had declined. The old man had married a second time, to retrieve his fortunes. Now he was dead and everything was gone to the dogs, there was nothing but debt and threatening.

For months, Mabel had been servantless in the big house, keeping the home together in penury for her ineffectual brothers. She had kept house for ten years. But previously, it was with unstinted means. Then, however brutal and coarse everything was, the sense of money had kept her proud, confident. The men might be foul-mouthed, the women in the kit-chen might have bad reputations, her brothers might have illegitimate children. But so long as there was money, the girl felt herself established, and brutally proud, reserved.

No company came to the house, save dealers and coarse men. Mabel had no associates of her own sex, after her sister went away. But she did not mind. She went regularly to church, she attended to her father. And she lived in the memory of her mother, who had died when she was fourteen, and whom she had loved. She had loved her father, too, in a different way, depending upon him, and feeling secure in him, until at the age of fifty-four he married again. And then she had set hard against him. Now he had died and left them all hopelessly in debt.

She had suffered badly during the period of poverty. Nothing, however, could shake the curious sullen, animal pride that dominated each member of the family. Now, for Mabel, the end had come. Still she would not cast about her. She would follow her own way just the same. She would always hold the keys of her own situation. Mindless and persistent, she endured from day to day. Why should she think? Why should she answer anybody? It was enough that this was the end, and there was no way out. She need not pass any more darkly along the main street of the small town, avoiding every eye. She need not demean herself any more, going into the shops and buying the cheapest food. This was at an end. She thought of nobody, not even of herself. Mindless and persistent, she seemed in a sort of ecstasy to be coming nearer to her fulfilment, her own glorification, approaching her dead mother, who was glorified.

In the afternoon she took a little bag, with shears and sponge and a small scrubbing brush, and went out. It was a grey, wintry day, with saddened, dark-green fields and an atmosphere blackened by the smoke of foundries not far off. She went quickly, darkly along the causeway, heeding nobody, through the town to the churchyard.

There she always felt secure, as if no one could see her, although as a matter of fact she was exposed to the stare of everyone who passed along under the churchyard wall. Nevertheless, once under the shadow of the great looming church, among the graves, she felt immune from the world, reserved within the thick churchyard wall as in another country.

Carefully she clipped the grass from the grave, and arranged the pinky-white, small chrysanthe-mums in the tin cross. When this was done, she took an empty jar from a neighbouring grave, brought water, and carefully, most scrupulously sponged the marble headstone and the coping-stone.

It gave her sincere satisfaction to do this. She felt in immediate contact with the world of her mother. She took minute pains, went through the park in a state bordering on pure happiness, as if in performing this task she came into a subtle, intimate connection with her mother. For the life she followed here in the world was far less real than the world of death she inherited from her mother.

The doctor's house was just by the church. Fergusson, being a mere hired assistant, was slave to the countryside. As he hurried now to attend to the outpatients in the surgery, glancing across the graveyard with his quick eye, he saw the girl at her task at the grave. She seemed so intent and remote, it was like looking into another world. Some mystical element was touched in him. He slowed down as he walked, watching her as if spell-bound.

She lifted her eyes, feeling him looking. Their eyes met. And each looked again at once, each feeling, in some way, found out by the other. He lifted his cap and passed on down the road. There remained distinct in his consciousness, like a vision, the memory of her face, lifted from the tombstone in the churchyard, and looking at him with slow, large, portentous eyes. It *was* portentous, her face. It seemed to mesmerise him. There was a heavy power in her eyes which laid hold of his whole being, as if he had drunk some powerful drug. He had been feeling weak and done before. Now the life came back into him, he felt delivered from his own fretted, daily self.

He finished his duties at the surgery as quickly as might be, hastily filling up the bottles of the waiting people with cheap drugs. Then, in perpetual haste, he set off again to visit several cases in another part of his round, before teatime. At all times he preferred to walk, if he could, but particularly when he was not well. He fancied the motion restored him.

The afternoon was falling. It was grey, deadened, and wintry, with a slow, moist, heavy coldness sinking in and deadening all the faculties. But why should he think or notice? He hastily climbed the hill and turned across the dark-green fields, following the black cinder-track. In the distance, across a shallow dip in the country, the small town was clustered like smouldering ash, a tower, a spire, a heap of low, raw, extinct houses. And on the nearest fringe of the town, sloping into the dip, was Oldmeadow, the Pervins' house. He could see the stables and the outbuildings distinctly, as they lay towards him on the slope. Well, he would not go there many more times! Another resource would be lost to him, another place gone: the only company he cared for in the alien, ugly little town he was losing. Nothing but work, drudgery, constant hastening from dwelling to dwelling among the colliers and the iron-workers. It wore him out, but at the same time he had a craving for it. It was a stimulant to him to be in the homes of the working people, moving as it were through the innermost body of their life. His nerves were excited and gratified. He could come so near, into the very lives of the rough, inarticulate, powerfully emotional men and women. He grumbled, he said he hated the hellish hole. But as a matter of fact it excited him, the contact with the rough, strongly-feeling people was a stimulant applied direct to his nerves.

Below Oldmeadow, in the green, shallow, soddened hollow of fields, lay a square, deep pond. Roving across the landscape, the doctor's quick eye detected a figure in black passing through the gate of the field, down towards the pond. He looked again. It would be Mabel Pervin. His mind suddenly became alive and attentive.

Why was she going down there? He pulled up on the path on the slope above, and stood staring. He could just make sure of the small black figure moving in the hollow of the failing day. He seemed to see her in the midst of such obscurity, that he was like a clairvoyant, seeing rather with the mind's eye than with ordinary sight. Yet he could see her positively enough, whilst he kept his eye attentive. He felt, if he looked away from her, in the thick, ugly falling dusk, he would lose her altogether.

He followed her minutely as she moved, direct

and intent, like something transmitted rather than stirring in voluntary activity, straight down the field towards the pond. There she stood on the bank for a moment. She never raised her head. Then she waded slowly into the water.

He stood motionless as the small black figure walked slowly and deliberately towards the centre of the pond, very slowly, gradually moving deeper into the motionless water, and still moving forward as the water got up to her breast. Then he could see her no more in the dusk of the dead afternoon.

"There!" he exclaimed. "Would you believe it?"

And he hastened straight down, running over the wet, soddened fields, pushing through the hedges, down into the depression of callous wintry obscurity. It took him several minutes to come to the pond. He stood on the bank, breathing heavily. He could see nothing. His eyes seemed to penetrate the dead water. Yes, perhaps that was the dark shadow of her black clothing beneath the surface of the water.

He slowly ventured into the pond. The bottom was deep, soft clay, he sank in, and the water clasped dead cold round his legs. As he stirred he could smell the cold, rotten clay that fouled up into the water. It was objectionable in his lungs. Still, repelled and yet not heeding, he moved deeper into the pond. The cold water rose over his thighs, over his loins, upon his abdomen. The lower part of his body was all sunk in the hideous cold element. And the bottom was so deeply soft and uncertain, he was afraid of pitching with his mouth underneath. He could not swim, and was afraid.

He crouched a little, spreading his hands under the water and moving them round, trying to feel for her. The dead cold pond swayed upon his chest. He moved again, a little deeper, and again, with his hands underneath, he felt all around under the water. And he touched her clothing. But it evaded his fingers. He made a desperate effort to grasp it.

And so doing he lost his balance and went under, horribly, suffocating in the foul earthy water, struggling madly for a few moments. At last, after what seemed an eternity, he got his footing, rose again into the air and looked around. He gasped, and knew he was in the world. Then he looked at the water. She had risen near him. He grasped her clothing, and drawing her nearer, turned to take his way to land again.

He went very slowly, carefully, absorbed in the slow progress. He rose higher, climbing out of the pond. The water was now only about his legs; he was thankful, full of relief to be out of the clutches of the pond. He lifted her and staggered on to the bank, out of the horror of wet, grey clay.

He laid her down on the bank. She was quite unconscious and running with water. He made the water come from her mouth, he worked to restore her. He did not have to work very long before he could feel the breathing begin again in her; she was breathing naturally. He worked a little longer. He could feel her live beneath his hands; she was coming back. He wiped her face, wrapped her in his overcoat, looked round into the dim, dark-grey world, then lifted her and staggered down the bank and across the fields.

It seemed an unthinkably long way, and his burden so heavy he felt he would never get to the house. But at last he was in the stable-yard, and then in the house-yard. He opened the door and went into the house. In the kitchen he laid her down on the hearthrug, and called. The house was empty. But the fire was burning in the grate.

Then again he kneeled to attend to her. She was breathing regularly, her eyes were wide open and as if conscious, but there seemed something missing in her look. She was conscious in herself, but unconscious of her surroundings.

He ran upstairs, took blankets from a bed, and put them before the fire to warm. Then he removed her saturated, earthy-smelling clothing, rubbed her dry with a towel, and wrapped her naked in the blankets. Then he went into the dining room, to look for spirits. There was a little whiskey. He drank a gulp himself, and put some into her mouth.

The effect was instantaneous. She looked full into his face, as if she had been seeing him for some time, and yet had only just become conscious of him.

"Dr. Fergusson?" she said.

"What?" he answered.

He was divesting himself of his coat, intending to find some dry clothing upstairs. He could not bear the smell of the dead, clayey water, and he was mortally afraid for his own health.

"What did I do?" she asked.

"Walked into the pond," he replied. He had begun to shudder like one sick, and could hardly attend to her. Her eyes remained full on him, he seemed to be going dark in his mind, looking back at her helplessly. The shuddering became quieter in him, his life came back in him, dark and unknowing, but strong again.

"Was I out of my mind?" she asked, while her eyes were fixed on him all the time.

"Maybe, for the moment," he replied. He felt quiet, because his strength had come back. The strange fretful strain had left him.

"Am I out of my mind now?" she asked.

"Are you?" he reflected a moment. "No," he answered truthfully, "I don't see that you are." He turned his face aside. He was afraid now, because he felt dazed, and felt dimly that her power was stronger than his, in this issue. And she continued to look at him fixedly all the time. "Can you tell me where I shall find some dry things to put on?" he asked.

"Did you dive into the pond for me?" she asked.

"No," he answered. "I walked in. But I went in overhead as well."

There was silence for a moment. He hesitated. He very much wanted to go upstairs to get into dry clothing. But there was another desire in him. And she seemed to hold him. His will seemed to have gone to sleep, and left him, standing there slack before her. But he felt warm inside himself. He did not shudder at all, though his clothes were sodden on him.

"Why did you?" she asked.

"Because I didn't want you to do such a foolish thing," he said.

"It wasn't foolish," she said, still gazing at him as she lay on the floor, with a sofa cushion under her head. "It was the right thing to do. *I* knew best, then."

"I'll go and shift these wet things," he said. But

still he had not the power to move out of her presence, until she sent him. It was as if she had the life
of his body in her hands, and he could not extricate
himself. Or perhaps he did not want to.

Suddenly she sat up. Then she became aware of
her own immediate condition. She felt the blankets
about her, she knew her own limbs. For a moment
it seemed as if her reason were going. She looked
round, with wild eye, as if seeking something. He
stood still with fear. She saw her clothing lying
scattered.

"Who undressed me?" she asked, her eyes resting
full and inevitable on his face.

"I did," he replied, "to bring you round."

For some moments she sat and gazed at him
awfully, her lips parted.

"Do you love me then?" she asked.

He only stood and stared at her, fascinated. His
soul seemed to melt.

She shuffled forward on her knees, and put
her arms round him, round his legs, as he stood
there, pressing her breasts against his knees and
thighs, clutching him with strange, convulsive
certainty, pressing his thighs against her, drawing
him to her face, her throat, as she looked up at him
with flaring, humble eyes of transfiguration, triumphant in first possession.

"You love me," she murmured, in strange transport, yearning and triumphant and confident. "You love me. I know you love me, I know."

And she was passionately kissing his knees, through the wet clothing, passionately and indiscriminately kissing his knees, his legs, as if unaware of everything.

He looked down at the tangled wet hair, the wild, bare, animal shoulders. He was amazed, bewildered, and afraid. He had never thought of loving her. He had never wanted to love her. When he rescued her and restored her, he was a doctor, and she was a patient. He had had no single personal thought of her. Nay, this introduction of the personal element was very distasteful to him, a violation of his professional honour. It was horrible to have her there embracing his knees. It was horrible. He revolted from it, violently. And yet—and yet—he had not the power to break away.

She looked at him again, with the same supplication of powerful love, and that same transcendent, frightening light of triumph. In view of the delicate flame which seemed to come from her face like a light, he was powerless. And yet he had never intended to love her. He had never intended. And something stubborn in him could not give way.

"You love me," she repeated, in a murmur of deep, rhapsodic assurance. "You love me."

Her hands were drawing him, drawing him down to her. He was afraid, even a little horrified. For he had, really, no intention of loving her. Yet her hands were drawing him towards her. He put out his hand quickly to steady himself, and grasped her bare shoulder. A flame seemed to burn the hand that grasped her soft shoulder. He had no intention of loving her: his whole will was against his yielding. It was horrible. And yet wonderful was the touch of her shoulders, beautiful the shining of her face. Was she perhaps mad? He had a horror of yielding to her. Yet something in him ached also.

He had been staring away at the door, away from her. But his hand remained on her shoulder. She had gone suddenly very still. He looked down at her. Her eyes were now wide with fear, with doubt, the light was dying from her face, a shadow of terrible greyness was returning. He could not bear the touch of her eyes' question upon him, and the look of death behind the question.

With an inward groan he gave way, and let his heart yield towards her. A sudden gentle smile came on his face. And her eyes, which never left his face, slowly, slowly filled with tears. He watched the strange water rise in her eyes, like some slow fountain coming up. And his heart seemed to burn and melt away in his breast.

He could not bear to look at her any more. He dropped on his knees and caught her head with his arms and pressed her face against his throat. She was very still. His heart, which seemed to have broken, was burning with a kind of agony in his breast. And he felt her slow, hot tears wetting his throat. But he could not move.

He felt the hot tears wet his neck and the hollows of his neck, and he remained motionless, suspended through one of man's eternities. Only now it had become indispensable to him to have her face pressed close to him; he could never let her go again. He could never let her head go away from the close clutch of his arm. He wanted to remain like that for ever, with his heart hurting him in a pain that was also life to him. Without knowing, he was looking down on her damp, soft brown hair.

Then, as it were suddenly, he smelt the horrid stagnant smell of that water. And at the same moment she drew away from him and looked at him. Her eyes were wistful and unfathomable. He was afraid of them, and he fell to kissing her, not knowing what he was doing. He wanted her eyes not to have that terrible, wistful, unfathomable look.

When she turned her face to him again, a faint

delicate flush was glowing, and there was again dawning that terrible shining of joy in her eyes, which really terrified him, and yet which he now wanted to see, because he feared the look of doubt still more.

"You love me?" she said, rather faltering.

"Yes." The word cost him a painful effort. Not because it wasn't true. But because it was too newly true, the *saying* seemed to tear open again his newly-torn heart. And he hardly wanted it to be true, even now.

She lifted her face to him, and he bent forward and kissed her on the mouth, gently, with the one kiss that is an eternal pledge. And as he kissed her his heart strained again in his breast. He never intended to love her. But now it was over. He had crossed over the gulf to her, and all that he had left behind had shrivelled and become void.

After the kiss, her eyes again slowly filled with tears. She sat still, away from him, with her face drooped aside, and her hands folded in her lap. The tears fell very slowly. There was complete silence. He too sat there motionless and silent on the hearthrug. The strange pain of his heart that was broken seemed to consume him. That he should love her? That this was love! That he should be ripped open in this way!—Him, a doctor!—How they would all jeer if they knew!—It was agony to him to think they might know.

In the curious naked pain of the thought he looked again to her. She was sitting there drooped into a muse. He saw a tear fall, and his heart flared hot. He saw for the first time that one of her shoulders was quite uncovered, one arm bare, he could see one of her small breasts; dimly, because it had become almost dark in the room.

"Why are you crying?" he asked, in an altered voice.

She looked up at him, and behind her tears the consciousness of her situation for the first time brought a dark look of shame to her eyes.

"I'm not crying, really," she said, watching him half frightened.

He reached his hand, and softly closed it on her bare arm.

"I love you! I love you!" he said in a soft, low vibrating voice, unlike himself.

She shrank, and dropped her head. The soft, penetrating grip of his hand on her arm distressed her. She looked up at him.

"I want to go," she said. "I want to go and get you some dry things."

"Why?" he said. "I'm all right."

313

"But I want to go," she said. "And I want you to change your things."

He released her arm, and she wrapped herself in the blanket, looking at him rather frightened. And still she did not rise.

"Kiss me," she said wistfully.

He kissed her, but briefly, half in anger.

Then, after a second, she rose nervously, all mixed up in the blanket. He watched her in her confusion, as she tried to extricate herself and wrap herself up so that she could walk. He watched her relentlessly, as she knew. And as she went, the blanket trailing, and as he saw a glimpse of her feet and her white leg, he tried to remember her as she was when he had wrapped her in the blanket. But then he didn't want to remember, because she had been nothing to him then, and his nature revolted from remembering her as she was when she was nothing to him.

A tumbling, muffled noise from within the dark house startled him. Then he heard her voice:—"There are clothes." He rose and went to the foot of the stairs, and gathered up the garments she had thrown down. Then he came back to the fire, to rub himself down and dress. He grinned at his own appearance when he had finished.

The fire was sinking, so he put on coal. The

house was now quite dark, save for the light of a street-lamp that shone in faintly from beyond the holly trees. He lit the gas with matches he found on the mantel-piece. Then he emptied the pockets of his own clothes, and threw all his wet things in a heap into the scullery. After which he gathered up her sodden clothes, gently, and put them in a separate heap on the copper-top in the scullery.

It was six o'clock on the clock. His own watch had stopped. He ought to go back to the surgery. He waited, and still she did not come down. So he went to the foot of the stairs and called:

"I shall have to go."

Almost immediately he heard her coming down. She had on her best dress of black voile, and her hair was tidy, but still damp. She looked at him—and in spite of herself, smiled.

"I don't like you in those clothes," she said.

"Do I look a sight?" he answered.

They were shy of one another.

"I'll make you some tea," she said.

"No, I must go."

"Must you?" And she looked at him again with the wide, strained, doubtful eyes. And again, from the pain of his breast, he knew how he loved her. He went and bent to kiss her, gently, passionately, with his heart's painful kiss.

"And my hair smells so horrible," she murmured in distraction. "And I'm so awful, I'm so awful! Oh, no, I'm too awful." And she broke into bitter, heart-broken sobbing. "You can't want to love me, I'm horrible."

"Don't be silly, don't be silly," he said, trying to comfort her, kissing her, holding her in his arms. "I want you, I want to marry you, we're going to be married, quickly, quickly—to-morrow if I can."

But she only sobbed terribly, and cried:

"I feel awful. I feel awful. I feel I'm horrible to you."

"No, I want you, I want you," was all he answered, blindly, with that terrible intonation which frightened her almost more than her horror lest he should *not* want her.

A Tree. A Rock. A Cloud.

It was raining that morning, and still very dark.
When the boy reached the streetcar café he had
almost finished his route and he went in for a cup of
coffee. The place was an all-night café owned by a
bitter and stingy man called Leo. After the raw,
empty street the café seemed friendly and bright:
along the counter there were a couple of soldiers,
three spinners from the cotton mill, and in a corner
a man who sat hunched over with his nose and half
his face down in a beer mug. The boy wore a helmet
such as aviators wear. When he went into the café he
unbuckled the chin strap and raised the right flap up
over his pink little ear; often as he drank his coffee
someone would speak to him in a friendly way. But
this morning Leo did not look into his face and
none of the men were talking. He paid and was leaving the café when a voice called out to him:

'Son! Hey Son!'

He turned back and the man in the corner was
crooking his finger and nodding to him. He had
brought his face out of the beer mug and he seemed

suddenly very happy. The man was long and pale, with a big nose and faded orange hair.

'Hey Son!'

The boy went toward him. He was an undersized boy of about twelve, with one shoulder drawn higher than the other because of the weight of the paper sack. His face was shallow, freckled, and his eyes were round child eyes.

'Yeah Mister?'

The man laid one hand on the paper boy's shoulders, then grasped the boy's chin and turned his face slowly from one side to the other. The boy shrank back uneasily.

'Say! What's the big idea?'

The boy's voice was shrill; inside the café it was suddenly very quiet.

The man said slowly: 'I love you.'

All along the counter the men laughed. The boy, who had scowled and sidled away, did not know what to do. He looked over the counter at Leo, and Leo watched him with a weary, brittle jeer. The boy tried to laugh also. But the man was serious and sad.

'I did not mean to tease you, Son,' he said. 'Sit down and have a beer with me. There is something I have to explain.'

Cautiously, out of the corner of his eye, the paper

boy questioned the men along the counter to see what he should do. But they had gone back to their beer or their breakfast and did not notice him. Leo put a cup of coffee on the counter and a little jug of cream.

'He is a minor,' Leo said.

The paper boy slid himself up onto the stool. His ear beneath the upturned flap of the helmet was very small and red. The man was nodding at him soberly. 'It is important,' he said. Then he reached in his hip pocket and brought out something which he held up in the palm of his hand for the boy to see.

'Look very carefully,' he said.

The boy stared, but there was nothing to look at very carefully. The man held in his big, grimy palm a photograph. It was the face of a woman, but blurred, so that only the hat and the dress she was wearing stood out clearly.

'See?' the man asked.

The boy nodded and the man placed another picture in his palm. The woman was standing on a beach in a bathing suit. The suit made her stomach very big, and that was the main thing you noticed.

'Got a good look?' He leaned over closer and finally asked: 'You ever seen her before?'

The boy sat motionless, staring slantwise at the man. 'Not so I know of.'

'Very well.' The man blew on the photographs and put them back into his pocket. 'That was my wife.'

'Dead?' the boy asked.

Slowly the man shook his head. He pursed his lips as though about to whistle and answered in a long-drawn way: 'Nuuu—' he said. 'I will explain.'

The beer on the counter before the man was in a large brown mug. He did not pick it up to drink. Instead he bent down and, putting his face over the rim, he rested there for a moment. Then with both hands he tilted the mug and sipped.

'Some night you'll go to sleep with your big nose in a mug and drown,' said Leo. 'Prominent transient drowns in beer. That would be a cute death.'

The paper boy tried to signal to Leo. While the man was not looking he screwed up his face and worked his mouth to question soundlessly: 'Drunk?' But Leo only raised his eyebrows and turned away to put some pink strips of bacon on the grill. The man pushed the mug away from him, straightened himself, and folded his loose crooked hands on the counter. His face was sad as he looked at the paper boy. He did not blink, but from time to time the lids closed down with delicate gravity over his pale green eyes. It was nearing dawn and the boy shifted the weight of the paper sack.

'I am talking about love,' the man said. 'With me it is a science.'

The boy half slid down from the stool. But the man raised his forefinger, and there was something about him that held the boy and would not let him go away.

'Twelve years ago I married the woman in the photograph. She was my wife for one year, nine months, three days, and two nights. I loved her. Yes ...' He tightened his blurred, rambling voice and said again: 'I loved her. I thought also that she loved me. I was a railroad engineer. She had all home comforts and luxuries. It never crept into my brain that she was not satisfied. But do you know what happened?'

'Mgneeow!' said Leo.

The man did not take his eyes from the boy's face. 'She left me. I came in one night and the house was empty and she was gone. She left me.'

'With a fellow?' the boy asked.

Gently the man placed his palm down on the counter. 'Why naturally, Son. A woman does not run off like that alone.'

The café was quiet, the soft rain black and endless in the street outside. Leo pressed down the frying bacon with the prongs of his long fork. 'So you have been chasing the floozie for eleven years. You frazzled old rascal!'

For the first time the man glanced at Leo. 'Please don't be vulgar. Besides, I was not speaking to you.' He turned back to the boy and said in a trusting and secretive undertone: 'Let's not pay any attention to him. O.K.?'

The paper boy nodded doubtfully.

'It was like this,' the man continued. 'I am a person who feels many things. All my life one thing after another has impressed me. Moonlight. The leg of a pretty girl. One thing after another. But the point is that when I had enjoyed anything there was a peculiar sensation as though it was laying around loose in me. Nothing seemed to finish itself up or fit in with the other things. Women? I had my portion of them. The same. Afterwards laying around loose in me. I was a man who had never loved.'

Very slowly he closed his eyelids, and the gesture was like a curtain drawn at the end of a scene in a play. When he spoke again his voice was excited and the words came fast—the lobes of his large, loose ears seemed to tremble.

'Then I met this woman. I was fifty-one years old and she always said she was thirty. I met her at a filling station and we were married within three days. And do you know what it was like? I just can't tell you. All I had ever felt was gathered together around this woman. Nothing lay around loose in me any more but was finished up by her.'

The man stopped suddenly and stroked his long nose. His voice sank down to a steady and reproachful undertone: 'I'm not explaining this right. What happened was this. There were these beautiful feelings and loose little pleasures inside me. And this woman was something like an assembly line for my soul. I run these little pieces of myself through her and I come out complete. Now do you follow me?'

'What was her name?' the boy asked.

'Oh,' he said. 'I called her Dodo. But that is immaterial.'

'Did you try to make her come back?'

The man did not seem to hear. 'Under the circumstances you can imagine how I felt when she left me.'

Leo took the bacon from the grill and folded two strips of it between a bun. He had a gray face, with slitted eyes, and a pinched nose saddled by faint blue shadows. One of the mill workers signaled for more coffee and Leo poured it. He did not give refills on coffee free. The spinner ate breakfast there every morning, but the better Leo knew his customers the stingier he treated them. He nibbled his own bun as though he grudged it to himself.

'And you never got hold of her again?'

The boy did not know what to think of the man, and his child's face was uncertain with mingled curiosity and doubt. He was new on the paper route; it was still strange to him to be out in the town in the black, queer early morning.

'Yes,' the man said. 'I took a number of steps to get her back. I went around trying to locate her. I went to Tulsa where she had folks. And to Mobile. I went to every town she had ever mentioned to me, and I hunted down every man she had formerly been connected with. Tulsa, Atlanta, Chicago, Cheehaw, Memphis . . . For the better part of two years I chased around the country trying to lay hold of her.'

'But the pair of them had vanished from the face of the earth!' said Leo.

'Don't listen to him,' the man said confidentially. 'And also just forget those two years. They are not important. What matters is that around the third year a curious thing begun to happen to me.'

'What?' the boy asked.

The man leaned down and tilted his mug to take a sip of beer. But as he hovered over the mug his nostrils fluttered slightly; he sniffed the staleness of the beer and did not drink. 'Love is a curious thing to begin with. At first I thought only of getting her back. It was a kind of mania. But then as time went on I tried to remember her. But do you know what happened?'

'No,' the boy said.

'When I laid myself down on a bed and tried to think about her my mind became a blank. I couldn't see her. I would take out her pictures and look. No good. Nothing doing. A blank. Can you imagine it?'

'Say Mac!' Leo called down the counter. 'Can you imagine this bozo's mind a blank!'

Slowly, as though fanning away flies, the man waved his hand. His green eyes were concentrated and fixed on the shallow little face of the paper boy.

'But a sudden piece of glass on a sidewalk. Or a nickel tune in a music box. A shadow on a wall at night. And I would remember. It might happen in a street and I would cry or bang my head against a lamppost. You follow me?'

'A piece of glass . . .' the boy said.

'Anything. I would walk around and I had no power of how and when to remember her. You think you can put up a kind of shield. But remembering don't come to a man face forward—it corners around sideways. I was at the mercy of everything I saw and heard. Suddenly instead of me combing the countryside to find her she begun to chase me around in my very soul. *She* chasing *me*, mind you! And in my soul.'

The boy asked finally: 'What part of the country were you in then?'

'Ooh,' the man groaned. 'I was a sick mortal. It was like smallpox. I confess, Son, that I boozed. I fornicated. I committed any sin that suddenly appealed to me. I am loath to confess it but I will do so. When I recall that period it is all curdled in my mind, it was so terrible.'

The man leaned his head down and tapped his forehead on the counter. For a few seconds he stayed bowed over in this position, the back of his stringy neck covered with orange furze, his hands with their long warped fingers held palm to palm in an attitude of prayer. Then the man straightened himself; he was smiling and suddenly his face was bright and tremulous and old.

'It was in the fifth year that it happened,' he said. 'And with it I started my science.'

Leo's mouth jerked with a pale, quick grin. 'Well none of we boys are getting any younger,' he said. Then with sudden anger he balled up a dishcloth he was holding and threw it down hard on the floor. 'You draggle-tailed old Romeo!'

'What happened?' the boy asked.

The old man's voice was high and clear: 'Peace,' he answered.

'Huh?'

'It is hard to explain scientifically, Son,' he said. 'I guess the logical explanation is that she and I had fleed around from each other for so long that finally we just got tangled up together and lay down and quit. Peace. A queer and beautiful blankness. It was spring in Portland and the rain came every afternoon. All evening I just stayed there on my bed in the dark. And that is how the science come to me.'

The windows in the streetcar were pale blue with light. The two soldiers paid for their beers and opened the door—one of the soldiers combed his hair and wiped off his muddy puttees before they went outside. The three mill workers bent silently over their breakfasts. Leo's clock was ticking on the wall.

'It is this. And listen carefully. I meditated on love and reasoned it out. I realized what is wrong with us. Men fall in love for the first time. And what do they fall in love with?'

The boy's soft mouth was partly open and he did not answer.

'A woman,' the old man said. 'Without science, with nothing to go by, they undertake the most

327

dangerous and sacred experience in God's earth. They fall in love with a woman. Is that correct, Son?'

'Yeah,' the boy said faintly.

'They start at the wrong end of love. They begin at the climax. Can you wonder it is so miserable? Do you know how men should love?'

The old man reached over and grasped the boy by the collar of his leather jacket. He gave him a gentle little shake and his green eyes gazed down unblinking and grave.

'Son, do you know how love should be begun?'

The boy sat small and listening and still. Slowly he shook his head. The old man leaned closer and whispered:

'A tree. A rock. A cloud.'

It was still raining outside in the street: a mild, gray, endless rain. The mill whistle blew for the six o'clock shift and the three spinners paid and went away. There was no one in the café but Leo, the old man, and the little paper boy.

'The weather was like this in Portland,' he said. 'At the time my science was begun. I meditated and I started very cautious. I would pick up something from the street and take it home with me. I bought a goldfish and I concentrated on the goldfish and I loved it. I graduated from one thing to another. Day

by day I was getting this technique. On the road
from Portland to San Diego——'

'Aw shut up!' screamed Leo suddenly. 'Shut up!
Shut up!'

The old man still held the collar of the boy's
jacket; he was trembling and his face was earnest
and bright and wild. 'For six years now I have gone
around by myself and built up my science. And now
I am a master. Son. I can love anything. No longer
do I have to think about it even. I see a street full of
people and a beautiful light comes in me. I watch a
bird in the sky. Or I meet a traveler on the road. Everything, Son. And anybody. All stranger and all loved!
Do you realize what a science like mine can mean?'

The boy held himself stiffly, his hands curled
tight around the counter edge. Finally he asked:
'Did you ever really find that lady?'

'What? What say, Son?'

'I mean,' the boy asked timidly. 'Have you fallen
in love with a woman again?'

The old man loosened his grasp on the boy's
collar. He turned away and for the first time his
green eyes had a vague and scattered look. He lifted
the mug from the counter, drank down the yellow
beer. His head was shaking slowly from side to side.
Then finally he answered: 'No, Son. You see that is

the last step in my science. I go cautious. And I am not quite ready yet.'

'Well!' said Leo. 'Well well well!'

The old man stood in the open doorway. 'Remember,' he said.

Framed there in the gray damp light of the early morning he looked shrunken and seedy and frail. But his smile was bright. 'Remember I love you,' he said with a last nod. And the door closed quietly behind him.

The boy did not speak for a long time. He pulled down the bangs on his forehead and slid his grimy little forefinger around the rim of his empty cup. Then without looking at Leo he finally asked:

'Was he drunk?'

'No,' said Leo shortly.

The boy raised his clear voice higher. 'Then was he a dope fiend?'

'No.'

The boy looked up at Leo, and his flat little face was desperate, his voice urgent and shrill. 'Was he crazy? Do you think he was a lunatic?' The paper boy's voice dropped suddenly with doubt. 'Leo? Or not?'

But Leo would not answer him. Leo had run a night café for fourteen years, and he held himself to be a critic of craziness. There were the town characters and also the transients who roamed in from the night. He knew the manias of all of them. But he did not want to satisfy the questions of the waiting child. He tightened his pale face and was silent.

So the boy pulled down the right flap of his helmet and as he turned to leave he made the only comment that seemed safe to him, the only remark that could not be laughed down and despised:

'He sure has done a lot of traveling.'

Summer-time

The most foolish things happen to people in the summer. For instance, this summer a most foolish thing happened to Mr Joseph Laurel, and yet, of course, in a way it was a revelation too.

After playing tennis with Beatrice Hammond most of June and July, he went down to stay with her sister in the country. He dislikes tennis very much, but at the courts where they play there are on a sloping bank some lovely rhododendrons, and some large yellow flowers rather like them, growing on bushes, and with petals thick like wax and a heavy scent like honeysuckle. After about one set Mr Laurel flings his racquet on the grass and himself on the bank, and, with his hands under his head, he looks up at the sky or at the people on the courts. And there is something particularly luxurious about this, which the other players appear not to understand.

Beatrice is an extraordinarily good player. I suppose she plays to keep young, because she is well over thirty. Tennis is, if one might say so, very becoming to her. She is tall and dark, and it always seems like a sudden revelation of her personality to see her in white. And she moves like a winged fury behind the nets, and shoots stinging balls at people in a way that Mr Laurel can quite understand other people finding rather fascinating.

She told him that her sister had invited him, but I should think the invitation really came from her. She said that they wanted someone to make up a set with her niece and her niece's cousin, and that she did not dare invite anyone who played well, because Leonora played so badly. And Mr Laurel, who prides himself on his bad tennis, decided to go.

He had been there before when the sister's husband was alive. They had a rather charming house, with a nice tennis court. The daughter, Leonora, had rather curious pale brown hair, the colour of smoke in a modern painting. When he saw her first she wore it down her back in ringlets. Now this time she had put it up in a rather old-fashioned way, which made her look older than she was. She had only just left school. The cousin who was there was also very young, a tall dark boy, very alert, and only just out of the sixth form.

Beatrice drove Mr Laurel down, and he was a little bored at first, but they had tea outside in the garden. Leonora sat opposite him in a green basket chair, near a rose tree, whose pink roses made her hair look strange. The cousin sat on the grass, handing the cake-stand round by balancing the whole thing from underneath on his hand, and though Mrs Chalen asked Mr Laurel one or two tiresome questions, all the same the charm of the garden began to make an impression on him.

"I want to ask your advice about Leonora," said Mrs Chalen, turning anxiously to him. "I don't know what to let her do."

"Has she any particular talents?" he asked.

"None that I know anything about," said her mother, looking at Leonora severely.

Mr Laurel looked at Leonora too, and she smiled back to him. She had a curious small, square smile, which was very attractive, though perhaps also a little heartless.

"She can't dance," said Basil, her cousin, not intending to insult her, but simply to eliminate one possibility.

"Or play tennis," said Beatrice a little impatiently.

"Will you have some more chocolate cake?" said Leonora.

"Thank you," said Mr Laurel, taking some. "I think she should go to an art school," he said to her mother.

"Do you really think so?" said she. "Can you paint, dear?"

"I don't know," said Leonora.

"Oh, that doesn't matter," said Mr Laurel, smiling at her. "Some artist will marry her because he wants to paint her hair, and they will live happily ever afterwards."

"Yes," said Leonora, with innocent approval.

"You really think so?" said her mother, smiling a little doubtfully.

"Undoubtedly," said Mr Laurel.

And thus her fate was decided, for sure enough she has gone to art school.

"I am going to be a dancer," said Basil.

Mr Laurel does not remember much what happened that evening, but it was very delightful to see the darkness come slowly down over the garden and the roses.

However, that night, just as he was dropping off to sleep, he heard a little tap at his door, and then it slowly opened and Leonora's head appeared.

"Can I come in?" she whispered.

"Yes," he whispered back.

She came in, and Basil came after her.

"We are a deputation to you," she said.

"We are pleased to hear you," said Mr Laurel, leaning back on his pillow. "Switch on the light."

She sat on the edge of his bed. She wore a pink dressing-gown with lace on it, over her pyjamas, and looked very charming.

"Look here, Your Majesty," she said, "when Aunt Beatrice is here we have to play tennis all the time, and we don't want to."

"In truth," said Basil, balancing himself on the bedpost, "we, your liege subjects, flatly refuse to waste our time, and yours too, in such an unintellectual pastime."

He put his hands on the bed-rail and threw his legs high into the air, coming down lightly on the carpet.

"Now you have a good deal of influence with Aunt Beatrice," said Leonora, applying herself more seriously to the deputation.

"Sweet lady," said Mr Laurel, smoothing down the collar of his sleeping-jacket, "it shall be as you wish. We consider that the game is too frivolous for a royal pursuit, and will play it only when the Lady Beatrice, over whom we have no authority, absolutely insists."

"Good," said Basil. "Come, Leonore. Try to exit backwards. Good-night, Your Majesty."

But Leonora did not for the moment move from the bed.

"Is that your dressing-gown?" she asked. "Isn't it lovely? May I try it on?"

"A present from the Emperor of China," Mr Laurel remarked. "You may."

She walked up and down the room in the brightly coloured thing.

"It is curious how few colours suit you," said he.

She looked at him reproachfully and put the dressing-gown on the bed. Basil switched the light off and went out.

"But when colours do suit you, they do," said Mr Laurel, laughing, and taking hold of the end of her dressing-gown. It slipped a little off her shoulder and she nearly left it behind with him, like the princess in the fairy tale, and she went out.

"Isn't he decent?" he heard her whisper to Basil outside the door.

Just as he was falling asleep it occurred to him that it was not a fairy tale at all, but Potiphar's wife. What an amusing thing!

The next morning he went into the garden before breakfast. They had breakfast very late there. The grass was still wet with dew, and the top of the tennis net was wet too. He drew his hand along it as he passed. Then he sat down in the sunshine.

Leonora and Basil came running down on to the lawn. She wore a navy blue jersey and knickers, while Basil looked very tall and rather diabolical in a black jersey and tights.

"We do our exercises now," he shouted in explanation.

They proceeded to do the more gymnastic dance steps. Basil seemed to be able to spring perpendicularly into the air with very little expenditure of energy. Leonora was agile, but there was nothing conscious about her movements. Basil turned a somersault on to his feet and said, "She helps me a lot, you know. I have to practise lifting her."

And he lifted her in various ways and into various positions, and finally, carrying her high above his head, he ran the whole length of the court with her.

"Bravo," said Mr Laurel, with genuine admiration.

"Do you really think it is good?" said Basil, coming back; "and it would be much easier with a proper dancer, you know."

"Yes," said Mr Laurel. "Have you any definite plans?"

"Well, not exactly," said Basil. "I have lessons every vac., you know, and now I can have them all the time. I shall have some money when I am of age, and Aunt Margaret is lending me some until then."

"Perhaps I can help you in some way," said Mr

Laurel. "I know one or two dancers. Would it be any use your meeting them?"

"Oh yes, please," he said, and grasped Mr Laurel's hand. "Of course there is a lot I can't do, you know," he added. "There are many things I can't practise with Leonore. Look, put your hand there."

He placed Mr Laurel's hand on his spine and bent back very far indeed.

"Good," said he.

"Now do it to Leonore," said Basil.

He obediently put his hand on Leonora's spine and she bent back rather stiffly. If one could judge by touching it, her spine must have been very pretty. It is a funny thing, but there really is something very attractive about the thought of the skeletons of red-haired people. These are the only kind of skeletons one would not mind meeting at night. How deliciously intimate it would have been to have a conversation with Leonora's skeleton!

"You see, she does not press on you at all, as she should," said Basil, and Mr Laurel recalled the object of the experiment.

There was only one fault that could be found with the tennis court there, and that is that there was a glasshouse full of yellow roses just a little too near. When Mr Laurel does return a ball he usually endeavours to return it to heaven, whence at the beginning all things came, and on one of these occasions, after a short sojourn in the upper air, it fell through the roof of this glasshouse.

Leonora ran from her side to fetch it, and he, entering at the other end, contemplated for a moment the lovely picture she made among the yellow roses.

"How nice you look!" he said, forgetting to look for the ball.

She smiled. "Like what?" she asked.

I do not know why it is impossible to expound an æsthetic appreciation to a schoolgirl.

"Like the apricot and the pineapple in a fruit salad," he said.

She turned away, and as they both saw the ball and reached for it he pressed her hand, and the child blushed most furiously and ran out.

The curious thing is that he does not remember noticing Beatrice much during all this time. At least, they walked along together the day they went for a picnic, but she talked about the things they always talk about when they meet in town, and she rather got on his nerves, so completely had he given himself up to the atmosphere of the country and the garden and the roses, and Leonora with them. They were going to picnic on a little hill near, where some young birch trees grew near the top, rather like a regiment of young amazons, novices who, after the first battle, had been forced to retreat up the hill, but had retired in perfect order. A much older, larger tree among them added to this effect; but no, indeed, it made them look also rather like a party of schoolgirls with a mistress on guard, and they presented a most terrifying phalanx of virginity. Mr Laurel laughed.

They all sat in the shadow of the first of the birch trees and had tea, and afterwards he lay looking up at the sky and at the feathery little branches above his head, and listened to the sound of Leonora's voice making Basil arrange the things as she wanted them in the basket. Afterwards she came and sat by him, and began to fan him with a fern.

"The gnats are coming," she said.

Basil looked towards them, but seeing her occupied, called Beatrice.

"I say, Aunt Beatrice, if you could only hold this branch a moment," and he went out of Mr Laurel's field of vision into the big tree. But Beatrice on her way there cast at Mr Laurel a little smile of malice and veiled amusement, for which he saw no occasion then.

Leonora looked down at him and smiled, saying something or other, and he shut his eyes, and imagined himself making love to one of those birch-maidens, and slipping an arm around her slender silver waist. But as soon as he tried to imagine her virtuous reaction to such behaviour she turned back into a tree, with her little leaves and her branches swaying inaccessible above his head. He opened his eyes and looked at Leonora. She was looking at him and she blushed a little. He wondered what she would have done if he had slipped an arm around *her* waist instead; but not for worlds would he have had anything happen to dispel the delightful languor of that afternoon under the pale blue sky, so he contented himself with holding a corner of her green dress as he might have plucked a leaf of the birch tree.

They went home, not straight down the hill, but along the side of it, by a path winding between the trees. And he was no less charmed with Leonora and the birch trees than with Basil, walking between the trees balancing the basket on his head, as dark and graceful as a young slave.

By the time they reached the road it was growing dusk. Basil and Beatrice walked on in front, and Leonora and Mr Laurel slowly followed them. Leonora talked.

"I am so glad you have stopped teasing me," she said, and she told him all about school, and her dearest friend Judith, with whom she had only lately had a terrible quarrel, and about the mistress whom they both adored, Judith, it appeared, with a fierce and flaming passion, Leonora, so he was led to believe, with a calmer but more eternal devotion. And he learnt also how serious a step she felt leaving school was, and then he thought what a large gulf there was between them, but not so wide that he could not help her to balance across it, perhaps on a thin plank that shook and dipped down in the middle. Not, you know, that he was nearly forty and she seventeen, but merely that he had left school a term before her.

It was nearly dark when they arrived home, and on the way into the garden Basil began to sing, beating time with a dusty branch in his hand, and Leonora joined in. Mr Laurel did not know the song, but he joined in too, singing anything to the tune. And again he caught Beatrice looking at him with a malicious little smile, which he resented without quite knowing why. It was a well-known fact that he did not always sing in tune, but he was not sensitive about that.

After this it poured with rain for three days without stopping. There was no tennis. Mr Laurel sat about indoors and read, and he spent one morning playing dances for Basil. One evening Leonora sang

Elizabethan songs in a rather sharp, high voice. She stood in the middle of the carpet and sang without an atom of self-consciousness.

> "You are more fresh and fair than I,
> Yet stubs do live when flowers do die,"

said her voice, and the piano played a little dance measure to it. Really, it was all very charming.

The next morning the rain was over and the sun was shining through its tears. Mr Laurel went out into the garden. The grass was sodden with rain; three days' rain had fallen on it. The little posts on the tennis court were wet, and each rose in the garden was full of rain. There is something quite strange about a garden after the rain. A field wakes up fresh and strong like a peasant. Three days' rain is nothing to it. But a garden lies exhausted, like a young girl who has tasted too much the pleasures of love. There is no describing the voluptuous feeling a garden gives one.

Mr Laurel went and sat in a little summer-house and looked up at the house over the sloping lawns. And there he began carving a rose on the wooden table with such engrossment that he did not see Basil and Leonora come down to the garden, and they did not see him, but stood near a little rose tree.

Leonora smelt a flower, and Basil handed her a handkerchief to wipe the raindrops off her nose.

He looked down at the flowers and suddenly round at Leonora. Then he looked up towards the house, but it never occurred to him to look in Mr Laurel's direction.

"Leonore, come over here a minute," he said, pointing to the glasshouse.

She looked up at him, but obediently followed.

Against the side of the glasshouse some freshly cut squares of turf were piled up. He pointed to them, and she sat down, looking up at him, and probably expecting some new trick. Now he was out of sight of the house. He bent down, put his arms round her shoulders, and kissed her, on the cheek though, not on her mouth.

Mr Laurel could see from where he was how she blushed. Basil laughed, and felt, I dare say, awfully wicked and daring. But he was a little embarrassed too. For lack of anything to say he kissed her again, and she hid her face against his macintosh. They sat down side by side, and could not even look at each other. Then Basil said something with a casual air, nonchalantly turned a cartwheel somersault on the wet grass, and they walked out through the gate, looking straight ahead of them, and with the mark of the brown turfs across the backs of their macintoshes.

And as they passed out of the gate it seemed to Mr Laurel that his youth vanished with them. He watched them walk along the road until they disappeared, and he was left behind with the rain-sodden garden. He felt an overwhelming melancholy within his soul, and yet it seemed, too, as if he were on the threshold of a thought that would console him, when, looking up, he saw Beatrice sitting reading just outside the house. She was in white again, ready to play when the grass was dry. He suddenly began to see why she had smiled with such malice. It was at the spectacle of him fatuously running after a schoolgirl, anxiously watching each little blush, as though blushes were not simply a physical characteristic of schoolgirls. He nearly blushed himself at the thought. It would have been far more appropriate if he had carried on a flirtation with Beatrice, who was nearer his own age. He suddenly felt even more alarmed. He recalled the number of times he had played tennis with Beatrice and taken her out, without ever having considered that she was of a marriageable age. But now that he had discovered that he was himself middle-aged, he began to see that he had behaved in a most compromising manner. He almost ran across the lawn, intending in

a few moments' conversation to efface his unconscious behaviour of years. But he stumbled up the
steps, and when he got to her he felt a little embarrassed, perhaps not unnaturally.

Beatrice looked slowly up from her book as
though she believed he had come especially to tell
her something. This put what he had meant to say
out of his head, and after a moment's embarrassing
silence he hurriedly looked down the garden and
said, "It will soon be dry enough for tennis."

"Yes," said Beatrice, and after a moment looked
down again at her book. And as he went in he saw
her smiling to herself, so that he felt awfully foolish.

She took absolutely no notice of him for the next
few days, except on one morning, when Basil and
Leonora were out together she made him play tennis
with her. He felt unusually tired and weary. When
Beatrice played with him she always played without
exerting herself, so that he did at least touch the ball
now and then, but this time she exerted herself to
play. Balls seemed to be hurled at him from every
direction, and everyone of them seemed to be
expressing contempt. She served balls that sped low
along the ground, and he felt that he had forfeited
her respect for ever. If only he had had the strength
to return one of them! But the racquet hung heavily
in his hand and he felt profoundly depressed.

Only the day before they were to go he thought of the long drive home with her, and he felt that it would be an ordeal too terrifying to be borne. He walked downstairs thinking of it with dread.

"A letter for your Imperial Highness," said Leonora, waving it to him and laughing.

Mr Laurel opened it, and, though there was nothing important in it at all, said with an expression of great consternation, "I must go home to-day."

"But we were going to give you a farewell feast to-night," said Leonora. "Oh, please, don't go."

"I am so sorry," he said, "but it is very important."

There was no mistaking her disappointment. And she and Basil paid him the utmost attention during lunch, but he was not to be deceived a second time. And then they took him to the station, and sat on the wooden fence and waved him affectionate and admiring good-byes.

Now he has decided to go abroad for the winter, because he finds that his diary is full of engagements with Beatrice, and he is only waiting to keep some quite inevitable ones and to take Basil to lunch with the dancers, and then he will escape.

MACMILLAN COLLECTOR'S LIBRARY

Own the world's great works of literature in one beautiful collectible library

Designed and curated to appeal to book lovers everywhere, Macmillan Collector's Library editions are small enough to travel with you and striking enough to take pride of place on your bookshelf. These much-loved literary classics also make the perfect gift.

Beautifully produced with gilt edges, a ribbon marker, bespoke illustrated cover and real cloth binding, every Macmillan Collector's Library hardback adheres to the same high production values.

Discover something new or cherish your favourite stories with this elegant collection.

**Macmillan Collector's Library:
own, collect, and treasure**

Discover the full range at
macmillancollectorslibrary.com